wife for the weekend

a Sugar City novel

OPHELIA LONDON

Entangled Publishing, LLC
2614 South Timberline Road
Suite 109
Fort Collins, CO 80525
Visit our website at www.entangledpublishing.com.

Bliss is an imprint of Entangled Publishing, LLC. For more information on our titles, visit http://www.entangledpublishing.com/category/bliss

Edited by Stacy Abrams
Cover design by Heather Howland
Cover art from Shutterstock and iStock

Manufactured in the United States of America

First Edition March 2016

Bliss

To Kevin. My leap of faith.

Chapter One

To say the line was "out the door" wasn't correct, since the door in question led to the tarmac and was definitely not headed that way.

If Jules had taken that course at the Mystic Center on how to read lips, she'd at least know what was going on. The outlook was pretty grim, though, due to the combination of the late hour, the electrical storm lighting up the runway, and the intuitive loathing in her stomach that had nothing to do with the long line.

The last flight out of Las Vegas was going to be canceled.

Jules cinched her beaded carry-on over one shoulder when it looked like the line was about to move, all the while eyeing the first customer at the airline's counter. He did not look happy. But, hello? Were any of the other fifty would-be passengers in line overjoyed?

No one seemed as worked up and stressed out as the guy in the dark blue suit. He pounded a fist on the counter. Sheesh, even the back of his neck look tense.

What he needed was a good massage, full body, classic

Swedish. Maybe she should slip him her business card and tell him to come see her when he came back to Vegas. Whoops. After giving her notice at the spa last week, she didn't have cards anymore.

Anyway, Jules didn't want to think about work or the potentially canceled flight or where she was supposed to be flying tonight.

Instead, she simply closed her eyes and breathed, allowing her brain to drift to another place...full of golden retriever puppies and wind chimes and never-ending blank canvases waiting to be covered in thick brushstrokes.

Nothing could be done about the delay. Not even shouting and pounding fists could stop Mother Nature from being a meanie. At least Jules lived in Vegas and could turn around and go home. Surely they'd put her on the first Pennsylvania-bound flight in the morning.

Blue Suit said something gruff to the airline attendant, then gestured to the length of the line. *No need to get agitated, sunshine. Take a breath and find your happy place.* The guy ran a hand through his hair, picked up his slick leather carry-on, and stepped to the side.

A second later, FLIGHT 3318: CANCELED flashed in bold red across the screen.

In unison, the line groaned. The attendant got on the loudspeaker and said the airline was automatically rebooking the passengers individually online, and they would receive an email within the next hour about tomorrow's flights.

Another group groan, though Jules was just a tiny bit relieved.

Until guilt struck.

The canceled flight was only prolonging the inevitable. She'd eventually jet to Harrisburg, then grab a bus to Hershey. One side of her brain looked forward to returning to her summer stomping grounds, though it was coupled with sadness—Grams wouldn't be there this time. Not to mention Jules would have to deal with that semi-huge, ridiculous clause in Grams's will…

The other side of her brain was surprised by how much she was dreading the trip.

If only she were the type of girl to drink away her problems. But ever since that night in ninth grade when she and her best friend, Kate, had sneaked shots from Kate's parents' liquor cabinet, Jules and alcohol never really got along.

Wedding parties were her thing, though. Despite how she wasn't a fan of the whole "till death do us part" crap, she loved them, all the color and flowers and sparkles and smiles. It wasn't like she was hung up on Vince or anything. They'd dated one summer when they'd been fifteen, and that was eight years ago.

It was her yearly summer trips to Hershey to visit Grams that had kept them so tight over the years. And she loved Vince—as a friend. His fiancée was even cool, and very suited to marry into the über-rich, finely pressed Elliott family.

Shouldn't she be excited to celebrate their marriage?

Marriage. Ugh. Whatever. Not only had her best friend just gotten divorced, but Jules's own parents split up right after she was born, and her mother had remarried three times before she died. For many reasons, Jules was far from gaga over the conventional institution.

At the conclusion of the airline agent's announcement, the people in line began drifting away. Jules was about to join when she was nearly run over.

"Ow." She gasped, moving to rub her shoulder where she'd been bashed. But somehow—midbash—the arm of the other person slid between her arm and the strap of her carry-on, tangling them together. As she tried to pull back, her purse strap joined the tangling party.

"Pardon me," her assailant said, now trying to disentangle

himself from her by something close to a complicated swing dance move. "Sorry—wait, this way."

It was the guy in the blue suit, the one with the attitude. When he lifted his arm and tried to lead her under it, Jules glanced at his lowered head. Nice hair, dark and with curls, probably hints of auburn under natural sunlight. A way more conservative cut than she preferred, but not tragic.

He exhaled a low laugh, thankfully not as frustrated as he'd been at the counter. And what was that mouthwatering aftershave, for heaven's sake? He smelled how she imagined George Clooney would.

"Hold on," Jules said, when it seemed Clooney Blue Suit was making their predicament worse. "Let me just..." She released her grip on her purse and carry-on, and they immediately dropped to the floor.

But she still wasn't free from Clooney Blue Suit, since his jacket button had snagged the bodice of her peasant top, twining them together—front to front.

"Don't move," he said.

Like she could or *would*. This was her favorite shirt and she wouldn't let a designer suit ruin it, even one that smelled like Cloonz. He moved a hand between their bodies, and when his finger expertly looped around the knotted fringe, it touched skin, causing her breath to catch. Was he trying to cop a feel on the sly or be a gentleman?

"Almost...got it..." he said.

Since Jules didn't reach five three, he was nearly a head taller, and she inconspicuously lifted her eyes to see a chin speckled with a twelve o'clock shadow. When she realized she'd been holding her breath, she was forced to take in a deep inhale, helplessly aware that the front of her low-cut shirt strained extra tight, and that the guy could probably see directly into cleavage.

Don't think about it, don't think about it, she inwardly

chanted. *It was an accident and most likely the guy isn't an airport creeper.* Although it did seem to be taking an awfully long time for him to undo the snag.

"I have scissors in my—"

"There!" he said, then blew out a breath. As he stepped back, Jules almost swayed forward to follow him, a bit off balance. "I'm so sorry about that," he added, stooping to pick up her bags. "I was trying to figure out what to do about my flight, and wasn't looking where I was going."

"No harm done. Have a good night. Namaste." She reached out to take her purse from him. When she tried to pull it back, it wouldn't move because he was holding it in place.

Clooney Blue Suit was staring down at her. His eyes were blue, with the longest lashes she'd ever seen. When he blinked and a notch formed between his eyes, he totally reminded her of…someone.

"Jules Bloom?"

She almost said, "Vince?"

It couldn't be him, though. Her childhood ex was in Hershey preparing to get married. But the canceled flight they'd both been booked for was going to Harrisburg, right across the river from Hershey.

"Isn't that your name?"

Jules nodded, still in a blank haze, but about to come out of it any second…

"Oh. Hi," she said, after inspecting him from a different angle.

No, it wasn't Vince, but definitely one of his brothers. Which one? He had three, and they looked alike—dark-haired and chiseled and skyscraper tall. This was even the case when they'd all been kids.

She quickly ran each Elliott brother through her head. Wasn't Danny, Vince's twin. He had a scar on his eyebrow.

Wasn't the oldest, Luke. He was built more like an NFL quarterback than the other brothers. That left...

Jules considered his lingering hand on her tangled shirt fringe and knew *exactly* which brother this was.

"Dexter." She took a full step back, away from those handsy hands. "Hey."

"Hey." He motioned to the gate. "You were on this flight, too?"

She nodded. "Sucks that it's canceled."

"I know." He ran a hand through his hair. It was really rather nice, despite the unadventurous cut. "You're going to the wedding?"

The question was surprising. Though she and Vince hadn't been a couple for ages, everyone in his family knew they were friends. Jules knew this because she knew how close the Elliotts were. They were in and out of each other's personal lives like the characters on *Friends*. Jules never understood that. The only happy family memories she had were with Grams.

Now that was gone.

It wasn't that big families intimidated her; she'd just rather stay free and do her own thing.

"Of course I'm going to the wedding," she replied. "Why wouldn't I?"

Dexter loosened the knot of his gray-and-black-striped tie. "Strange you'd come to your ex's wedding." He shrugged. "I think we even had a bet going about it at one point."

"Hmm." Jules knew about the betting, too. The Elliott siblings were always daring each other to do crazy stuff. Even Roxy, the only daughter in the family, was into it. Jules recalled when Roxy lost a bet and had to hitchhike home from a party in Philly.

Again, Jules didn't get that kind of family dynamics, but it worked for the Elliotts, and what did she know about nondysfunctional families, anyway?

"Looks like we're stuck here for a while," Dexter said, glancing around the airport as the place emptied out.

"Not me. I live here."

He slid his hands in his pants pockets. "That's right."

His "that's right" wasn't because he actually knew her, but because of the *Friends* relationship. In fact, it had been years since she and Dexter had seen each other. Which was fine — they'd never meshed. He was all stiff and analytical, bored her to tears. Right after high school, he'd moved to Manhattan for college and to work in the family's tech business. Vince was always making fun of his brother's power suits and high-roller business lunches.

The persona fit Dexter. He was born wearing a dark suit. Reincarnated Alex P. Keaton in the flesh.

There were other things about him that Jules knew. Starting from when she'd met him that first summer, eighteen-year-old Dexter Elliott already had a reputation for being a major serial dater. If the rumors were true — which they were! — his womanizing behavior had grown over the years.

Any woman involved with a known player like Dexter deserved what she got.

Jules never asked for that kind of hassle. Her life was about freedom and beauty, living your dreams, following your passions, no matter where they led. Personally, her dreams revolved around oils and watercolors, and painting whatever she wanted, wherever she wanted. Of course her favorite place to paint was on Grams's back deck facing the lake. It had better light than any studio she'd ever used. Since art didn't pay the bills, massage therapy was her fallback.

But she was done with the safety of a fallback.

"Do you have a car here?" Dexter asked.

"I took the bus."

He sighed and raked a hand up the back of his head.

"Damn. Then we're both stuck."

"Why?"

Instead of answering, he gestured to the window, at the light show rivaling Independence Day. "The weather caused wrecks up and down the freeway," he said. "No buses, and apparently the taxi queue is more than an hour wait. I was on the phone before the cancelation was announced and not even the car services I use can make it out here until close to midnight."

"That's not for two hours."

He nodded. "I made a reservation, though. The first car available."

"Seriously?" She bit the inside of her cheek and tugged the fringe on her shirt. "How will I get home?"

"I can drop you off, if you don't mind waiting. Not that you have much choice. You can always sleep in the terminal."

They both let out a weary laugh. "Not when I have a nice bed at home."

Dexter glanced over his shoulder. "There's a Mexican restaurant by gate three. Open late and good service. We can wait it out there."

Skeptically, Jules took in his hair, his blue eyes, the tailored suit. Okay, she could see how *some* women fell for it. His basic looks weren't unappealing at all—to those *other* women.

"Sure. Why not?"

Dexter turned in that direction, reaching for her carry-on. Yeah, he might be a big old player, but at least he had good manners. When he bent to pick it up, Jules got a healthy eyeful of his butt. The guy could certainly fill out a suit like Clooney—he had that going for him, too. Add the amazing Elliott good looks and no wonder he was a lady-killer.

Good thing Jules was big-time against his type, right down to the suit and Bluetooth earpiece.

"Thanks," she said as they headed through the terminal.

They must've made a ridiculous pair. Dexter in tailored Armani and polished shoes strolling beside Jules in her fringy peasant top, flowy vintage skirt that hit the floor, and lace-up sandals. People probably thought he was her social worker.

This made her want to laugh. She didn't give a flip what other people thought. That was one of the first lessons Grams had taught her, and it completely saved Jules from becoming an insecure preteen bound for neurosis and low self-esteem.

One thing Grams hadn't taught her was how not to lose her independence when she fell in love. Even though it was more than three years ago, the memory of how she'd lost her identity, herself, by becoming so unhealthily entwined in someone else's life still haunted her. A rock-solid reminder to never let that happen again.

Even if that meant never falling in love. No long-term relationships—period…to be on the safe side.

She loved her life and what she'd become. And she'd never lose that again over a man.

They didn't speak as they walked. Dexter was reading his phone, tapping the screen, adjusting the earpiece. All business, all day. When did he have time to be that notorious ladies' man?

Sure, he was hot—in the traditional, *GQ* magazine way. But except for the tangled fringe, he hadn't given her so much as an appraising look. She was a female, however, and judging from past experiences, she wasn't at all on the uninteresting-to-men side.

As an amateur student of the human psyche, Jules was curious about when he'd turn on his legendary, supposedly-panty-dropping charm.

"Here okay?" he asked as they got to the restaurant, gesturing toward two stools at the end of the bar. He waited for her to sit first, which was a nice gesture, but certainly not enough to make her start tearing his clothes off.

"Are you with the canceled flight?" the bartender asked, sliding coasters in front of them.

"Yes." Dexter dropped his carry-on and put his phone in his pocket.

"First round's on me, then."

"Round of what?" Jules asked.

The bartender was filling a pitcher with something green and foamy. It smelled strongly of citrus and something sharp. "A special for passengers who really need it," he replied. "I call it the Vegas Sunrise. Takes the edge off, smooths the corners. I should start charging the airlines for it."

"Sounds perfect," Dexter said with a sigh. He probably did need a massage, and definitely needed a drink more than she did. But she'd sip to be polite.

The bartender filled two glasses and pushed them across the bar. "Tell me what you think. I'm Shoopy," he said, leaving to help another customer.

"Your name is Shoopy?" Dexter said under his breath, then winked at Jules.

"My neighbor had a hamster named Shoopy," she replied, her voice just as low. "It died a horrible death *during* a Vegas sunrise. I'm sure that's just a coincidence."

They laughed quietly, then Jules turned to her drink, sniffing it suspiciously. She couldn't detect any alcohol besides rum, but she'd seen the bartender add shots from miscellaneous bottles.

"Cheers." Dexter held up his glass.

Jules clinked hers against it. "Bottoms up," she said, making Dexter choke on his first sip. "Does it taste that bad?"

"No." He wiped his mouth with a napkin, blue eyes twinkly and boyish. Charming. "Haven't heard that toast in a while. And you said it so straight-faced."

"I take drinking with strange men very straight-faced." Though she couldn't help smiling.

Dexter smiled back. And yeah, okay, it was slightly swoony. "We're hardly strangers," he said. "Here's to rekindling friendships in random places, and to *you,* Juliet Bloom, and those funny strings on your shirt that brought us together." He clinked her glass again, eyes grazing the front of her top.

It made her stomach flip. Butterflies? Nervous? Intimidated? Curious?

Instead of replying, she dipped her chin and took two deep gulps of the cocktail. Why not? She wasn't driving, and if she was hanging with Dexter Elliott for the next two hours, her regular "oms" wouldn't be sufficient. She'd need a buzz on.

He smiled at her over the top of his glass, so she took another long gulp. By the time she set down her half-empty glass, her head was definitely abuzz.

• • •

Dexter had been so annoyed, he'd been ready to blow his top. Who knows what would've happened if he hadn't run into Jules. Literally run into her. His fault, of course, as he'd been too absorbed in getting the hell out of Vegas.

When the run-in had resulted in getting completely tangled in the straps of her bags, he couldn't help laughing. Miraculously, he'd even felt less annoyed about the canceled flight.

Small world that it was Jules, a girl he hadn't seen in years.

"Whoa, easy there," Dexter said as Jules set her glass on the bar.

She smiled, licked the corner of her mouth, and glanced away. Huh. He'd never noticed she had green eyes. And her long, unruly hair was what his sister, Roxanne, would've called strawberry blond. Maybe she was Irish.

Aye, a wee bonny Irish lass to fit nicely upon me lap.

Or maybe this drink was unusually strong. Random Irish-accented thoughts about Jules on his lap shouldn't be in his head.

"I'll let Vince know I won't be in tonight. Do you need to make a call?" he asked, after pulling out his phone, noticing Jules eye it with interest. No, not interest—distaste. "Anyone you need to let know?"

Seemed like a strange question, since she obviously had her own cell.

Or did she?

Come to think of it, those summers she was in Hershey when they were kids, she never used a cell, didn't have a MySpace account. She'd been social media-ly challenged then, and probably still was.

She also still dressed like a vintage store shop window from the '70s. All hippie-type, flower-child, flowy stuff that left way too much to the imagination for a guy who didn't like to take time to imagine.

Pretty face, though. He looked away, then grabbed his drink and took another gulp. Brutal stuff. What the hell was in this thing?

He tapped a quick text to Vince, then set his phone on the bar. "So," he said.

"So," Jules said. "You're close to your family?"

"Mm-hmm. You know this, though, because of Vince. You two are tight."

She shrugged and a lock of her hair fell across one shoulder. Because of all the hair, he hadn't noticed her shoulders were bare. *Kind of a lot of skin for a plane ride*, he couldn't help thinking…like an older brother.

If he thought about it, that was how he'd always felt toward her, since she'd been Vince's girlfriend way back in the day. It made him feel like a snake now, as his gaze lingered on her bare shoulders, his mind wondering if the skin felt as smooth as it looked.

"We stayed friends," she replied. "I spent most summers in Hershey before and after we dated."

Dexter remember that, too. She was always running around barefoot, eating yogurt tacos instead of Hershey bars, and constantly wanting to paint his portrait. Not just his, anybody's. And not just portraits. Jules wanted to paint everything.

"Why was that?" he asked. "Do you have family there?"

She held her hair back and nodded with an appealing, open smile that made Dexter want to smile, too, and keep looking at her face. After taking another drink, he noticed Jules's gaze had drifted into the middle distance, smile fading.

"My grandmother," she said.

"She lives in Hershey?"

"Lived."

Ah. Dexter understood the cloudy eyes. "Sorry. I hadn't heard."

"Thanks. It wasn't sudden; she was sick for more than a year. But it feels sudden anyway."

The ridiculous impulse to hold her hand suddenly flooded his mind. He went as far as glancing at them on the bar. She had blue stains under her nails. Paint. She was still an artist.

How…interesting?

He cleared his throat and took a drink. "I'm sure that's common," he said, to have something to say instead of thinking about other ways she could be interesting.

"I know. Anyway, the memorial was two months ago and I'm meeting with Grams's estate lawyer tomorrow. Just a formality. I know she left me her house."

"In Hershey?"

"Mount Gretna."

"Nice." Dexter watched as she took a slow drink. He pulled at the knot of his tie. Was the airport getting warmer?

Or was it him?

"Grams knew I loved it." She smiled, as if recalling a happy memory. Man, when the girl smiled, it transformed her whole damn face.

"Ah. So, that's the *real* reason you're going to Hershey?" He held up his glass. "I'll be sure and tell my brother it's not for his wedding."

"No, *no!*" She gasped in a loud voice and grabbed his arm. "Don't do that. Of course the reason is Vince. I swear."

"I'm joking." When she drew away her hand, he laughed to hide his disappointment. "Um. But even if I wasn't, we wouldn't want to mess with Vince's ego at a time like this."

She exhaled a low, feminine giggle, crossing her legs. Thanks to her long gypsy-like skirt, Dexter could see only the tips of her toes, not even an ankle.

Maybe the woman was sexually repressed. Maybe he should do something to help her break free from that. He was a giver, after all…

Dude. Don't even think about it. Vince would have your head.

Plus, it wouldn't be a one-nighter then go—which was the kind of "relationship" he preferred—because they were both on their way to Hershey. He'd see her all weekend.

No. Just no.

"Vince doesn't have ego issues," Jules said. "Though I do know he could use more support than he's gotten."

Don't picture her legs under that skirt. "What makes you say that?"

"He tells me things he doesn't tell you."

"Impossible." Dexter scoffed. "My brothers and I tell each other everything."

"Everything?" She arched an eyebrow in a very appealing way. Maybe even flirtatious?

"Well, obviously not everything. *I* don't, at least."

For example, he hadn't told anyone that he'd given his father notice a week ago and was leaving Elliott Technology. Dad hadn't said much, and Dexter had felt like a tool bag for doing it over the phone, but he knew it had to happen before the wedding weekend. A knot clenched in Dexter's stomach at the thought of facing him.

"Certain things a guy never shares," he added.

"Hmm." Jules glided a finger along the rim of her glass. "I've heard plenty of those stories about you."

It wasn't even an insult. Dexter wasn't ashamed of his personal life on any level. He was living exactly how he wanted to—unrestricted and happy and with zero attachments.

Romantic attachments were for suckers who couldn't handle his kind of freedom.

"No need to get into what you may or may not have heard. But I am interested in something else you said." He took a drink, then sat forward. "Does Vince think we don't support him getting married?"

"Well." She pressed her lips together and swiveled her barstool. "I obviously know their engagement was really short, even though he's been with Maddie for four years. Didn't help that Luke's engagement was even shorter."

It shouldn't have surprised him that Jules knew about his older brother's relationship. The news had spread like a wildfire. "Practically nonexistent," Dexter corrected. "Luke came to town to work on a clinical trial, fell hard for the head of the research team, and the next thing we knew, he quit his job in Philly to stay in Hershey. They got married three months later. Totally insane."

"Don't you like her?"

"Natalie?" Dexter said. "Yeah, she's great—great for Luke."

"Ahhh. It's the marriage thing you're against." She nodded sagely, like she now knew everything about him.

"Committing matrimony isn't something I intend to take part in, at least not for another twenty years."

"A lot of wild oats to sow?" She didn't sound or look judgmental. In fact, she laid another smile on him, like she understood or didn't care what he did with his life. In addition to being an artist, seemed Jules was also still that same free spirit. Live and let live.

Dex was totally down with that.

"Maybe." He winked, then was surprised when it made her blush. Hmm. Nice. Very nice. And damn sexy. "Marriage is fine in the abstract, and I don't begrudge Luke taking the plunge…or Vince or my parents or *you*."

"Me?" She snorted, then covered her grin with both hands. So damn charming. "I may not be out wildly sowing my oats, but that doesn't mean I'm ever getting married."

"Why not?"

She took a drink, emptying her glass. "Lots of reasons."

Dexter was curious, but he didn't press the issue. It wasn't his business why Jules wasn't interested in marriage, though they did have it in common.

Sometimes, he wondered why he took such a strong anti-relationship stance. His parents had been happily married for more than thirty years, and both sets of grandparents were still together.

But they weren't the only examples in Dexter's life…

Not too many years ago, he'd seen Luke through an awful divorce. His oldest brother, whom he'd always looked up to as a superhero, had been broken in half, emotionally gutted and bled out over a woman. Not only that, his younger brother Danny was constantly putting himself out there, always hopeful, only to experience one bad relationship after another.

And then there was Roxy. His baby sister might not know how she'd been lied to, played, and manipulated by a guy she'd blindly trusted, but Dexter knew. To save Roxy from embarrassment and heartbreak, he'd do everything he could to keep the ugly truth from her.

No wonder Dexter wanted none of it. Seemed like most relationships around him were falling apart. Why would he willingly volunteer to be slaughtered?

Work came first, and always would. The one thing he could depend on.

"My family is currently obsessed with marriage," Dexter said. "First Luke, now Vince. In fact, a couple months ago, right after Vince got engaged, my idiot siblings bet that I'd get married before Vince, assuming I'm so anal that I couldn't stand it if we don't stay in order by age to keep natural symmetry…or something dumbass like that. It's obviously a joke 'cause not even someone like me who hates losing even one bet would get married for the hell of it."

"No one special in your life these days, Dexter Elliott?"

He snorted now, and it made them both laugh. Daaamn. Was he drunk?

That absurd bet. Knowing he was going to lose it did gnaw at him. He was too competitive for it not to. Maybe if he hadn't been so busy lately that the bulk of his social life had been put on ice, one of the women he'd seen more than once would agree to a quickie marriage.

Okay. He was definitely drunk to even engage the thought. He shouldn't have taken the bet in the first place, shouldn't have allowed such high stakes, but his brothers really knew which buttons to push.

"Honestly, though…" Jules continued, reaching for the pitcher.

Dexter slid it her way. "Sure you want another?" he asked, holding her glass while she refilled.

"It's good, don't you think? I usually don't like alcohol, or it doesn't like me."

He drained his own glass, then set it on the bar. Jules filled it to the rim, grinning the whole time. "Honestly, though?" he prompted.

"Huh?" she replied after taking a sip, leaving behind a foamy green mustache on her top lip.

Imagining how he'd remove it made Dexter feel light-headed, hot-blooded. She was a woman after all, and not on the non-sexy side. All that wavy hair and hidden skin, those lips and…

Duuuude.

"You said, 'honestly though,'" he repeated, "but didn't finish the sentence."

"Oh, yeah. Well"—she paused and leaned toward him—"and this is just between you and me… I don't get the whole whirlwind marriage thing. With Vince, though, and then with Luke, when you think about it, it wasn't really whirlwind. Luke and Natalie knew each other since high school. Before then, even."

"Vince really does tell you everything."

The movement was slow, as she shrugged and used her hands to push her hair off both shoulders, holding those strawberry-blond waves in a high ponytail, only to let them spill down like a waterfall. Her green eyes were glowing and mossy. She looked ethereal, like a damn mermaid.

"I guess I'm easy to talk to," she said. Dexter saw how she would be. Easy to look at, too. Easy to touch, probably. Maybe he should stop wondering and find out.

Or maybe he was way more buzzed than was healthy.

"Anyway," Jules continued, "even before Vince and Maddie got engaged, they talked about marriage all the time. When he got around to making it official, they didn't want to wait. See, so it's not strange their engagement was short. She didn't want a big wedding anyway." She took a drink, then blinked a few times, resting one elbow on the bar. Seemed her glass number two was stronger than number one.

"I'm sure my mother had a say in that."

"Do you think she bullied them into having this big wedding weekend at their estate?"

"Wouldn't surprise me. Eileen Elliott loves to throw a good party."

"Speaking of parties, isn't that why you're in Vegas? Vince's bachelor party?"

"Indeed." He nodded, then groaned at the memory. "I took the red-eye from JFK and made it just in time for the kickoff. Talk about an epic event for the ages."

"It ended two days ago, and Vince is already in Hershey. Why are you still here?" When he didn't answer right away, she rolled her eyes. "Ohhh. Got it. Never mind. Of course *that's* why you're still here. Why would a guy like you leave Sin City earlier than he has to?"

Dexter laughed, pushed his glass away, but then pulled it back and took a drink. "I might buy a summer home here for that very reason." The idea of being holed up in a suite at the Bellagio with one of the women he'd met at the bachelor party was certainly tempting, but two solid days of uninterrupted work was the real reason he hadn't left with the others.

"My neighbor's a real estate agent if you need one."

"She hot?"

Jules giggled and nearly spilled her drink. "Very hot—if you're into five-foot-two brunets with beer bellies. I'll give Larry your number."

Dexter laughed and put a hand on her arm. When was the last time he'd laughed so much or been so chill with a woman? He couldn't remember. Though he did remember where his hand was and stopped laughing.

He hadn't meant to touch her—it was a reflex.

And she hadn't moved away or even flinched. *Curious...*

Slowly, investigatively, he slid his hand up her arm, to the inside of her elbow, running his thumb across the soft skin. He heard her breathing turn heavier, so his hand traced higher, touching the tips of her hair. She leaned forward, and then *he* was breathing heavy. In five seconds, he'd—

His phone beeped with a text.

In unison, they sucked in a breath, and Dexter removed his hand, blinked hard, and stared at his cell, trying to focus, to remember where he was and why.

"The car's here."

"Already?" She nibbled her bottom lip. "Feels like we just…started. We only finished one pitcher."

"It's probably enough." *Enough for me, that's for sure.* "My assistant made a reservation at a hotel. Not sure where." As he drained the rest of his drink, his head got fuzzier. "Come on, I'll have the driver drop you off at home first."

"Cool."

Jules was a petite thing, and when she slid off the stool, she wobbled as her feet hit the floor. Dexter took her around the waist to steady her…to confirm that she did indeed have womanly curves under all those clothes.

"You okay?" he asked.

"I feel great." Her hair spilled back as she tipped her chin to look up at him. When she gave him a bright, slightly crooked smile, Dexter felt it in his chest, stomach, everywhere.

They made their way outside to ground transportation. "The car should be waiting by baggage claim," he said, holding the door open for her. It was pouring outside and Jules stopped walking and folded her arms across her chest like she was cold. He immediately took off his suit jacket and draped it around her shoulders. As he held it while she slid her arms through the sleeves, he let his hand linger on her shoulder. For nearly two hours when they'd been at the bar, he'd become obsessed with what it felt like.

Smooth and warm like the rest of her.

She glanced at him over her shoulder, green eyes locked on his. He was three damn seconds from wrapping his arms around her, tilting her head, and satisfying another obsession about what her lips felt like.

Instead, he sort of patted her on the back and hated himself. Maybe being women-free for two months had taken away his game.

"Thanks." Had he just imagined her gaze dipping to his mouth?

"For what?"

"For this." She lifted an arm, displaying the sleeve of his jacket that was so huge on her that it swallowed her hand.

"Welcome. Uh, anytime." He pulled at his collar. Why was it so damn hot in Vegas, even at midnight? "Here's the car." He pointed to a black sedan with his last name on a white card showing through the windshield.

Her eyes widened. "It's a limo."

"I asked for the first thing available."

"I've never been in a limo," she said, grinning like a little kid, making him grin, too.

"Well then." Before the driver could get out from behind the wheel, Dexter opened the car door. "After you." He waved to the driver over the hood. It was Carl; he'd known him for years.

"Woo-hoo, thanks!" On her way into the backseat, she picked up the bottom on her mile-long skirt to keep it from getting wet, displaying one leg. One long and toned and smooth leg. Getting a look at the other became his new obsession.

Once Dexter was inside, Carl peeled away from the curb. Jules was in the middle of a laugh when thunder crashed so loudly it made the car shake, causing her to squeal and jump.

"Don't you just love electrical storms?" she said, staring out the window wide-eyed. A bolt of lightning made her jump again—practically onto his lap.

"S-sorry," she whispered, squeezing his arm, tilting her chin to look at him.

He took in a slow breath and inhaled the scent of her. Fruity and sweet. "Don't be," he replied, sliding a hand up to her shoulder.

Was it the electricity of the storm, the pounding rain on the car, or the lightning illuminating her face that made it absolutely necessary to follow his next impulse?

Right as she flinched at another crash of thunder, he wrapped an arm around her, pulled her to him, and kissed her.

For a moment, his heart stopped. The rain stopped. Time stopped.

Before he could regret the action, or even repeat it, Jules hitched up her skirt, fisted his lapels, and pulled herself onto his lap, legs straddling him. He ran his hands over the silky skin of her knees, their lips connecting again.

A different electrical storm raged through his body and mind, then completely took over.

· · ·

Dexter blinked at the light. It made his head throb. And what was that damn beeping? When he tried to move, his head pounded harder. More beeping. His cell. Okay. He groaned, and his hand followed the sound across the bed. He was in a bed. A pile of pillows that he must've kicked away during the night lay on the other side. His cell was buried down by his stomach.

Squinting, he rolled over and tapped the face. Fifteen new texts. Hell. What was so important? He clicked on the most recent. It was from Luke, three hours ago.

Daaaamn bro. And you thought I was fast.

As always, Luke made no sense. Dexter clicked on the next most recent, from Roxy, a line of smiley faces and heart icons. His sister was insane. Finally, he scrolled to the top. Huh. All the texts were from his siblings in reply to a text he'd sent just after one o'clock. Besides Vince to tell him about the flight cancelation, he had no recollection of texting anyone last night.

It must've been a butt dial, but then he clicked the text and a photo popped up. Him and a woman, blurry, like a selfie taken with a shaky hand. Or maybe *he* was blurry—his eyes were sandpaper dry and could barely focus. A caption was sent with the picture.

Suck it. I won the bet!

Bet? The only current bet Dexter could think of was…

More alert now, he scrolled to the photo again. Yes, it was him and a woman. They were cheek to cheek, beaming at the camera like insanely happy idiots, and were each holding up one hand, showing off a pair of wedding rings.

Suck it. He reread the caption, slowly. *I won the bet.*

Suddenly, the pile of pillows on the bed beside him yawned and moved.

Chapter Two

Jules's mouth tasked like death, and why were her eyes superglued shut? She tried to move, but when she got as far as flexing her back, it felt like she was riding the Tilt-A-Whirl. Suddenly, it was as if someone turned the lights on. A second later, it was dark. But the return of darkness was accompanied by a curse word that sounded like it came from the other side of a tunnel.

What was going on?

At least now she was awake enough to realize she was lying stomach-down in bed. Out of habit, she yawned and stretched her arms to touch the carved roses on her headboard. Instead, her hands met something cold and metallic. Come to think of it, where was her memory foam mattress?

Slowly and with held breath, she let her foot wander toward the middle of the bed. When it brushed something solid—something that recoiled from her as quickly as she'd recoiled from it—she threw off the covers and sat up.

"Who the hell are you?" she shouted, glaring at the owner of the other foot. A man with messed-up dark hair, lying on his back, bare-chested, one arm thrown over his face. "I said, *who are you*? And why are you in my bed?"

"This isn't your bed," the man muttered.

"Of course it—" She cut herself off. It wasn't her bed or her bedroom. "Where am I?"

"Please stop yelling. I have a headache."

Well. Who did this guy—this creepy stranger—think he was? She was ready to reach for the pepper spray in her bedside drawer, but then remembered.

Her head pounded. Had she been drugged and kidnapped? Was she in a cult?

Sucking in a deep breath, she was about to scream for help at the top of her lungs when the guy moved his arm and she saw his face. "What the…? Dexter?"

He moved his arm all the way off and stared up at the ceiling. "You were expecting someone else?"

"I wasn't expecting…" She stopped, and for a moment, just held her head. "What happened?"

"You don't remember?"

"Flight was canceled. We went to a bar. I think there was rain. I *know* there was rum."

"That's as far as my memory goes, too."

"How did I get here?" she demanded.

"I told you." He rolled his head on the pillow to look at her. "I can't rememb—" His eyes bugged out of his skull. "Do you know you're…?" His bug-eyed stare slid from her face and traveled south.

Only then did Jules realize she was sitting up in bed, covers thrown off, stark naked. After she yelped in holy bloody horror, grabbed a fistful of sheets, and yanked them to her chin, she checked under the covers and…yep, stark naked down there, too.

Dexter laughed. He actually *laughed* at her.

"Shut up!" she insisted. "Get out of this bed."

"Fine." He pushed into a sitting position, his bare chest all…there and bare…and moved to the edge of the bed.

"Wait. Are you…um?"

"*Desnudo*?" he asked, way too calm. "Completely."

"Stay covered, and…keep on your side of the bed."

His mouth quirked into a smile. How dare he smile?

"This isn't funny—at all. *I've* never done anything like this." She pressed fingers to her forehead and massaged. "Never ever."

"You think I have?"

"Please." She rolled her eyes. "Everyone knows you wake up with a different woman every other night. Your reputation's no secret."

"Not what I meant when I said I've never done this."

Ugh. The guy was getting all Dexter-analytically annoying. Her brain was too fuzzy to deal with that. She needed strong tea, extra peppermint, a scalding shower, and then three hours of hot yoga until she detoxed whatever poison she'd ingested last night.

"What did you mean, then?"

"Look at your left hand."

Jules was way too hungover to play guessing games. But she sighed and pulled her hand free from the sheets. Everything went into slow motion as she blinked and stared at the ring on her third finger. "What's…?"

"I believe it's a—"

"I *know* what it is. What's it doing on *my* finger?"

Wordlessly, Dexter lifted his left hand and displayed a matching ring.

The room tipped and spun, whirred and whirred. "Are we…?"

"Yeah," he said, and pulled out his phone, displaying a picture of them together, goofy-grinning and showing off the rings.

"That doesn't mean—"

"There's more." He flipped to his camera app. The most recent photo was the one of them and the rings, but the first one gave Jules a shiver. It was them, all smiley, but on her head was a…a frickin' bridal veil. In the next photo they were facing each other while holding hands, standing before a mystery guy with tacky Elvis muttonchops and slicked-back hair. The three of them stood under a white arch.

"Wait a minute—"

"Look at the rest."

Before she did anything, she took a breath—in through the nose, hold, out through the nose—and flipped to the next photo. They were kissing and she was holding flowers. The next was just Dexter, holding a piece of paper. Jules touched the screen to stretch the photo, even though her sinking, intuitive gut already knew what it was.

"This doesn't just *happen* like on TV. There are *laws*, even in Vegas. A couple can't be issued a license while under the influence!"

"Tell that to our marriage license," Dexter said, pulling out a piece of wrinkled paper from under his pillow. "It's dated today, both of our names. Signed. And lower your voice. Are you always this loud?"

The license looked legit. And legal. Holy Hare Krishna. "This can't be."

"Oh, it be." He leaned against the headboard, looking way too chill and relaxed, and way too much like a naked man with an incredible body in her bed.

It was too late to stop herself from flushing all over.

"I already emailed my lawyer. The most recent applications for Nevada marriage licenses are online. We're on there. This is real."

"Then why aren't you *freaking out*?" Jules said, trying to look him in the eyes and not elsewhere. "This is epically horrible."

"I realize that," he replied so serenely she wanted to punch him. "And I did freak out. I was awake for fifteen minutes before you—freaking the hell out."

"At least we're on the same page about that."

What a mess, a drunken mistake that should never have happened. Of all people to wake up married to, Dexter Elliott was so far down the list she'd run out of ink. Last night, through alcohol goggles, she might've been irrationally attracted to him. And maybe something inside thought about that absurd clause in Grams's will, and how even a tawdry midnight Vegas wedding would fix it.

Jules was always up for fun adventures, but the thought of even her drunken subconscious wanting womanizing, workaholic Dexter as a husband for any reason was insane.

Obviously her cocktail-soaked self had been on hormone autopilot. Sure, fine, Dexter was hot and she'd been slightly attracted to him at the bar, but not nearly enough to want to peel off her clothes and...

"Um, so I have a question," she said. "I know we're undressed in a bed and whatever, but that doesn't necessarily mean we...you know."

Dexter furrowed his brow. "I assumed we did."

"Well, I assume we *didn't*. I *know* we didn't. Even plastered out of my head, there's no way I'd randomly have sex with you."

"One way to find out." Dexter slid to the edge of the bed. Jules was ready to tell him to stop before he showed the rest of his three-piece-suit-less body, but she looked away instead. And waited.

"Oh. Ohhh. No more assuming."

"Why?" She hesitantly glanced his way. Thankfully, he'd pulled on a pair of black boxer briefs. Now if she could find her own clothes. When Dexter turned around, he was holding an empty condom wrapper. "At least we were safe."

"No. Oh, no no no." She felt her whole face go hot with embarrassment; even her ears were burning. "Fine, it happened once—"

"Twice." He held up another empty wrapper. "No, wait—three times. And they were definitely used, um, properly."

"*Three*?" she shrieked. "Since one a.m.? How are you not broken in half?"

"You're confident three times with you in one night would break me?"

Jules couldn't help shrugging coyly. "I take vitamins."

Dexter laughed. He stood there—in black boxer briefs with flat abs and what some women who weren't in touch with their spiritual selves might call a perfect body—and laughed like they were friends sharing a joke.

"Come to think of it, I am exhausted. Starving, too, like I just finished an extra-rigorous workout at the gym."

"Dexter—stop." But she couldn't help laughing under her breath in helpless horror. "This isn't funny. It's not like we can stay married. We have to undo this right now."

"Yeah, about that…"

The way he rubbed his square jaw messed with her mental balance, but also made her keenly aware that they were both pretty much naked. Which made her a different kind of unbalanced.

"After I finished freaking out," Dexter continued, "I started thinking." He sat on the foot of the bed. "Jules, we have to stay married."

• • •

Dexter didn't expect her to throw her arms in the air and exclaim that she absolutely agreed. But he didn't expect the explosion.

"What?" Jules's eyes were huge and bloodshot, making them appear even greener. "What the hell are you saying? What are you even talking about? What…"

Jeez, she's loud. Her mouth never stops.

"Hear me out."

"No! Don't!" When she held up a hand, the sheet covering her slipped, and Dexter caught sight of a good amount of skin. After using three condoms last night, he was a little surprised when his chest felt hot at seeing so much of her now. Jules obviously noticed his stare because she quickly covered up.

"Listen for one minute." He waited for her to stop yelling and calm down. "We're married—that's a fact, and there's nothing we can do to change that right now. My lawyer's looking into an annulment, though I don't know if that's, um, possible." He glanced at the pile of wrappers. "I don't know the laws; we'll just have to wait."

"I guess we have no choice, but it doesn't mean we're *married*. We're not a couple. It was a mistake."

"A big one."

She crossed her arms and pushed her full red lips into a pout.

Dexter looked away. Now was a very bad time to study her lips. "My family already knows." He held up his phone. "And they seem really, sincerely happy about it—happy for us. They know you. They like you. Doesn't appear they know we were wasted, though."

"Clearly."

"This is my brother's big weekend. All the attention should be focused on Vince and Maddie. The last thing I want is to cause a bunch of drama at his wedding."

No reason for the family to think I'm more of a screwed-up relationship-phobe than they already do. Plus, the damage is done, no reason to lose a bet I don't have to…

"You're going to the wedding anyway. You'll be in

Hershey all weekend, right?"

She shifted on the bed, narrowing her eyes. "You're not actually thinking we should pretend to be a happily married couple."

"Just for the weekend. Just until we can get a quickie divorce. I'll take care of everything, and it'll only affect your life while you're here. Just because I'm not into marriage doesn't mean I want to ruin my brother's wedding."

Jules was nibbling a thumbnail. What he was suggesting — as crazy-ass as it seemed — was starting to make sense to her.

"You're saying we fake it for the weekend?"

He held his breath and nodded, knowing how insane the whole thing was. "Just through Sunday. Three days."

"Well... Hey, wait!" Those pouty lips were suddenly frowning. "You got married, which means you won the bet."

"So?"

Her frown deepened as she closed her eyes, her shoulders dropping as she exhaled a slow breath. "Just tell me," she said, eyes still shut. "Did you do this on purpose? To win?"

The accusation didn't surprise him. After all, five seconds ago he'd wondered the same thing. "Absolutely not," he said, hoping it was the truth.

She opened her eyes and fixed her scrutinizing gaze on him. "I guess I have to believe you."

"Thanks for the vote of confidence." Internally, though, he had to admit that, as completely warped as it sounded, something about winning a huge bet made him want to give himself a fist bump.

"What were the stakes?" she asked.

"Five grand."

"Seems pretty steep for a friendly—"

"Five each, which makes it twenty."

"What?" she blurted, staring at him unblinking. "You just won twenty thousand dollars?" Her expression puzzled him.

It wasn't envy, exactly, but close.

Hold on. Maybe she needed money, and their accidental marriage—with a 20K prize attached—was a blessing in disguise for her.

"Which I'll split down the middle with you," Dexter was quick to add, hoping that would sweeten the deal. "You've obviously earned it." When she opened her mouth, probably to protest, he held up a hand. "Think of it as an early divorce settlement. I'll have my lawyer write it up."

Seconds ticked by as her mouth hung open.

For the first time since he'd known her, Juliet Bloom was speechless.

"I…" she finally uttered. "I mean, I could definitely use it, but—no, no, I can't."

"No rash decisions. Besides, talking about money is vulgar. We won't discuss it again after you give me your bank information, or I can just write you a check. If you don't want to keep it, give it to charity, but it's yours, okay?"

She nibbled another nail, one stained with blue paint. "If I agree, it's not only because of the money. Vince is one of my best friends and I definitely don't want to screw up his wedding. That'd be awful."

While a glob of guilt and last night's Vegas Sunrise crawled inside his gut, he waited for her to agree, or to tell him to sit and spin. He wasn't sure which answer he was dreading the most.

"I hate lies of any kind, Dexter. Lies ruin lives, no matter how justified."

He almost had her. He just had to reel in slowly. "Don't think of it as lying. We're…postponing an unpleasant truth. After a month or so, we'll be divorced and the whole thing will be over. No one will care by then."

"Your family will. They're good people. I've always liked them. You say they're happy for us now, but what about when we break up? Roxy's a huge romantic—she'll be devastated. So will your mother."

She had a point. "I'll tell them I cheated on you," he replied logically. "With my rep, they'll believe that, and they won't blame you." He shrugged, even though the idea left a very bad taste in his mouth. In the abstract, maybe once he'd seemed like a guy who'd cheat. Dexter had done a lot of things, but never that.

"They'll be pissed at me for a while," he added, "but I can handle that. We just have to get through the weekend."

Jules was still chewing that nail. "I'm actually staying in Hershey longer than the weekend," she said after a moment. "I've got legal things to take care of with my grandmother's estate."

Dexter remembered her saying something about that last night, or this morning. He was still having a hard time putting events in chronological order—the few events he could actually remember. Most of last night was a big blank.

"That's fine," he said. "On Sunday, I go back to Manhattan and you'll stay in Hershey. My family will assume you left with me."

"But I don't live in New York."

"No one knows that."

"Vince does."

He shook his head. "Vince will be on his honeymoon. After the wedding, no one will notice you."

She cocked her head to the side. "You're a real *charmer*, Elliott, ya know that?"

He paused his smart-ass reply, registering her hurt/ annoyed expression. "Sorry. I meant, since you and my family don't exactly run in the same social circles." He thought of the billowy skirt and fringy shirt she'd worn last night—definitely not found in his mother's country club clique.

"I should tell you…" But she didn't finish. Instead, she

shifted and tugged a strand of hair.

"What should you tell me?"

Her eyes widened but quickly glanced away, like she'd been caught having evil thoughts. "Um…that I'm…a terrible liar. I turn hyper red-faced and get hiccup attacks and—"

"I'll do all the talking," he said. "Since neither of us seems to remember anything, we might never know whose fault it is that we're in this mess."

Although Dexter knew it sure the hell hadn't been him. Nothing would've possessed him to ask any woman to marry him. Not even his inebriated subconscious would pick someone as hippie-dippy and flat-out *noisy* as Jules.

So the question was, if he wasn't the instigator, why did he go along with it? A riddle like that could drive him loco, and he was too hungover to get philosophical.

"I guess that's true," Jules said. "Okay, for the sake of Vince's wedding, I can pretend."

Before either of them could say another word, his phone beeped. He grabbed it and read the new message. "They booked us a direct flight to Harrisburg. We have an hour to get to the airport. Did you get the same message? Check your phone."

"I don't have one."

Of course you don't, Flower Power.

"I have a cell," she corrected, "but not a smartphone. No internet. It's probably dead, anyway. I never use it."

Dexter didn't have the brain energy to probe into that. "I'm sure we're on the same flight, but I'll make a call." He stood to begin searching the room for his clothes. "We'd better get going."

"Um, okay." Still on the bed wrapped in a sheet, Jules was biting her lip and glancing around, as if contemplating what to do next.

If he were the gentleman his mother raised him to be,

he'd offer to leave the room or at least turn around. But he didn't. Instead, he was a hungover scoundrel and stood in the middle of their hotel bedroom in nothing but his shorts.

"Do you mind?" she finally said.

"Not at all." He smirked.

She huffed, blew the hair out of her face, and snapped, "*Fine*." Keeping the sheet tightly wrapped around her like a mummy, she scooted to the end of the bed and stood.

Okay, maybe there was an interesting body under all those long, loose-fitting clothes. At least that was what the fitted sheet showed. Or didn't show. Suddenly, he felt a bit overheated, as if his body was reacting to a memory his brain didn't know.

Pretending to look for his clothes, he turned around and scanned the room. What he focused on did nothing to lower his body temperature.

"I suppose this belongs to you?" With one finger, Dexter hooked the strap of a black bra that was hanging over the lampshade and held it up. "Not my size."

Jules huffed angrily, shuffled over, and grabbed it. The way her cheeks glowed like two red apples made him chuckle.

"Easy. I wasn't going to try it on."

"It's new," she said, hiding it behind her back.

"It's nice. Want me to help you track down the rest?"

"No, I want you to stand right there and not move while I find my clothes."

"Why didn't you say so?" he said, still laughing. Then he was a gentleman and turned around. It probably wasn't fair that he could see her reflection in the window. But it wasn't like she dropped the sheet and started swinging from the bedposts. She shuffled around the room, long hair falling over her face, while she picked up items of clothing that had apparently been torn off, then thrown into corners. By him? Her?

By the time he'd stopped imagining that, she'd disappeared into the bathroom.

After staring at the closed door, he found his white button-down wadded in a ball behind the armchair. It was wrinkled beyond hope, four buttons missing, and the left sleeve had a major rip.

What the hell happened last night?

Chapter Three

Without time to shower and scrub her body clean of ickiness and blocked-up chakras, Jules used the entire bottle of hotel mouthwash and brushed her teeth with a finger. Though nothing took away the "morning after" eck factor.

Fully clothed, she took a second to stare down her reflection. Since it was a little late to go into a full-on self-lecture about the obvious dangers of drinking too much, she simply pointed at the mirror and scowled like a schoolmarm.

"Are you decent?" she asked, opening the bathroom door a crack.

"Depends who you ask."

She closed her eyes and blew out a long, cleansing breath, taking time to breathe back in slowly. How did she get involved with a man-whore like Dexter? "Are you clothed?"

"Yes."

Dexter was dressed all the way down to the gray power tie hanging loose around his neck. He sat on the end of the bed tying his shoes. When he glanced up, he stopped. And stared.

"Don't look at me like that," she said, feeling the need to cover up.

"Like what?"

"Like you've seen me naked."

"I have." He rubbed his jaw and sat back. "Even if I can't remember."

The reply shouldn't have made her stomach experience a microscopic flutter. Besides his good looks—which she was already immune to—Dexter Elliott had nothing that appealed to her.

"Just keep on *not* remembering. I might be small and a pacifist, but I'm not afraid to use my fists." She glanced around the room.

"What are you looking for?"

"Somewhere to sit."

Wordlessly, he patted the spot on the bed next to him.

"No."

"If I have cooties, you've already got them."

Why bother arguing the point? Instead, she sat beside him and picked up her sandals, which he must've moved at the end of the bed. After all, why would her shoes be in place when the rest of their clothes had been strewn around the room like they'd been caught in a sex tornado?

"Thanks." Without having to look his way, she felt the weight of his eyes as she wrapped the laces around her ankles. "Dexter. Stop."

"What am I doing?"

When she finally glanced at him, sure enough, his man-whore eyes were glued on her. If he was supposed to be about one night then bye-bye, why was he looking at her like…he wanted more?

"Hey, stud. If we go by this plan of yours for the weekend, you can't do that."

"Do what?"

Ugh, he was exasperating. "You can't flirt or leer or give me your playboy eyes or look at me or—"

"Might be difficult to pretend we're married if I can't look at you."

She exhaled and tied the last lace in a double knot. "You know what I mean. Stop."

At last, his heavy gaze was replaced by a smirk. She could handle Dexter's smirks. "Fine. Whatever." He stood and offered his hand. "We have a plane to catch."

For a second, she stared at his hand, feeling stubborn and defiant. Maybe, though, the offering was an olive branch, symbolically starting over.

So she took his effing hand. His grip was strong and warm, more calloused than she'd expect from someone who came from piles of money and worked in an office.

Speaking of money… The shock of how much he'd won in a sibling bet hadn't worn off. Neither had Dexter's offer to give her half. She really shouldn't. She really, really shouldn't. But with Grams's cottage needing renovations, and with Jules barely scraping by as a now-unemployed massage therapist and starving artist, ten grand was a lifesaver.

Plus—and she couldn't help feeling loads of guilt over it— suddenly being married was an even huger lifesaver. Legally.

"Do you know what happened to our carry-ons?" she asked, picking up her purse that was looped over the doorknob.

"Still in the car from last night," Dexter said. "Apparently, we couldn't be bothered. Carl's waiting outside."

"Right. Okay." Jules nodded and tried not to feel nauseous. Good thing she had a complete change of clothes in her bag, and more in her suitcase. But who knew when she'd see that again? Hopefully she'd get a chance to change before the flight, otherwise she'd be queen of commando city for the next seven hours.

Peering in his direction, Dexter's eyes suddenly dashed away from her, like he'd been reading her mind and knew last night's underwear was stashed in her purse.

Man-whore, she muttered internally. If she didn't have to see Grams's lawyer, she wouldn't bother going to Hershey now, despite the wedding—he'd understand if she bailed. She was a bailer, after all. Vince knew that better than anyone. Which meant Dexter probably knew, too. Freaking Elliotts.

Dexter ushered her into the limo at the curb and chose not to sit in the furthermost corner. She needed a few quiet moments cleansing her aura and not getting stressed out about a man so buttoned up, he probably never left the house without a perfect side part in his hair or walked barefoot.

And she was married to him.

Om shant shant shant…

As the car zoomed down the freeway, she stared out at the traffic, slowly rotating her neck from side to side. Muscles she didn't know existed were strained and sore. If she'd had time, she would've gone into the spa and had Alexandra or Emory work on her. Trading off massages was one of the perks that came with her day job. *Ex*-job.

The restrictions of a nine-to-five made it impossible for her to love-love her job, but it paid the bills. *Someday…* she told herself time and time again like a mantra, *someday soon my art will totally support me and I'll live the way I've always dreamed, the way Grams dreamed for me.*

At the thought, her heart squeezed and dropped, and a sob sat in her chest. Two months, and she still missed Grams like crazy. It was a wonderful blessing that she'd left Jules the lake cottage, but Jules would rather her grandmother be alive than to inherit a house—even one she loved.

More than anything, Jules hoped this return to Hershey would break her free from the artistic block since Grams's passing. After all, what kind of a painter was she if she wasn't painting?

It wasn't that she didn't want to. She just…couldn't.

Her heartbeats remained slow and heavy when they got to the airport, checked in, cleared security. It felt like she was coming out of a daze when she blinked and found herself sitting in first class next to Dexter. Had he paid for her upgrade or had it been included because of their canceled flight? She was about to ask, but he wore earbuds and was tapping on a laptop.

Like so many other people, workaholic Dexter was glued to technology. Whatever, she didn't want to have a conversation with him, anyway. Who cared if he paid for her upgrade? Because of what he'd obviously talked her into last night, he owed her way more than a plane ticket, or ten thousand dollars. Right?

She glanced at the simple gold band on her finger, then slammed her eyes shut. Her brain ached as she strained to remember. Okay, maybe in this condition, she couldn't blame him 100 percent, but she was sure it wasn't her fault, no matter how fortunate the monetary and legal outcome.

At least the seats in first class were comfortable. When she heard a sound, she opened her eyes. A tall Bloody Mary sat on her tray table. Dexter had one, too, with three extra celery sticks and no olives.

"Hair of the dog that bit you," he said, clinking his glass against hers, earbuds still in place. When he winced at his first sip, it made her smile. She relished his flappable moments. It reminded her that he was human.

Then she took her own sip and felt like wincing, then dying. Whatever they'd drunk last night was the most potent thing she'd ever consumed.

After draining half the glass, she passed it off to the flight attendant, closed her eyes, folded her arms, and tried to sleep. Every time she moved, her thumb brushed against that ring.

. . .

Despite his head being in a fog, Dexter got a lot of work done. Damn good thing—the meeting with the investors from Three Jacker Media was only six days away. For months, he'd been prepping for this, balancing the demands of his day job with this new venture. Finally, it was within reach.

Not that he hadn't enjoyed working at Elliott Technology; he was great at his job as VP of product management. Nor was he ungrateful for everything his father had done for him, but surely Dad didn't begrudge his own son for wanting to go out on his own. If he could get this one last investor, the dream might become reality.

He gave himself a mental fist bump, then closed his eyes, fingers still on the keyboard out of habit. Now, if he could also manage to catch a few winks before landing—

A snuffled snore at his side startled him awake. Jules was curled in a ball. Her legs pulled in, bare feet on the seat, arms encircling them, while resting a cheek on one knee. How could she possibly be comfortable? In fact, how could she possibly bend into a position like that? Was the woman a contortionist?

Huh. He couldn't help feeling a little cheated that he couldn't remember a damn thing that happened in that hotel room. What if she'd done contortionist tricks on him?

She snored again, sucked at her bottom lip, and pulled in her chin, causing a curtain of that mermaid hair to fall over her face. It was thick like a heavy blanket. Could she breathe through it? Without thinking, Dexter swept her hair to one side of her face. A few strands caught on the corner of her mouth, so he ran a finger across her cheek, pulling those strands away. She shifted and made a soft noise. Not a snore, more like a sigh of contentment. On autopilot, he brushed her cheek, then dragged a thumb beneath her bottom lip.

Her eyelids fluttered. Dexter blinked out of a daydream and jerked his hand away. Her green eyes slowly opened and looked at him, closed again, then another sigh, like she'd been expecting to see him there…pleased, even.

"Mmmm, that was nice," she whispered dreamily. "Really, really…" Before she could finish, her eyelids sprang open. "What are you doing?"

"Nothing."

She released her knees, and her bare feet hit the floor. Wearing a confused expression, she looked to the side, up at the ceiling, then down at her lap.

"We're on a plane," he said reassuringly. For all he knew, she had a fear of flying and was gearing for a meltdown. "On the way to Hershey for Vince's wedding, remember?"

"Of course I remember, but…" She broke off and blinked rapidly, rubbing a fist over one eye. "I guess I was…dreaming."

"Must've been one hell of a dream."

"Yeah, it…" With noticeable hesitation, she lifted her chin and met his eyes. "It was."

"Who's the guy?"

"Guy?"

"In your dream." He couldn't help smiling while he shut his laptop. "The way you were sucking on your lip and sighing, I figured there was a guy involved."

She stared at him and blinked again, like she was trying extra hard to focus. "There was no guy."

"Oh." He crossed his arms and grinned. "Even better."

Jules rolled her eyes and fidgeted with the tassels on her shirt. "For your information, I was dreaming about, um, cookies—chocolate chip, to be exact. I was eating cookies and…and getting a hot stone massage."

"In your dream."

She nodded firmly, but her cheeks were bright red and a pinkish marble pattern was creeping up the flesh of her neck.

Talk about a liar's tell.

"Sounds like one lucky cookie."

Her cheeks turned that deep apple red again. "Um, yeah."

Damn man. One lucky cookie, indeed.

"Anyway, we land in an hour."

"Already?" She unbuckled her seat belt, leaned toward him and over his lap to look out the window.

Her hair smelled clean like citrus and girl. Did the rest of her body have the same scent? Suddenly, his mouth went dry, and it wasn't exactly comfortable to have Jules leaning across his lap.

"You, uh, slept most of the way," he said in a louder than necessary voice, hoping it would make her return to her own seat.

"Really?" Finally, she did sit back and encircled the place on her wrist where there probably used to be a watch. "I guess I was exhausted after—"

"Yeah," he said, not needing her to finish.

"Did you get any sleep?"

"Not really. I was working."

"The whole time?"

"I have a meeting at the end of next week. It's important."

She propped an elbow on the arm rest. "So those stories are true, too? You really do work all the time. Vince said you're a workaholic and that's why you don't date properly."

"Only so many hours in the day."

She tugged at her hair, then tucked some behind an ear. "You don't think it's important to make time for personal relationships?"

"Oh, I always make time for those."

She blew out a dramatic groan and rolled her eyes to the ceiling. "I mean real human connections, not meaningless sex."

He cocked an eyebrow. "Meaningless?"

"That's what it is for you, right?" Her volume amplified. "I'm not talking *specifically* about what we did in the hotel last night—*that* was a drunken mistake. And a pretty wheels-off passionate one, judging by how my bra was hanging from the lampshade."

"Shhh." He placed a hand over hers to get her to lower her voice, but she slid it away.

"You're pretty uptight, you know? You can *have* a promiscuous lifestyle but you can't talk about it?" She pulled her knees into her chest. "I'm not judging, I'm just saying."

It was as if the woman was speaking into a live microphone.

"Anyone ever tell you your voice carries?"

"How you live is none of my business, but all those women…"

"You make me sound like James Bond."

"Aren't you?"

He sat up a little taller and straightened the knot of his tie. "Well, I don't want to brag."

"Never mind."

Dexter was done talking, too. It was fun to tease Jules about it, but honestly, last night wasn't a joke. Waking up married in Vegas. How clichéd was that? If it had happened with one of those "other women"—someone he didn't know, but who might actually hold him to those vows—he would've been in deep shit.

Not like this whatever-marriage would last long. The best attorney in Manhattan already set the wheels in motion to fix it as quickly and quietly as possible. Then he'd never have to think about Lady Juliet again, or that black bra, or those sounds she made when she dreamed.

Chapter Four

When Jules went for her bag, Dexter was already carrying it. "Thanks, but I can manage."

"Quiet, little one," he said, a bit ruffled, though letting her go first as they deplaned.

That casual sex talk must've really gotten to him. Why live the life if you're too neurotic to be proud of it? Not her business. Though it was amusing to watch him squirm.

"Luke offered to make the airport run today," Dexter said, "but I told him we'd cab it."

"We?"

"Yes, we," Dexter replied patiently. "Since everyone thinks we're newlyweds, don't you think we should show up together?"

"Right." She nodded. "It's just… I'm not used to people planning or taking charge."

"Independent woman?" he asked with a crooked grin that might've been cute.

"I have to be. Now, especially."

"Why? Because I'm a guy who likes to take charge if only

to make his companion's life easier?'"

She shrugged, even though he'd hit the nail on the head. "Relationship-wise, I don't allow myself to get entangled anymore. It's messy, and I've learned my personality is a bit too codependent." She sighed, wondering why she'd disclosed all that. "So I just don't let it happen. End of story. Self-reliant, self-sufficient."

"And always at a distance," he inserted while studying her face.

Jules was relieved he didn't say more. She didn't need the guy to delve into her screwed-up psyche.

"Baggage claim is this way."

"I know," she said, feeling irritable. Who was she irritated with? Herself? "I've been flying into this airport alone since I was ten."

"Okay, okay." Some of his perfectly combed dark hair was falling across his forehead. For a second, she imagined her fingers pushing it into place, then running through his hair to the back of his head.

Ugh, no. She tried to shoo the image away. It was too similar to the one she'd been mentally replaying as they'd walked through the terminal. Just a snippet from the dream she'd had on the plane. It had felt so real that—even after she'd realized she was awake, and Dexter was beside her, looking at her, just like in the dream—it was almost like it was still happening.

She balled her hands into tight fists, then released them, concentrating on feeling her blood flow, though that didn't stop the movie in her mind from replaying over and over: Dexter Elliott kissing her, sliding his hands up her back, down her ribs, covering her hip bones. The short scene was playing on a loop.

No way had she dreamed that on her own. The only explanation was…

She was remembering last night.

"Jules?"

"Huh?"

Dexter was watching her, and they were at baggage claim. Sure, Jules was great at zoning out and did it pretty frequently, but today she couldn't seem to stay in the here and now even when she'd tried.

"I asked if that's yours." He pointed at the bag on the conveyer belt coming their way. "It matches your carry-on."

"Yes," she said. And again, before she could make a move, Dexter had it.

Calm down, Jules. Do you have to be self-reliant about everything? Allow him to be a gentleman.

"Why don't you get in line for a taxi while I wait for my bag?"

Great plan. She wanted to be away from his pleasing good manners.

The April afternoon air had a chill to it. Jules was so used to the no-sleeves-year-round weather of Las Vegas, she had to think if she brought a jacket. A few minutes later, Dexter appeared, wheeling both suitcases down the walkway. She couldn't help laughing at the way he was talking to himself, probably muttering how he had to be seen with her beat-up beaded suitcase with the peace sign patch.

It did make him look cute, and so comically uncomfortable.

The cuteness and her smile disappeared when she realized he was talking on his Bluetooth. Seriously, could the man not take five minutes off from work? How tedious must life be if it revolved around a job and pitching the next great deal, or hitting the top of the next list or...well, Jules didn't really know what Dexter did for a living, not specifically—a lot of Vince's family info went right out of her head. What she did know was he was the youngest VP at Elliott Tech, and was in line to take over when Braxton Elliott retired.

"Yo! We're next!" she hollered in a loud voice, even though he was obviously trying to listen to the other end of his Bluetooth.

He held up one finger but didn't reply.

Exasperated, she blew out a breath and got in the cab. Still on the phone, Dexter slid in the backseat beside her. "Hershey," he said to the driver. "Derry Woods Hill."

"Not there!" She clutched his arm.

"What?" He peered at her, then said into his Bluetooth, "I'll have to call you back," then took off the earpiece. "It's my parents' house. Where the wedding party is right now. They're probably just finishing lunch."

"We need to make a stop first."

"Why?"

"Because I need to change my clothes."

"You look fine." Dexter punched the back of the front seat. "Let's go," he said to the driver, and the car took off.

"I do not look fine. My shirt is torn." Jules displayed a rip in her sleeve and that the seams at the front of her neck hole were pulled apart. "I'd like to wash my face with my own cleanser, and I'm not wearing any—" She cut herself off.

"Not wearing…?"

She squirmed in her seat and knew she was about to blush, cursing her fair complexion. "Forget it."

He cocked a brow as his eyes traced down her body, making Jules feel warm but uncomfortable under his heavy blue-eyed gaze.

"I asked you to please not do that," she said, crossing her arms, replacing embarrassment with attitude.

"I'm not doing anything."

The image of that dream kiss flashed through her mind, made breathing slightly more difficult. "Let's just get this over with. I have other things to do."

"Don't we all." He sat back and loosened the knot of his tie.

"You missed a button, Mr. Bond. Two, actually. Your tie

was covering it."

"I didn't miss them. They're gone."

"Where?"

He shrugged. "The floor of the limo, maybe. Our hotel room. In the bed."

"Oh. You mean *I* tore open…" It was too mortifying to finish.

"Seems that way." He rested his head back on the seat and closed his eyes. "But I won't charge you for it, since I tore your shirt, too."

Good gracious. What had they done to each other last night? And why couldn't she remember? *Actually, maybe it's better I don't.*

"That's fair," she said.

"Might be a bit awkward when we first get to the house, but it'll be over quickly. I was thinking we should act like we planned on surprising them all along. That way, they'll politely congratulate you, while my brothers give me hell until they've had their fill."

"Sure you can handle that?"

"I've handled rougher. Haven't I?" He nudged her arm. "Oh, and Vince'll threaten to give me a pounding for marrying you."

"He'd beat you up? Why? We haven't dated in eight years and *he's* getting married."

"Big bad player like me corrupting a sweet young thing like you?"

Jules couldn't help chuckling. "How has some woman's older brother not broken your face?"

He touched his nose. "Twice."

"Seriously?"

"Never by an older brother. First time was in college during a mixed martial arts class. And I'm totally cool with that because it was the instructor who's a level-five black belt badass."

"And the second time?"

"Um." He cleared his throat. "That happened at the end of a…bad non-date."

"*Non*-date? What—" She waved a hand. "Never mind. Please go on about the broken nose." She grinned and laced her fingers under her chin.

"I must've said something she didn't like and she probably wanted to pick up a wineglass and splash it in my face, but we were at Starbucks, so she threw her oversize mug at me."

"You mean the coffee in it?"

"No, the whole damn mug. Broke my nose in three places."

"Impressive."

"Worse thing is, it was hot chocolate. No dude deserves to get his nose broken by whipped cream." He shook his head. "I'd been trying to shake off Hershey for years, then cocoa breaks my face."

Jules threw her head back and laughed. Dang, Dexter Elliott was one hilarious big bad player. "So listen, we'll go to your parents' and do the meet-and-greet thing." She paused to breathe through the sudden nervousness in her stomach. "I want to see Vince, of course, and Roxy and Luke, but I have to get to my grandmother's attorney's office. I told him I'd come today. Where's the closest bus stop to your house?"

"How about I take you to the lawyer, then to your grandmother's. But aren't you staying at the house? I thought all the close family guests were. There's plenty of room."

Yes, she'd been officially invited by Vince and Eileen to stay at the Elliott estate all weekend, but she hadn't planned on it. The plan was to stay at Grams's house—*her* house. She'd better start thinking of it as her house, otherwise, signing the official papers would be too painful.

She loved the cottage. Even though the inside had been falling apart for years, it was her favorite place on earth. Everything from the screen-less windows and antique kitchen fixtures to the breakfast nook with the breathtaking view of the lake though the wall of windows. Her favorite place to paint.

If she ever found the inspiration to paint again.

During Jules's last visit, Grams suggested—for the hundredth time—that Jules turn the nook into an art room. It would make a perfect studio thanks to the all-day natural light. Even though Jules had already decided to do it, the thought of gutting the nook now squeezed her heart so much she could cry.

"I already have a place to stay," she said, answering Dexter. "It's not right in Hershey so I'll need to pick up Grams's car. One of her neighbor's kids has been driving it so the battery won't die."

"Why don't you call to say you won't be picking it up today?"

She rubbed her nose. "I don't use my phone unless it's an emergency."

"Oh." Dexter blinked about a hundred times, and wore the same expression everyone wore when she told them she was pretty much technology-free. Dexter flipped his cell in his hands, then rested it on his knee, as if the need to stay connected 24/7 made him keep his phone in sight at all times.

So what if she couldn't Facebook mobile-ly or map app the nearest gastropub? She was doing just fine.

They were quiet the rest of the drive. Even sleeping for almost the whole flight hadn't made her rested or energetic. She was still fighting the hangover and needed a session of yoga like nothing else. When the cab made a sharp left and headed up the hill, her stomach tightened.

"Here we go," Dexter said. "Just remember, this is Vince's weekend—I bet no one pays much attention to us."

"Cool," Jules replied with a nod. She was great with people, could talk to anyone about anything, even the Elliott parents, who seemed so scary when she was a kid. As she got older and realized she was reacting to their big house and money, Jules was never intimidated by them again. Having loads of money didn't mean you were a better person or a kinder person or more artistic or happy.

Jules couldn't think of a happier person than herself, and she didn't have an extra dime to her name. All of her savings would go toward fixing up the cottage. With an extra ten thousand, or twenty times as much, would that make her happier?

Her thoughts were derailed when the cab pulled to a stop. Dexter tucked a credit card into his wallet and was out the door before she could take a breath of preparation. She double-wrapped the strap of her purse around her wrist and followed him to the driveway. Their bags were already on the porch.

"Thanks again," Dexter said to the cab driver, slipping him a bill. "I know it was a long drive." She couldn't see the currency from where she was, but by the way the guy's eyes lit up unbelievingly, it was probably a Benjamin.

At least Dexter believed in taking care of the little people. It always sucked when Jules put her whole body's effort into giving someone an amazing massage, only to get tipped 5 percent.

Dexter walked to the porch. Jules leveled her chin and followed. Without a word, he pushed open the door, placed a hand on the small of her back, and steered her inside the house. Thank goodness she didn't give a crap about money; the sheer size of the place was enough to intimidate a Rockefeller.

But, wait… Would the Elliotts think she was a gold digger for marrying Dexter, overlooking his zillion man-whore red flags?

Too late to consider that now. Instead, she breathed in the welcoming smell of wood polish, candles, and something homey baking.

"They're in the yard," Dexter said.

Jules let him lead her past the living room, down the

hallway, and into the huge, industrial-sized kitchen. He dropped his hand from her to unlatch a set of French doors that opened into the green and spacious backyard. Jules saw only the backs of people—maybe twenty—gathered around an outside bar.

"Oh, my ever-lovin' crap! Look!"

"They're finally here!"

"Time for us to pay up."

Dexter swore under his breath. And Jules really, really wished she was wearing underwear.

· · ·

"Hi," Dexter said with a wave, his confidence slipping a notch. "Hi," he repeated, "um, everyone."

"*Hi?* That's all you have to say?" The next second, he was shoved out of the way by one of Roxy's bony elbows. "Jules, this is too much awesome! Why didn't you tell me?" His sister captured Jules in a bear hug.

Dexter hadn't known they were close friends. Probably should've asked.

"Rox, hey!" Jules said, her voice high-pitched but lacking the usual volume. "Did we totally surprise you or what?"

"Brother." Suddenly, Dexter was enfolded in his own bear hug. Even if he hadn't seen it was Luke, his nose would've known. His recently married brother always smelled like chocolate these days, thanks to his Hershey-employed wife, Natalie. "Congrats. We're all in shock."

"That was our plan," Dexter replied.

"You fooled us all." His brother Danny was now slapping him on the back. "Sneak-attacking at the eleventh hour while hiding a legit, respectable girlfriend. Why does that sound like you?"

"Right?" Dexter forced a big smile, waiting for everyone

to get the congratulatory BS out of their systems.

"Well, well. *Brother*," Vince said, coming up from behind. "I should kick your ass right now. Do you have any idea what you've done?"

"Dude, no." Dexter's muscles clenched. He'd joked with Jules earlier about Vince being pissed, but never considered he'd really care. "It's not what you... Let me explain—"

All three of his brothers busted out in laughter.

"We're just giving you hell, man." Vince grinned. "When did you become such an easy target? I tell ya, though, if it wasn't Jules, I'd think this is a setup so you'd win the bet, but she's one girl who can't be bought, and she's the worst liar ever."

Though Dexter was still miles away from feeling comfortable, they hugged again, while he offered his own wedding congratulations. After all, not screwing up Vince's weekend was the whole point of keeping the Vegas mistake a secret.

At the thought, he scanned the patio. He'd kind of forgotten about Jules.

She was still with Roxy, smiling, though she looked a little freaked around the eyes. Roxy was touching Jules's hair, pointed at her skirt. Girl-talking about what Jules had worn to the wedding.

The same outfit she has on now.

"Dexter."

After plastering on another smile, he turned toward the voice and stepped forward. "Mom," he said, bending down to kiss his mother's cheek.

Before he could unbend, she had his face between her hands and stared him straight in the eyes. "How could you do this?" Her tone was harsh, exactly like the time he'd been busted for throwing an all-night pool party. "I can't believe it."

"Mom, I'm..." he stammered, ready to apologize for...

something.

"Dexter," she said, voice catching. He was horrified when she blinked back a tear. "Oh, Dex. I'm so happy."

"You are?"

"Of course!" She pulled him into a hug and squeezed tight. His mother hadn't hugged him so close or so hard since high school graduation when he'd been valedictorian. Something about that gave him pause.

Had Mom not had reason to be proud of him since then? Not until he came home married to Jules?

"Dex."

The knee-jerk, infantile reaction to the new voice was to emotionally cower. But Dexter was a grown man who made grown-man decisions, so he squared his shoulders and stepped up.

"Hi, Dad," he said, not sure if he should hug him or offer his hand to shake. They hadn't spoken since that phone call a week ago when Dexter had told him he was leaving ET.

In the end, Dexter didn't have to decide how to greet his father, because Dad stuck out his hand—the cold, formal greeting he'd dreaded. Disappointed and swimming in irrational guilt, Dexter forced a smile and civilly shook his father's hand.

"Can we talk?" he asked, leaning forward and dropping his voice. But Dad shook his head an inch and looked the other way. Dexter might've forced the conversation, but Luke and Vince were pounding him on the back again.

So much for no one paying attention.

For the next few minutes, he smiled and bumped fists, accepted more slaps and "you had us so worried" congratulations. Even people from town offered congrats. Eventually, it was just the family again while the rest of the party guests returned to their conversations on the other side of the lawn. The family, except for his father, who'd disappeared.

Dexter had to get him alone sometime in the next two days.

"So? How did this happen?" Mom asked, sparkly eyed.

"How did what happen?" Dexter asked. Like a moron.

"You know." Mom patted the side of her hair. "You and Juliet—*Roxanne*," she snapped across the patio. "Stop monopolizing your new sister-in-law. They've only been married one day, I'm sure she's missing her husband."

Husband? Their eyes found each other. Jules looked as weirded out as Dexter felt. He hadn't even thought the word "husband" yet. Let alone "wife."

Holy hell—he had a damn wife.

"Aww, look at them," Roxy cooed. "They're so cute, staring at each other like no one else exists. Jules, you're shaking. You must sincerely not want to be away from Dex. That's so adorbs, I might vomit."

"Um, yeah," Jules said, hiding her hands behind her back.

Dexter noted the pink marble flush creeping up her neck, so he quickly moved to her side. "Babe, um, sweetheart, I'm here," he said, putting an awkward arm around her, like he'd never touched a woman before. He didn't know what to do next, so he glanced at Luke and Natalie, then at Vince and Maddie, to see how real couples behaved.

Following their lead, he let his arm drop to Jules's waist, pulled her into his side, and absently kissed the top of her head. "All better now?"

"Um-hmm," she exhaled, but he could tell she was biting the inside of her cheek, felt her shaking.

Hold it together, Flower Power.

"So," Luke said, "tell us everything. None of us knew you were dating. Hell"—he paused to chuckle—"I can't think of a more unlikely couple than you two."

"No doubt," Roxy added.

"And I thought we were friends," Vince chimed in, pointing at Jules. "You've been totally holding out on me." He scratched his head. "How long have you been together?"

"Uh." Dexter ran a knuckle over his chin, no idea what to say. He and Jules hadn't discussed their backstory. Like an idiot who didn't know his own family's tendencies, he hadn't counted on the relationship twenty questions game. "Since, um...since..." He glanced at Jules, who'd gone pale.

"Yeah." Roxy grinned. "When did you first hook up?"

"Roxanne," Mom scolded. "Don't pry."

"Mom, it's fine. We're family. Right, Jules? Tell us all the romantic details." Roxy lowered to sit on the grass, eyes glowing. His twenty-one-year-old sister needed to stop watching chick flicks. "Come on, dish!"

"Well," Jules began, "we ran into each other in...in—"

"Vegas," Dexter cut in, figuring they should stick as close to the truth as possible, less chance to slip up. "I was there on business, and we just, kind of, were both there."

"When?" Roxy asked.

Jules opened her mouth, but for a moment, no sound came out. "Sept— um, Oct—Noctober!" she blurted.

Oh, man. This was not good. Jules had warned what a bad liar she was. Here they were fielding questions from the nosiest people in Hershey, and they hadn't come up with fake dating tales to feed them.

Stick close to the truth.

"Last November," Dexter said. "At the airport. We kind of got, um, tangled up." He gave her a squeeze, hoping it would get her to stop shaking. "Remember?"

She nodded noncommittally at first, but then he felt her release a deep breath, tense muscles relaxing. "His cufflink got caught on my shirt." She snorted a little laugh, right on cue. "We couldn't get separated."

"A shirt like you're wearing now?" Roxy asked, pointing

at Jules. "With the fringe?"

Jules tugged one of the strings. "Kind of."

More like the *exact* shirt she had on. There were still fragments of those fringes around his button.

"Did you ask her on a date right then?" Natalie asked, looping an arm through Luke's.

"We went to a bar."

"Restaurant," Jules was quick to correct. "Tex-Mex."

Dexter couldn't help chuckling. "Tex-Mex," he agreed. "Will you ever forget that drink the bartender made for us?"

Jules rolled her eyes dotingly. "How could I?"

"That was potent stuff."

"I'll say. What did the bartender call it?"

"Vegas Sunrise. But it should've been called the great black hole."

Jules snorted again, charmingly. "You could wallpaper a room with that stuff."

He lifted an eyebrow. "We kind of did. I think. Shoopy," he whispered with a wink.

"Shoopy," she whispered back, smiling, her creamy fair cheeks turning an enchanting shade of pink.

Dexter traced his fingers up her spine, under her hair, until he touched skin, until he knew she'd stopped breathing.

Out of the blue, he had a memory flash. Not of the airport or the bar, but of that same square of skin, and how he'd swept her hair away so he could touch it with his mouth. The image was so vivid he had to blink hard to clear it.

When he opened his eyes, Jules's chin was tilted up at him, causing unexpected heat to burn through his chest.

"What about your second date? The big follow-up?"

Dexter blinked again. For a second there, he'd forgotten where he was. He'd been in a bubble with Jules, with just the moment of that memory. He glanced at Roxy, racking his hungover brain for an answer to her question.

"Tell us about it, Jules," Roxy added, a gossip-hungry look in her eyes. "Where'd he take you? Did he come to Vegas or fly you to New York?"

Jules bit her lip as that betraying marble crept up her throat.

"I bet New York," Luke said.

"No, babe," Natalie retorted. "Ten bucks says he took her to Paris on a private plane."

"You think?"

"Wouldn't you do that if you had access to the company jet?"

They both turned to Jules, waiting for an answer.

Dexter was no help, since he couldn't think of the last time he'd been on a proper date, let alone a second date.

"Was it Paris?" Natalie asked, leaning into Luke's side.

"Um," Jules tried again. "Um, yeah. Well, no it was…uh, yuh—*yoga*."

"Yoga?" Roxy said. "Like a class?"

"In Paris?" Natalie added.

"Mmm." Jules nodded.

"You took her to a yoga class on a date?"

"Hold on, back up," Vince said. "The more important question is, Dexter can do yoga? That I *can't* believe."

"Of course he can," Jules said with sudden energy in her voice. "I'd never be with someone who doesn't love yoga as much as I do."

Everyone was gawking at Dexter now, wearing expressions of pure bafflement. Not like he couldn't go along with it now, not after what Jules just professed.

"I love yoga, obsessed with it." He gave her shoulder a pat. "I'm an expert at those, ya know, poses." He quickly flipped through his memory files. "The crane, the warrior, and the uh, the bridge pose."

"The bridge?" Roxy said. "Isn't that the one when you lay

arched on your back, and your pelvis is all the way up? Like *you're* the bridge?"

Yikes. Had Dexter just admitted in front of his brothers that he could arch his damn pelvis?

"Exactly," Jules said, linking her arm through his. "That's his most advanced pose. Right, sweetie?"

Dexter could be a gym rat, but he seriously doubted he'd ever be flexible enough to do that.

"Let's see it," Roxy said, clapping her hands like a happy seal. "Do the bridge pose on the lawn, Dex. Show us!"

No way in hell.

Dexter pinched Jules's back until she squirmed. "Not without my sensei spotting me," he said.

"*Guru*, not sensei, honey pie," she whispered. "Sorry, we're, uh, we're both pretty tired from last night. Isn't healthy to strain any more muscles."

Roxy's eyes went dinner-plate wide. "What muscles did you strain on your wedding night?"

Jules's face drained of more color. So...when the tables were turned, maybe she wasn't as free-speaking about sex as she claimed.

"Our third date was the important one." Dexter jumped in to fill the silence.

"Really?" Roxy grabbed a drink off the table and rose onto her knees. "Why?"

Ugh. He really needed to sit down with Jules and come up with a story. Their first ten dates should get them through this weekend.

Think, Elliott. Think. Where would a normal guy take a normal girl on a third date? "We went ice-skating. Jules loves ice-skating."

"In Las Vegas?" Mom asked.

Dexter swallowed. "Um, yeah. See, I flew into town really late, as a surprise, and the only place open in her neighborhood was an ice rink. It was just closing, actually, but…but I paid the guy to stay open for us, for just an hour." Dexter talked faster, on a roll, the details spilling out like he was watching them in a movie. "So there we were, in the ice rink, all by ourselves except for the Zamboni. Jules laced up her skates and got all bundled up, but since they didn't have my skate size, I jogged beside her around the rink." He high-kneed in place to demonstrate, terribly proud for coming up with something so original on the fly.

"That's a scene from *Rocky*," Luke said.

Crap.

"I did that on purpose—for the date. It's Jules's favorite movie."

"It is?" Mom asked. "A film about boxing?"

"Mmm," Jules said. "I love when he wins at the end."

Luke rubbed his chin. "Rocky loses in the first movie."

"Oh, right. I know." Jules waved a hand. "But I love it when he…he eventually wins. You know?" Her neck was getting alarmingly marbly. What did she say would come next? A hiccup attack?

He needed to end this fast.

"When did you know you were in love?" Roxy asked, toying with the straw of her iced tea. "Who said it first? And how did Dex propose?"

Since his sister had addressed Jules, Dexter figured it was her turn to come up with something. Hopefully not a scene from *Rambo*.

"Well, we knew we were in love at the, uh…" She ran both hands through her hair and held it back from her face, displaying her bright red ears. "And when he proposed, he just sort of…" Her sentence was cut off when she hiccuped three times in a row.

"Dear," Mom said, reaching a hand out to Jules. "Do you feel okay?"

"She's fine," Dexter said.

"Yes, fi—" Another set of hiccups shook her body.

She didn't sound fine, or look fine. The marble was covering her chest and throat, and if she had another hiccup attack, she might start hyperventilating.

"Dex, get her some water—she looks peaked," Mom said. "Have you eaten?"

Jules shook her head.

"For heaven's sake. Vincent, pass me that plate of canapés. Have one, dear." Mom picked up a cracker with something white and orange on top. "Open wide."

Then Dexter stood there and watched his mother literally hand-feed Jules.

"Better?"

Jules nodded as she chewed, but suddenly she slapped a hand over her mouth and dashed into the house. Silence hung in the air as they stared after her.

"We didn't eat on the plane and came straight here," Dexter explained, sliding his hands in his pockets. "She's just hungry or tired or…" *Or what?* "I'll go check."

He left his family and followed where Jules had run into the hallway. She was pacing in a circle, shaking out her hands and muttering at the floor.

"You all right?"

"No. I'm not." Her voice was so loud it echoed off the walls.

"Shhh. Come on, don't blow this."

"I told you I'm a terrible liar—it makes me physically ill, you saw that. I especially don't like lying to my friends. I had no idea what to say to them."

"That was my fault. We should've talked first." Now he was shaking out his hands like Jules. "We didn't take the time to figure out a story to tell them."

"Well, I can't do that now," she said, getting pink-faced

and twitchy.

"I couldn't agree more. It looks like you're having a meltdown. We can't let them see you like this." He thought for a moment. "Are you stable? Okay to drive?"

"Drive?"

"Come with me." He put an arm around her and ushered her to the front door, grabbing a set of keys from a long panel of hooks. "My car is the black Bimmer out front. Take it and drive around for a while, clear your head. Better yet, go to your lawyer's office. That's a logical excuse, at least, for why you're gone." He placed the keys in her hand. "Meet me back here and we'll find a private spot to figure out what to do next. Okay?" He waited for her to nod. "Go now before someone else comes to check on you."

The strain on her face relaxed, and she wasn't nearly as flushed. Though he did kind of like that flush.

"Thanks." She took the keys, grabbed her purse from another hook, and walked out without looking back.

Dexter watched from the front porch. He only cringed a little when she ground into second gear. After his car had disappeared down the driveway, he let out a long breath, brushed down the front of his jacket, squared his tie, and went to face the family. By now, they should be back to fawning over Vince and Maddie—the honored couple.

But the second he stepped onto the patio, he knew he was wrong. His parents and siblings, along with their significant others, stood in a line, staring at him.

"Sorry about that," Dexter said. "She's a little...we're both overwhelmed. I think it's best if you keep me and Jules and, um, *everything* a secret for now. Is that cool?"

His mom stepped forward from the group, holding both hands over her heart. "Dexter," she said, breaking into a smile. "Why didn't you tell us Juliet's pregnant?"

Chapter Five

Once Jules was down the hill, she finally took a deep breath, a few of them. *In through the nose, expand the belly, fill the chest, out through the nose.* Since no one else was on the road, she put the car in park at a four-way stop and just sat.

That was the most awkward situation she'd ever been in. They better get their story straight before she had to face the Elliotts again.

Though she'd never been good at lying, there were moments when it wasn't so bad. Like when she and Dexter had talked about their fake first date. The Tex-Mex restaurant, those drinks, and all the while, Dexter had slid his hand up her back, making her relaxed and calm and…something else.

Jules closed her eyes, thinking more about that touch, and how it had felt so familiar that she knew where his hand would go next. No doubt about it, she was remembering another part of last night.

Before her memory could advance any further, she jumped a mile when the car behind her honked. She jammed into gear and continued down the road, heart pumping fast, palms sweaty. Not out of fear, but from whatever that "something else" was.

There couldn't be a "something else" with Dexter. Well, apparently there had been for maybe five seconds last night when neither of them knew what they were doing. But there would never be again. Even if she wasn't already dead-set against falling in love or emotionally losing herself over a guy, that guy would never be womanizer Dexter.

No reason to think about his hands or that kiss.

Was it their first kiss? No, that had been in the limo. At least that was a solid memory.

Grrr. Doesn't matter. Stop thinking about it.

With one hand, Jules grabbed her purse and fished for the business card in the side pocket, refreshing her memory of where the law office of Quentin Sanders was located. It was right off Main Street, so Jules drove past the streetlights shaped as silver Hershey's Kisses, then hung a right on Cocoa Avenue. She pulled into the lot, making sure not to park too close to another car. Dexter's BMW was worth more than she'd make in a year doing massages.

The office suites were on the fourth floor, and she took the stairs, needing to burn off energy and get a little cardio in after sitting for so long. No joke, she really was sore from last night.

No one was in the lobby. No one at the reception desk either, though voices came from down the hall.

"Hello? Anybody home?"

"One second," someone answered back.

Out of habit, she smoothed down her hair that was always unsmoothable and played with the key ring until she heard footsteps. "Hi," she said to a guy in a suit. "My name's Juliet Bloom. I'm here to see Quentin Sanders."

"You're looking at him."

Jules eyed the guy. "The Quentin Sanders I spoke with on

the phone sounded a lot older."

"That must've been my father. I'm Quentin Junior. Call me Quent. Dad and I share a practice. Sorry, he doesn't have many clients left, so I assumed you meant me."

"Oh." Jules smiled, even though the nervous tremble in her stomach was still trembling away. At least now she wouldn't have to hire her own lawyer to fight that clause in Grams's will. "Is your father here? I just got into town and we had a standing appointment. He said I could drop in whenever I arrived."

Quent rubbed his chin. "When was the last time you spoke to him?"

"A week ago."

"Oh." He scratched his head. He was kind of a fidgety guy. "There's a problem. My father's in Reykjadalur."

Jules's mouth fell open. "Iceland?"

"The hot springs help his arthritis, so he goes whenever he… Sorry, anyway, Dad's not here. I'm sorry you came all this way."

"But I've got to sign papers. He's my grandmother's lawyer—or was. Grandma died and left me her house in the will. The reading was two months ago but I couldn't be here for that *and* the funeral—I couldn't be away from work that long. But I know Grams left it to me, we talked about it, then your father called and said there was one legal matter I had to see him about before I can take ownership."

Jules already knew what that one legal matter was…

Quent nodded. "If it's just that, your signature will be sufficient, and I can notarize. Just have to find your grandmother's folder. Come back to my office."

Feeling antsy, Jules followed him down a hall. If something went wrong with getting Grams's cottage, where would she live? She'd already given notice at the spa and told her landlord she'd be out at the end of the month. If she couldn't get the cottage, she'd be homeless.

And who goes to Iceland for arthritis therapy, anyway?

"Have a seat," Quent said. "Sorry, what was your grandmother's name?"

"Rosemary Granger."

"Rosy?"

"You knew her?"

"She was one of Dad's oldest friends. He was very sad about her passing. I'm sure he wishes he could be here to do this himself."

"Thanks," Jules said, touched.

"I'll find the files and be right back." A few minutes later, he reappeared and sat behind a big desk. "Okay," he said, flipping through papers in a folder. "Ah, here it is, and a Post-it with your name on it."

Quent ran a finger over the pages, mumbling as he read to himself. "Right. Okay. Rosy left one Juliet Bloom her primary residence at 32 Lakeview Drive. Oh wow, it's really close to the water."

"The back deck faces Conewago Lake." She couldn't help smiling, remembering the dozens of times she and Grams had dragged chairs all the way out to the shore and hung out at the lake all day.

"Are you going to keep it or sell?"

"Sell?" Jules was affronted. "I'd never sell Grams's house."

"I was wondering, because you could probably get the upper five hundreds for it. Depending on its condition."

This made Jules laugh under her breath. "The condition isn't great, but I don't care. It's been my summer home for as long as I can remember. What did you mean by upper five hundreds?"

"Five hundred thousand dollars if it was on the market."

Jules's jaw dropped.

"A place near the water in today's economy, people are buying vacation homes again, driving up prices."

Jules couldn't speak. Did Grams know she was sitting on a property worth half a million dollars? Probably not. Grams cared as much about money as Jules did—which was nothing.

"I plan on making some minor renovations," she finally said. "To make it my own. Grams wanted me to."

"Well then, let me finish reading the details of the will. You have your ID?"

"Driver's license, social security card, and birth certificate."

"Perfect. I'll, um… Oh, huh. This is odd."

Here it comes.

"There seems to be a, well there's a stipulation regarding your inheritance."

"Stipulation?" She hoped her voice didn't squeak.

"A rather specific one. Looks binding, though. It's in regards to your marital status. You don't get your grandmother's house unless you're married."

Showtime.

"Oh, that?" She waved a hand and crossed her legs. "Yes, Grams could be eccentric about some things. Old-fashioned. Who knows why she put that in the will. Moot point, though— I'm married." She held up her left hand, wiggling her fanned out fingers, that gold band flashing under the fluorescent lights.

Though it was technically a true statement, Jules felt her neck start to sweat, and her cheeks were probably bright red. If she started hiccupping, the guy would get suspicious.

Unfortunately, among other things, nerves made her overly chatty. At the worst possible times.

"We got married yesterday." She bit the inside of her cheek. "This morning, actually. We flew to Las Vegas. Well, no, *he* did, I live there, so we just sort of met up and…" Now her face was getting hot, and her neck was surely marbling like hell. "I have the license to prove it. Um, no, Dexter does. I'll show it to you."

"Dexter?"

"Elliott."

Quent sat back in his chair and dropped his pen on the desk. "*You* married Dexter Elliott. Today."

"Yes?" *Crap, crap, crap. At least sound sure about it.*

"I've known Dexter my whole life." His expression changed. Instead of a sweet estate lawyer, he looked like an ambulance chaser. "Well now. Small world."

Jules fidgeted in her seat. "Can I sign, and you give me the key to the house and…"

"You can sign now, sure, but I also need the signature of your husband. Bring him by next week. We're closed Monday."

Jules couldn't wait until next week. She had to take ownership of the house today, or blow unnecessary money on a hotel. She didn't have that extra ten grand yet, after all.

"Would it be possible to take the papers to him? I know it's Saturday, but he's just as anxious to get the cottage. I can sort of run them up to the house, have him sign, then bring them right back. Will that work?"

"No can do." Quent eyed her in a suspicious way, almost as if he wanted to bust her. "I have to be there as witness."

"Can you come with me? You expense mileage, right? Just bill me for however long it takes. It's not far from here— you can follow me."

"I know exactly where the Elliotts live."

"Please?" Jules tried not to sound as fretful as she felt. "It would mean so much to me." She smiled at him and tilted her head, but then remembered she was a married woman and wasn't supposed to be smiling like that at other men. "To the both of us, Dex and me."

He looked at her for a second, then finally nodded. "Sure. It's been a few years since I've seen old Dex. Wouldn't mind dropping in on the Elliotts. It's been even longer since I've been up to their place."

"Great! No time like the present!" Her voice was way too high and squeaky. She tried to calm down as she walked with Quent outside. He was parked in back of the office building and said he'd meet her at the house.

Jules slammed into reverse, knowing she needed to get to Dexter before Quent, needed two seconds to explain the situation. Would he totally flip out, thinking she'd planned to…what? Roofie him into marrying her so she could inherit a house? Why not? She'd suspected, on even a tiny level, that he'd done the same thing to win the bet.

The Bimmer roared down the street, tires screeching as she made a sharp left. At an annoyingly long red light, she fished through the bottom of her purse, feeling for her tiny flip phone. This was definitely an emergency. Crap, man—the thing was as dead as Hamlet. She tossed it on the passenger seat and floored it the rest of the way.

The space where the BMW was parked earlier was still open, so Jules pulled in, set the brake, then ran full speed up the driveway, nearly tripping over her long skirt. Tires crunched on gravel behind her. Shoot—Quent.

Without bothering to knock, she pushed through the front door.

Voices came from the kitchen, but she didn't hear Dexter's. Panting, she crept down the hall and peered out the window to the backyard. There he was, holding a beer and talking to Luke. This was her only shot, and managing to pull him away from one Elliott was better than a whole pack of them. With heart racing, she poked her head out the French doors.

"Psst. Dex." But he was oblivious. "Dexter," she called in a hissy whisper. As her excellent karma would have it, Luke punched Dexter's shoulder and walked off. Jules didn't waste a second before flying out the door, grabbing his arm and pulling him away. "I need to"—she paused to pant—"talk to you."

"Hey." His brow furrowed as he looked behind her. Her behavior must've made it seem like she was being chased. "Why do you look so—"

"Shhh. Shut up." She yanked his arm. This time he followed as she tugged him around the corner behind a tree. "Lawyer," she said, still out of breath. "Signature…yours… Iceland."

"Say what?" Dexter stepped back and stared. "What are you talking about?"

"The cottage. Grams…husband, you have to…sign."

"Oh." He ran a fist across his forehead, miraculously able to decipher her nonsentences. "Since we're married, I have to sign?"

Close enough. She held her breath and nodded.

"Okay, okay. Did you bring it with you? It's fine, I'll sign now and we'll figure out the legal stuff later. Oh, but first, there's something I have to tell you, and you're not going to like it." When he put his warm, heavy hands on both her shoulders, it slowed her down—the same way it did in her memory of them together. The strength of his hands. Their weight. "You know how you ran out of here earlier like you were about to be sick?"

"I was sick," Jules said. "Sick of lying."

"I know. Everyone saw that and now… It's kind of funny if you think about it, but they assumed you're—" He cut off and stared at something over her shoulder. That concerned look in his eyes was replaced by fury. "What the hell is he doing here?" he said in a voice so sharp she felt it in her spine.

Jules turned to see lawyer Quent coming around the corner.

"Well, well, Dexter Elliott. I hear congratulations are in order."

...

The moment he laid eyes on Quentin Sanders, a hot wrath burned under Dexter's collar that he hadn't felt in years.

"What are you doing here?"

Quent smiled like a used-car salesman. "Offering my best wishes," he said and extended his hand. Dexter didn't acknowledge it.

Maybe that was why Jules was acting so freaked—trying to warn him that Quent was here. But why would she think to warn him? How would she have any idea about their past? Vince didn't know. Had Roxy told her? Not possible. His sister still didn't know the truth.

Begrudgingly, Dexter stepped away from Jules and shook his hand, mainly because other people on the patio could see them now, and it wouldn't be good manners to punch the guy out in front of the mayor.

"Thanks," Dexter said. *Offering best wishes, my ass. The guy hasn't had a sincere bone in his body since high school.* "This is Jules."

"I've met your wife. We came from my office together."

"*Your* office?" He glanced at Jules. She wasn't red and marbly and hiccuppy like before, but there was definitely something urgent happening with her face.

He took a second to recall what she'd said when she grabbed him a minute ago, looking all flushed and breathless. For a moment then, he couldn't help staring into her eyes, big and green and earnest, her fingers digging into his arm. Something about Iceland and lawyers. Oh, right. She needed his signature.

"*He's* the attorney handling your grandmother's estate?"

"Yes," she said, sounding a little calmer.

"Okay." He cleared his throat and looked at Quent. "Do you have something for me to sign? Let's go inside to the study."

"I thought we should talk first," Quent said. "I've been practicing law less than a year, so I owe the estate and my firm due diligence."

"About…?"

He lifted another used-car salesman smile. "For all I know, your marriage is a sham."

Automatically, Dexter's stomach and jaw tightened. "Why would you say that?"

"Coincidental. Juliet *happens* to inherit a house worth an easy five hundred grand, but only if she married."

"Half a mil?" Dexter looked at her.

She was pale again and knotting the front of her shirt. Dammit. His new wife shouldn't look so uncomfortable around her husband. Not if Quent was watching their every move.

"Honey," he said, cupping her elbow, gazing as deeply into her eyes as he could.

Bring it down, Flower Power. Easy, easy. Do one of your yoga mantras.

"She told me you two got married in Las Vegas—this morning." Quent scratched under his chin. "This is where the coincidence gets real."

"So?" Dexter crossed his arms, widened his stance. "Do you doubt my *wife*? Or me?" He kept his eyes focused on the newbie lawyer he'd known for nine unfortunate years. "You know *I'm* not the one who tells false stories for kicks."

Okay, yes, Dexter was currently in the middle of a whopper of a false story, but the difference between him and Quent was that Quent told lies to hurt people on purpose.

Specifically—Roxy.

Quent didn't even blink at the comment. "Why should I believe you? There's a lot of money at stake."

"Five hundred g's?" Dexter scoffed. "You think that

amount means anything to me?"

"Hey, this has nothing to do with money," Jules said, annoyance in her voice.

Dexter put a hand on the small of her back and dipped his mouth to her ear. "Let me handle this," he whispered. "Okay, Shoopy?" It took a moment, but when she finally unclenched her teeth, Dexter slid his arm around her.

"Look," he said to Quent, "you have no idea about our relationship or how long we've been together. You come to this house and insult us on the day we get married, the day before my brother gets married, while my entire family is here."

"Your *entire* family?" Quent said, cocking an eyebrow.

That was it. Dexter saw red, and he was two seconds from throwing the guy out with his bare hands. "Don't," he snarled under his breath. "Do not go there."

Finally, Quent's smug expression flinched.

"If you have something for me to sign," Dexter added after a beat, "I suggest you hand it over, then get the hell off this property. You're trespassing."

"She invited me." He pointed at Jules.

"She didn't *know*."

Quent reached into the inside pocket of his suit.

"Not here," Dexter said. "In the study." He splayed his fingers across Jules's back and they all started to walk.

"Dex?" his mother called, stepping onto the patio, holding a drink and wearing a Kentucky Derby-type sun hat. "What's going on?"

"Nothing. Wedding present for us."

"Really?" Roxy followed Mom outside, and Dexter almost pushed his unwelcome guest out of sight. But it was too late. "Quent!"

More fiery red crowded his vision as he watched his little sister once more naively rush to Quent's side. He couldn't compute what they were saying to each other; maybe his brain was purposefully blocking it out.

What Dexter did know was at some point, he'd taken Jules's hand, and was probably gripping it past the point of comfort. She didn't say anything, only slid her free hand around his biceps, standing close.

Like a real wife would to offer support to her husband.

"Seems more congratulations are in order," Quent said, addressing Dexter.

"More?" Dexter said, concentrating harder on Jules's hand.

"The good news." He turned his attention to Jules. "You're pregnant."

"*What?*" Jules gasped.

"*What?*" Dexter barked, then looked at his mother. "I told you, I told everyone that wasn't why." When he felt Jules tug his arm, he explained. "You ran out of here earlier, all pale and nauseous, so naturally they jumped to the hastiest conclusion—like always."

"But…" Jules shook her head, still bewildered. "You weren't here then," she said to Quent. "Who told you?"

Quent didn't say a word, but his eyes slid to Roxy.

Oh, that's just great!

"Rox," Jules said like a disappointed big sister.

Roxy shrugged. "Sorry, I didn't mean to say anything."

"You've never been able to keep a secret," Dexter said impatiently. "Even one that isn't true."

"Sorry."

Despite how he'd told Roxy straight-up that Jules wasn't pregnant, his gossipy sister was already spreading the rumor like it was front-page news. And to the one person who definitely couldn't discover their marriage was indeed a sham.

Jules (and probably he) could be in a lot of trouble.

If he'd thought for a second that he could tell his family

the truth this weekend, he knew now there was no way he'd chance it.

"Anyway," Roxy said. "What is it?"

Jules sighed. "Neither, Rox. There's no baby. We just told you—"

"No." She giggled. "What's the wedding gift you're signing for?"

"My grandmother's cottage in Mount Gretna. But it's not a wedding pres—"

"The one on the lake?" Vince cut in.

Cool. The Elliott mob again. Super. For a second, Dexter wondered if he should repeat—again—that there was no bouncing baby on the way. Hopefully the topic would simply die off.

"She left it to me in her will."

"Jules was about to sign the papers." He squeezed her hand. "Quent was kind enough to personally deliver them so we can get it taken care of. The papers, Quentin?" Dexter prompted. No reason to duck inside, not while the gang was gathered.

Quent drew a few folded documents, smoothed them out, then handed a pen to Jules. She signed the four spots with signature flags and passed the pen to Dexter. If he had time to read through the whole thing, he would have, but right now, he wanted Quent the hell away from him, his family, and Roxy.

He signed the last page, then handed everything back.

"Thank you very much." Quent slid the pen into his pocket. "I'll bring the copies over."

"Fax them to my office," Dexter said.

Quent bowed his head. "You'll get them next week."

Dexter gave him a look he knew Quent would correctly interpret, and finally, without another word, the guy left.

"Thank you," Jules whispered under her breath.

He was about to say, *No, thank* you *for holding my hand*

and helping me not come unglued. But when he looked at her, she had so much gratitude in her eyes that he was taken aback. Now, he wanted to say, *You're welcome.* Then he wanted to…

Well, he wished they were in that Vegas limo, Jules on his lap, kissing the hell out of him.

"I totally remember your grandma's lake house," Roxy said. "It's so retro cool."

"I know, I love it," Jules said. "It's falling apart a bit, and I planned on doing a little renovating next year, but I think I can do it sooner now." Without her having to even glance at him, Dexter knew she meant that she could do it because of the bet money. Good, at least something positive would come of their mess. "I'm turning the back of the house into an art studio."

"For painting?"

It took a moment, but Jules finally nodded in acknowledgment. Seemed no one besides him noticed the split-second expression of fear that had crossed her face. Why did the thought of painting cause that? A moment later, however, she and smiled, her face illuminating so much that Dexter couldn't look away.

"Are you fixing it up to live there?"

Jules nodded again, and her expression slipped into that appealing dream state. It was almost contagious.

Dexter was halfway caught up in that look, until he realized something…

If his family knew Jules intended to live at the lake house, wouldn't they assume Dexter would live there, too?

It was impossible. He was pitching to the final investors on Friday, the meeting that for weeks he'd been preparing for…his big chance at breaking out on his own. He didn't have time to worry about a house or a wife.

They hadn't lasted one day and their plan was already unraveling.

Chapter Six

"Excuse us," Dexter said, taking Jules by the hand. "Baby and I need alone time."

It didn't take a book on "how to read Dexter Elliott's sarcasm" for Jules to interpret his tone. A little too cheerful with just a liiiittle too much edge. Before she could reply, he was dragging her into the house.

"I'm sorry," she said as she was being towed. "I tried to get here before Quent so I could explain."

"I don't care about that. I told you I'd sign anything."

"Oh, Dexter!" sweet Mrs. Elliott called. "Juliet!"

Dexter blew out a loud exhale, muttered under his breath, then turned around. "Yes, Mom?"

"So much for alone time," Jules whispered, then elbowed him in the ribs. "And be nice to your mother. Considering everything, she's being a trooper."

"Hi, you two." Mrs. Elliott smiled and straightened her enormous sun hat. "Before you disappear, I've made up your bedroom. Your father and I aren't so over the hill that I don't remember what it's like to be newlyweds, those early stages of passionate love.'"

"Mom…" Dexter cleared his throat and looked at the floor. Was Mr. Man-Whore blushing?

"I made space in the closet and the dresser. You're staying here with us all weekend, aren't you? For the wedding? Your bags are upstairs."

"I'm sorry, Mrs. Elliott, but—"

"Eileen," she corrected. "We're family."

Jules swallowed and felt on the brink of a hiccup attack. "Eileen, yes. It's sweet of you to offer, but I, um, *we'll* be staying at Grams's house—my house, um, ours. At the lake."

"Oh?" Eileen's happy expression crumpled like a wadded piece of paper. "So far away?"

"Mom, it's a fifteen-minute drive."

"What about the party? Cocktails at five. Surely it'll be easier to stay here tonight so you don't have to drive back and forth. No discussion—I insist. See, the caterers are already setting up. We have them all weekend. You know how jam-packed the next few days are." She touched Dexter's hand. "Don't upset your mother, and stay here tonight without a fuss."

"Well…" Dexter looked at Jules. "My sweetie was just telling me to be extra nice to you this weekend, so of course we'll stay."

Jules stiffened but knew she couldn't renege now. The giant monster, trapping her like this.

"Juliet, fresh towels are in the en suite, and call Mr. Decker through the intercom if you need anything ironed."

All Jules could do was nod, openmouthed.

"See you outside in an hour," Eileen added, happily sashaying toward the kitchen.

"Close your mouth, dear." Dexter put a finger under Jules's chin and pressed it up.

She knocked his hand away, but a masochist side of her

wanted to giggle at how their web of lies kept expanding. "What's your next bright idea? And who's Mr. Decker?"

"The butler, and keep it down—your voice goes through walls like a wrecking ball."

"This *is* me keeping it down."

He took her hand and gave a tug. She had no choice but to follow him up a switchback staircase, past the second-floor landing, and to the third floor. It was quite a hike. "Inside," he said, pushing open a door at the end of the hall.

"Whoa, looks like Sports Authority threw up in here," Jules said, scanning the sports memorabilia filling the room. "The Phillies, the Eagles and the 76ers I recognize." She stopped in front of a pendent. "But I've never heard of the Souls." She smiled over her shoulder at him. "If they're a professional team of athletic palm readers, I approve."

"Arena football, and they're pretty good." He pulled at the knot of his tie. "At least they were when I was in high school."

"You're not into sports anymore?"

"Don't have time to follow it all like I used to. I catch a few games with my brothers when I can, but it's been a while."

"You should make time for things like that. Enjoy life instead of spending it on a Bluetooth."

"Your opinion is noted, wifey dear." He slid off his tie and unbuttoned the cuff of his shirt.

Jules stepped back—this felt oddly familiar: Dexter by a bed, removing his clothes… "What are you doing?"

"What does it look like? It's my bedroom."

"Dexter." She exhaled patiently. "We might be stuck in here tonight, but that doesn't mean anything goes like in Vegas."

"Anything goes?" He cocked an eyebrow. "Are you starting to remember last night?"

"Not at all," she shot back. And huh, her pulse didn't even

stutter. Maybe she could lie without giving it away, after all. "I'm just saying, we have to have rules."

"I don't want to get into that now. What I really need is a shower."

Jules allowed herself to feel the grime of two days, and heartily agreed. "Me, too."

"Shall we?" He nodded at a door.

"Don't even, player. Hands off."

He snickered boyishly, the corners of his eyes crinkling. "Apart from the obvious string of messes, you've had me on the brink of laughing all day. You're easy to hang with, and you're a cool girl—*woman*, er, you know what I mean."

Without warning, Jules's heart fluttered, and her insides went kind of soft and gooey.

Gooey for Dexter? What the what?

"Okay, fine," he said. "I'll give you our bathroom and grab a shower down the hall." He took off his jacket, draped it over the back of a chair, then began unbuttoning his shirt until Jules saw his collarbones, chest hair, the lines of a flat stomach…

Finally, her heart rate took off.

"Then we'll meet back here and come up with our story," he added. "Okay?"

Jules swallowed and looked away, grabbing her bag. "'Kay." She fled into the bathroom, shut the door, locked it, then sat on the edge of the tub, trying to clear her mind. But every time she blinked, she saw Dexter taking off his tie, his coat, his shirt.

After she banished that vision, her thoughts took over… How sweet he was to his mother, the enviably close relationship he had with his siblings. Mostly though, Jules thought about how Dexter had reached for her hand when Quent had shown up. He'd squeezed it hard, and she hadn't even minded. Something about Quent being there had upset

Dexter, and he'd gone to her for emotional—though silent—support.

Making her go gooey all over again.

The hot shower felt amazing, and Jules took extra time to scrub every inch of her body clean. With her damp hair in a towel, she listened at the door to see if Dexter was back. Not a sound, so she entered the empty bedroom.

It really was a shame he wasn't into sports anymore. Why would he seemingly give up so easily something that he loved?

None of Jules's business, though. If she really were his wife, then maybe she'd worry, or do something to help fill that youthful void.

She pulled out the dress she was wearing tonight and hung it on the back of the closet door. It probably *could* use a steam from Mr. Decker, but the crushed cotton and velvet piping was supposed to look wrinkled. She flipped her hair out of the towel and was about to comb it out when the door swung open and Dexter's bare chest strode in.

Instead of shrieking like she wanted, she turned her back and made sure her towel was secure around her body. "Ever heard of knocking?"

"How would that look? We're married."

"I *know*." Slowly she turned around and tried very hard to not notice that he wore nothing but a towel around his waist. "I was just surprised."

She felt his eyes bore into the place where her towel was knotted, and then places where there was no towel. It made her feel tingly, and he wasn't even touching her.

Okay, fine, she was attracted to him. And unless she was reading him all wrong, he was attracted to her. So what? Even if she did have the occasional gooing-of-the-heart that had nothing to do with his looks, there was absolutely no way they could have a legit relationship—he was a man-whore and a workaholic, while she vowed to live free from emotional entanglements that came with love.

"Anyway," Dexter said, turning his eyes away. "While I was in the shower, I was thinking about what our story might be."

Jules certainly did not feel tingly again at the idea of Dexter thinking about her while in the shower. "Cool."

"Thus far, the only things people know are that we got together in November and had a few dates."

"Did you consider why we didn't tell anyone back then?" Jules asked, turning to the mirror to comb her hair before it dried completely. "Or is it common for you to date women and not talk about it? Oh, sorry—*non*-date." She glanced at his reflection to find him looking down and smiling.

"Correct, since I don't *date*, not with girlfriends and whatnot, no one asks who I'm seeing. I suppose we can go with that—since they didn't ask, I didn't tell."

"It'll never fly," Jules said. "You have a sister and mother who are totally into love and who's dating who. There's no way they haven't asked you about it in the last six months."

"You're right." He shrugged. "Though I don't pay attention to that."

"Too many women to count?"

He sat on the edge of the bed. "Maybe we can spin it that way. We'll say I didn't tell them about our raging love affair for fear of jinxing it."

"Not bad. I can use the same excuse for why I never told Vince or Rox. Your poor, cold, and dead relationship ego was so fragile, I didn't want to make any sudden movement and scare you away." She couldn't help laughing.

"Funny," Dexter said. "Okay, what comes next in a relationship?"

Jules had to think for a second. "Exclusivity. Love."

Dexter chuckled. "Like I have experience with either."

That was sad, actually. At least Jules had had experience

with both, even though they hadn't ended as good experiences.

"We're working with six months, right?" Dexter added, rubbing his freshly shaved jaw. Jules could smell the aftershave from clear across the room. Not because it was strong and repelling, but because it was mouthwateringly sexy. "How long are normal couples together, exclusively, before they get married?"

"I don't know," Jules admitted, dotting her face with tinted moisturizer. "A long time, I'd hope."

"We'll say we became exclusive after a month—"

"One month?"

"Too fast?"

She felt icy goose bumps break out on her skin. "For me, at least."

"We have to squeeze our whole dating life into six months. Should it be we fell in love fast then finally got married, or should it have happened gradually then we got married on a whim? Which seems more plausible?"

"Jeepers, you're so analytical. Can't we say we're going with the flow?"

"No," Dexter said while buffing an already-shiny black shoe with a towel. "You might be all flower-child free, but I'm not. No one would believe I'm 'going with the flow.'"

"Fine." She rubbed lotion over her elbows. "We'll say it happened fast, the falling in love part. That way getting married won't seem so..."

"Reckless."

She lifted her eyes to look at his reflection. "Exactly."

They were both quiet. Was he also pondering over how they'd been beyond reckless last night?

"Now that that's settled," Dexter said, "what should I know about you? Suppose I offer to get you a cocktail and I have no idea what you drink?"

"I don't drink all that often—despite my recent behavior.

I'd rather have water with peppermint oil."

"Oil?"

"Or lemon. Maybe lavender. Depends on my mood."

"Peppermint water. Hmm." He smiled. "That does sound nice. Heated?"

"That's how I usually take it. I'll make you some after the party."

"Yeah? Thanks." His smile broadened. "Now let's pretend for two seconds you're not the most peculiar woman alive and that you do enjoy a cocktail at a cocktail party. Wine?"

"Gives me heartburn. And I'm not *peculiar*. I'm a free spirit."

"What about beer, free spirit?"

She made a face.

"Scotch?"

"Do I look like a sixty-year-old congressman?"

"If I'm overly analytical, than you're peculiar and complicated."

"I'll take that as a compliment."

"We'll say you only drink champagne. That way you won't need a glass until the toast. We don't want to give credence to the pregnancy rumor, after all."

"Good thinking."

Dexter chuckled, looked away, then turned back. "You won't forget about making me the warm peppermint drink, will you?"

No, heart. No more gooing. In fact, tell the guy he can make his own nighttime hot toddy.

"Of course I won't forget."

• • •

It had been hard enough trying not to look at Jules at the hotel this morning. At least that sheet had left something to the imagination. But being in the same room with her while she wore nothing but a towel and her hair half damp hanging over her shoulders…

She was smart, too. Quick-witted, and she made him laugh, made him want to hold her hand and squeeze if he ever needed to.

He might not want to be married, but that didn't mean he minded hanging out with her, maybe share just one kiss—for old time's sake.

Suddenly, his childhood bedroom felt way too small and stifling.

"I'll just grab my stuff and get dressed in the bathroom."

"Why?" Jules was humming while running a comb through her long mermaid hair. Hell, she might as well be sitting on a rock singing a Disney song.

He swallowed. "Don't you want privacy?"

"It's fine. Not like I want to jump your bones, Dexter."

"I know…" He broke off and forced out a deep exhale. All right, so maybe *he* needed to be away from her towel-covered body more than she needed to be away from his. Fine. He'd been with top models in Manhattan. No need to get tied in knots over Jules Bloom.

And just like that, he dropped his towel. "Getting back to building our story," he said conversationally, "you were going to tell me about yourself. We've covered the champagne and your love of oils. What else should I know?"

"My birthday's June twenty-second, making me a Cancer, but I was two weeks late—you know what *that* means."

"Not a clue," Dexter said, pulling a clean and pressed shirt from his bag.

"It means I was born to be a Gemini." She paused to laugh and set down her comb. "I might be indecisive and talk too much, but nothing like a Gemini. Cancers can be tenacious, but our element is water not air, so obviously… *Dexter*!" She flung a hand over her eyes and spun around. "You can't walk around like that."

At her reaction, he felt a victorious smile curl his mouth. "Thought you didn't want to jump my bones."

"I don't!"

"So what's the problem?"

"Dexter." She pointed in the general direction of what his towel should be covering. "You're taking up my personal space." The parts of her face he could see were turning pink. The roguish tease in him enjoyed watching her unravel. When he did nothing to alter the cause of her complaint, she marched over to him, keeping tight eye contact, picked up the towel, and threw it at him.

It bounced off his stomach and hit the floor.

"Be polite," she growled, gripping the knot of her own towel.

This girl. Everything out of her mouth made him want to smile. "Oh, my not being polite is what this is about?"

"Dexter," she said, not using her inside voice. "Don't make me…"

"What?" he asked when she didn't finish. "That sounds like a challenge. I'll bet you—"

"Dex?" There was a knock. "Jules? Anything wrong?" Suddenly, the door was opening, and Dexter's sister was about to walk in on him wearing absolutely nothing.

Without thinking, he grabbed Jules around the waist and pulled her to his chest.

"What are you—"

"Shhh, hold on," he whispered, then fell backward onto the bed, Jules landing on top of him.

A second later, he heard Roxy squeak in alarm. "Oh, sorry! I'm sorry!"

Breath momentarily knocked out of him, Dexter answered in a hoarse voice. "What did you expect when you walk into two newlyweds' bedroom without knocking?"

"I did knock. I thought I heard...loud voices."

When Jules tried to roll off him, he was forced to hold her tighter to keep her in place. "That was us." He ran a hand down her spine, sliding it under the towel that had slid halfway down her back during their fall to the bed. "My little honey's used to thicker walls." Jules struggled, but her muffled protests were blocked by her thick hair. "No, no, you're not leaving me, sweet pea," he cooed, kissing the top of her head. "Roxanne didn't mean to disturb us. She's about to lock the door on her way out."

"Right, sorry."

He heard her turn the knob lock, then shut the door.

For a moment, neither of them moved. And for the first time, Dexter took in the feel of her skin against his in the places where no towel was between them. Now he really couldn't move.

Finally, Jules lifted her chin off his chest. Locks of strawberry-blond waves hung over her face, but he could see the glare in her green eyes, could almost hear what she was about to yell at him.

At the thought, he was already smiling.

"That was—"

"So she wouldn't see my junk," he said. "Self-preservation."

"Why didn't you just pick up your towel?"

"It wasn't the first thing that came to mind."

"Dexter," she moaned. But it wasn't the kind of moan he was used to when he was in this position with a woman. "I have to get off you. So just...don't look." Before he could reply, her hands were covering his eyes.

"What about *you* covering *your* eyes?" he asked.

"*I* can be trusted not to look."

"You don't trust me?"

His question made her laugh, made her body shake

against his. Damn, she better get the hell off or he'd be in big trouble.

Even though she was still covering his eyes, Dexter squeezed them shut tight, straining to picture Brent Celek's winning touchdown during the playoffs. Or Charles Barkley's most famous dunk. The next thing he knew, her soft weight was gone.

"Roxy's such a gossip, she'll tell everyone," Jules said, her voice coming from across the room.

Dexter counted to ten in his head, then sat up, thankful she'd thrown a towel over him. "I'm pretty sure people assume we have sex."

"Don't say that! Let's get dressed and get out of this room without another word. Think you can handle that?"

"No way," he said, catching her eyes in the mirror. "I'm not going downstairs and facing more questions without additional knowledge. You're liable to run out of the room again. I explained that away once, but they might not believe honeymoon exhaustion again."

"Someone actually bought that? Wait. Did you tell your brothers about the three condoms?"

Not wanting to make her mad by answering, he puffed out his cheeks and looked at the ceiling.

"Oh, man. Come *on*. I can't take much more of this."

He was about to ask her to please calm down, when she burst out laughing.

Hearing it made Dexter laugh, too. Any other woman would storm out and leave him hanging. Jules, though…she was cackling like a little kid. The sound made something shift in his chest, made him want to go to her so they could laugh together, but instead he said, "You get dressed over there and I'll get dressed over here, both facing our respective walls, okay?"

"Just keep that towel where it is until it must be removed."

He chuckled under his breath, took her dress off the hanger, and passed it to her. "You were telling me about being a Cancer, a water sign. Go on."

Dexter didn't have much interest in hearing about astrology, but he did want to hear Jules, find out more about what went on in that cute little head.

"It means I'm highly imaginative, creative, tenacious—about some things, but not work-obsessed."

"Not like me, you mean?" he said, already dressed to his pants, buttoning his shirt, but facing the wall.

"When's your birthday?"

"September third."

A new laugh exploded from her side of the room. It didn't make Dexter feel all that manly knowing the whole house thought they were currently doing the horizontal hoedown.

"Virgo," she said when she'd stopped hooting. "I could've told you that. You're practical, a critical thinker, all work and no play."

"I play some. And is that a bad thing?"

"Cancers and Virgos don't mesh, compatibility-wise. Heh-heh. Not like we didn't already know that."

"When someone brings that up tonight, I'll tell them flat-out that our love beats all odds." He heard the rustling of clothes and knew she was putting on her dress. The simple sound of a zipper made his chest feel tight. "Um, what else? Favorite food?"

"Pepperoni pizza with thick crust."

At that, he couldn't stop from turning around. "Really?"

She was adjusting the shoulder straps of a flowy turquoise dress that hit the floor. No sleeves, but she was sliding on multiple bracelets. "You're surprised?"

"No." He rebuttoned his cuffs to keep busy. "Seems too common for a free spirit."

"Someone like me should eat nothing but tofu and

sprouts?"

He smiled, enjoying when she got feisty, like a kitten who thought it was a lion. "Precisely. And I better not catch you wearing leather," he said as he brandished his cow hide belt, sliding it through his pant loops.

"You have no idea about me."

"Woman. That is why I'm asking questions." He sighed. "What's your biggest dream?"

Without a moment's hesitation, she said, "To make it as a painter. Throw everything into it and not look back, not second-guess myself. Total leap of faith." She folded her arms and ran her hands up to her shoulders as if she suddenly felt vulnerable. "It's complicated, though. Difficult." She dropped her chin. "And scary."

Dexter understood this on a level Jules couldn't have known about him. He was in the middle of doing just that… throwing everything into something new and complicated. Trying so hard to not second-guess. And being scared to death that every decision was wrong.

In a flash, he remembered the expression on her face earlier, when she'd been asked about painting, how anxious she'd looked. Why? Seeing her vulnerable and sincerely opening up made that wall in his chest shift again. The impulse screaming in his brain was to walk over to the woman in turquoise and just hold her, just be there like a friend, like a…something more he couldn't name.

"What's yours?" she asked. "Your biggest dream?"

He could've said the exact thing she had, only changed painter to entrepreneur. Was it odd that two people so different could have something so important in common?

"To make my father proud of me again."

"Dex," she said, tilting her head. "I'm sure he is."

Hearing his nickname while spoken in such a soft and caring voice made a lump unexpectedly block his throat. "I don't think he is. Not right now."

She took a step toward him. "Why?"

"Business stuff," he said, choosing not to share with her how he'd quit his job, disappointed Dad, and was one investor's meeting away from starting his own company. Or failing completely. Talk about a leap.

"I still don't know your favorite food," Jules said. Maybe she also sensed that the conversation was getting too intimate for two people who didn't believe in relationships. "What kind of wife am I?"

"Warm peaches."

"Dexter, stop flirting."

He took in her blushing expression and laughed. "That's my favorite food. Peach cobbler, peach pie, poached with a sprinkle of cinnamon. Any way I can get it."

"Oh." She blinked. "I thought you... Never mind."

More of that cute blushing. He chuckled under his breath as he tucked in his shirt. "College?"

"Two years at UNLV until my scholarship ran out. But I don't need a four-year degree."

"Pretty hard to get a job without one."

"Maybe in your prepackaged, super-shiny world. But I get along fine."

"Didn't mean to offend you."

She adjusted a long necklace studded with red and green jewels. "I'm used to people looking down on me."

Taken aback by the tweak in her mood, for once, he thought first before replying. "I...don't look down on you." Then he had to consider if that was the truth. "We're different, but it doesn't mean I think I'm better than you."

She rolled her eyes. "Keep telling yourself that."

He didn't want to argue the point. They were different, too different—period. Damn good thing she'd reminded him of that fact.

"Anyway, you know my immediate family," he said. "Both sets of grandparent are alive. Dad's father is a war vet who loves to talk about his kills. Don't let him corner you after he's had three beers—you'll have nightmares for a year. Mom's stepfather was raised by an actual British governess. Corporal punishment was big in those days, and he'll be quick to show you his scars."

"Don't let him corner me after three beers?"

That witty charm he'd grown used to was back, replacing the bitterness from a moment ago.

"He's a bourbon man who'll drink you under the table. Don't let him corner you at all. What about you? Parents in Vegas?"

"No." She turned to look in the mirror. "Mom died when I was sixteen. I was already working full time and got legally emancipated. I don't remember my father. He left right after I was born. In a way, Mom tried to make up for that by marrying three more times. She really wanted me to have a stable male presence, but none of them took."

"That sucks."

"It's not like they were mean or stole our money." She laughed it off, even though Dexter knew her well enough to suspect it was forced. "We didn't have any money to steal. Anyway, Grams has always been my family. She was more stable than anyone."

Judging by that marriage clause in her will that Jules had explained to him, Dexter seriously doubted Rosemary Granger was stable at all.

"It's after five," he said, glancing out the window. There were already twenty cars, and parking valets running up and down the driveway. "How soon will you be ready?"

Jules lifted her arms and let them fall. "I am."

She wasn't wearing any visible makeup, though, and her hair was just hanging in waves. He might've preferred her looking that way, all scrubbed and naturally glowy, but weren't women supposed to gussy up for these things? Bright red lipstick and with hair in some complicated style that would make her look untouchable?

"Okay. Great," he said, grabbing his jacket, making sure the knot in his tie was square and straight. It was a greenish-blue, coincidentally matching Jules's dress. "I'll wait while you put on your shoes."

"I'm not wearing any."

"Pardon?" He stared at her in confusion. "We're going downstairs, around people other than my family. You have to wear shoes."

"We'll be in the backyard, on the lawn. No one will notice." She lifted her dress, displaying her feet, toenails painted pink. She also wore a silver anklet with charms hanging off.

He'd notice her feet; they were sexy as hell—as far as feet went.

"We don't want extra attention on us, right?"

"Right…" She nodded slowly, waiting for him to go on. When he didn't, she rolled her eyes. "Fine, you want me to wear shoes tonight, I will." She plopped down on the bed and slid on the same sandals she'd been wearing all day. They laced up her ankles and tied in the back. "Am I *presentable* enough for you, Senator Uptight?"

She was joking. He hoped she was joking. "Presentable," he replied as he opened the door, letting her into the hall first. The scented cloud of her perfume or hand lotion or just *her* trailed behind as Dexter followed her out.

Chapter Seven

Senator Uptight could certainly fill a suit. Not that she didn't already know that. From now on, that's all she better see him in. No more lounging around wearing towels in confined spaces. Although a hand towel would've been nice when he'd been standing ten feet away, as naked as Michelangelo's David.

A tingle ran over her skin as they walked down the hall.

Then he pulled me to him, her disobedient mind replayed. *And we crashed onto the bed. For a split second, I thought he wanted to...*

She shut that particular door in her mind and bit the insides of her cheeks, thankfully halting all heart gooing. Dexter only looked on her as the hound dog he was. To him, she was nothing more than another female body.

"Hey," he whispered, nudging her arm. "We're about to go down the staircase, then we won't have one second of privacy. Ready?"

"Totally," she said in a positively firm voice. "Fire away."

"That's the spirit."

"What should I do if I'm asked something we didn't cover?"

"Smile." He shrugged one of those broad shoulders. "You can get through anything by smiling. See?" He gave her a toothy grin that looked anything but sincere, making her belly laugh. "Show lots of teeth, like this. Let's see yours."

Jules parted her lips like a snarling dog.

Dexter cracked up. "Close, but you gotta smile at the same time. Use the muscles at the corners of your mouth. Try again. Concentrate."

She hiccuped a laugh. "Gosh, it's really hard, though. How's this?" She gave her animated Joker's smile.

"Closer," he said, looking at her clinically. "But more like the dazzlingly beautiful woman you are, and less like a serial killer."

Jules's psychotic expression froze for a moment. He thought she was dazzlingly beautiful? As his eyes lingered on hers, she felt her expression changing. Her face muscles softened, her lips parted, the corners curling up, and her eyes widened.

Dexter stopped walking and stared at her. "Oh, um, yeah. That's, um…" He cleared his throat and pulled at his tie like it was suddenly too tight. "That's the one that'll work. Distracting as hell."

For the first time in years, Jules knew she looked dazzling, because she felt dazzling. All thanks to one look and tongue-tied reply from Dexter—which didn't exactly bode well when she was trying so hard not to go gooey.

At the top of the stairs, he took her hand and looped it through his arm. "If the smile doesn't work, try making people uncomfortable. That'll stop them from asking personal questions."

"Noted." Jules hadn't realized how noisy it was until they reached the ground floor. Though her free arm was immediately seized, she wasn't ready to leave Dexter. She felt safe with him, holding his hand, sharing private little jokes.

"I'm so sorry about earlier," Roxy said, tugging her away. "I could just die."

"It's fine." Jules shot a quick glance at Dexter. "I should learn to be quieter. But your brother just, ya know, drives me *insane*, and I can't bear—"

"Stop." Roxy put up a hand. "I don't want to hear the details. Ever. Let's talk about something else. What concerts have you seen lately? Oh! Did you see the new Emma Watson movie?"

Jules winked at Dexter, who was giving her the thumbs-up while being dragged away by a man she didn't recognize. She wanted to follow him, but knew she couldn't.

"Love your dress," Roxy said. "I could never pull off something like that."

They chatted casually as they made a loop around the perimeter of the party. Occasionally, Roxy would introduce Jules to someone, and when the questions started, Jules did the smile thing. If that didn't work, she casually slipped in something about what an animal Dexter was in the sack. That always derailed the conversation enough for her to escape.

"Don't hate me," Roxy said when they stopped behind a row of chairs, "but for a while today, I wondered if you guys were faking."

Jules's stomach turned to ice. Even when she tried the smile thing, so far, it hadn't worked on Roxy. Was their secret about to be discovered? Had Roxy already told people? Told Quent? Would she lose her house?

"W-why would we do that?"

"You know how my brothers are always betting and daring each other. I get in on it too, sometimes, but they get way out of control." She shrugged. "I thought maybe he paid you to pretend to be his wife."

"Just so he'd win a bet?"

"I told you, they're crazy."

For a moment, Jules felt like coming clean about the whole thing. If anyone in the Elliott family would understand, it would be Roxy. They'd known each other for years, and when she and Vince had stopped hanging out as a couple, Jules had spent a lot of her time with Roxy. They were friends, maybe closer friends than Jules had realized.

But she couldn't. Everyone knew it was impossible for Roxy to keep a secret. Jules had too much riding on this. Plus, she'd promised Dexter. She might be in the middle of the biggest lie of her life, but she would not break his confidence.

And of course, there was the money. Jules hated how that was an important factor. But there it was.

"Believe me, Rox," Jules said, linking their arms together. "We're not married so Dexter'd win a bet. Your brother has faults; I keep stumbling upon new ones, but eloping in Vegas is not one of them."

Roxy hugged her, nearly pulling Jules off her feet. "I'm so happy about that," she said, sounding choked up.

"Me, too."

It was strange—for the first time, that part didn't feel like a lie.

"Listen." Roxy's voice was low as she glanced sideways across the patio. "I want to hear more non-gross details later, but that hot intern from Dad's office just got here." She plastered a smile on her face. "Time to go spill a drink on him and see if he bites."

Jules laughed. "Good luck!"

She wasn't alone for long. First Luke and Natalie joined her. But they kept feeding each other little bites of a broken Hershey's bar, making Jules want to puke at the cuteness. So she fed them a detailed story about how she'd done a pole dance for Dexter and they'd torn the pole off the ceiling.

Leaving the couple with that visual, she meandered to the other side of the patio, smiling like a deranged maniac whenever anyone made eye contact. While cornered by one of Eileen's country club friends, someone scooped up Jules's hand.

"Sorry," Dexter said, "I need my darling Shmoopy."

"That's *Shoopy*," Jules corrected, glancing wistfully at a tray of wine flutes passing by. No, she wasn't about to start with the alcohol to calm her nerves. Hadn't she learned her lesson?

"What have you been telling people?" Dexter asked as soon as they were behind the rosebushes.

"Can you be more specific?"

"Things about me…what we do."

"Oh. That." She bit her lip. "I was doing what you said, making our story embarrassing to an audience."

He crossed his arms. "By telling my mother you threw yourself at me."

"It makes a more interesting story. Everyone's tired of hearing how you're a big bad lady-killer. I thought you'd be grateful."

"I'm not. No wife of mine should be throwing herself at anyone."

"Not even her husband?"

He frowned and pursed his lips, looking deep in thought. "I don't like it. You doing a pole dance while covered in strategically placed Hershey's Kisses?"

"Hey, I did not add that detail." She toyed with her bracelets. "But I like it. And I was *trying* to be inappropriately personal."

"Well, stop," he growled, but then dipped his chin and laughed. When he nudged her shoulder and winked, Jules laughed, too, trying so hard to not feel the desire to press herself against him until his arms wrapped around her.

"Anything *I* should know?" she asked.

"No." He looked down at the grass. "Oh, you do have a thing for waking me up in that special way every morning."

"*Every?*" Jules blushed at the idea, then tried not to imagine seeing Dexter's lazy, sleepy smile, his rumpled bed head, hearing him laugh with her and holding her at the beginning of every new day.

These were the exact kinds of thoughts that got her in trouble three years ago.

"Then *you* have a thing for scented bubble baths and Enya."

He closed his eyes and tightened his jaw. "Fine."

Jules smiled. "Now if you'll excuse me, I have more things to tell Roxy."

• • •

Dexter didn't like the idea of any further details getting to Roxy. Not only was his sister a gossip, but admittedly Jules wasn't the best liar in the world.

He watched her walk away, her long turquoise dress brushing the tips of the grass. Besides the telltale flush on her neck, she was doing pretty well with the make-believe.

But how twisted was that? Despite the kinky made-up stories, Jules was a nice girl. She was sweet and had a good heart. And sometimes when he'd see her on the other side of the patio, it took everything in him not to bolt from the conversation he'd been having, just so he could hear her voice, her laugh, put an arm around her because that's what husbands did. And because being with her made him feel…good.

He had no business training her to become a comfortable liar.

By the time Danny gave the best man's toast, Dexter was ready for the night to be over. When the first of the guests started to leave, he figured it was safe to head out, and was about to go upstairs when he saw Jules with Vince and Maddie. Soon enough, Luke, Roxy, and his parents joined her. Cornered again.

Being a good fake husband, Dexter headed straight over, ready to pull his severely blushing bride away. "Hey. What's the hot topic?"

"Jules was telling us about your honeymoon."

She glanced at him and bit her lip, failing to hide the fact that she looked remorseful. "They asked, sweetie."

Dexter didn't need details. Who knew what she'd cooked up?

"Time to say good night, honey," he said, and took her elbow.

"Speaking of honeymoons…" Roxy said, nudging Maddie until they both laughed.

Dude, she could be such a pain. Since they were obviously being scrutinized, he put an arm around Jules. It felt awkward, but who cared? He gave Vince a slap on the back, then waited for Jules to say good-bye so they could go.

Before they were three steps away, he heard Roxy say sotto voce, "They never kiss in public. Is that odd for newlyweds?"

Hot and sharp tingles swept up the back of Dexter's neck. After all they'd gone through today, he wasn't about to let his chatty sister blow their cover. So he did what any man would do.

Without warning, he stopped walking, took Jules around the waist, and pulled her in. He heard a gasp of surprise right before he planted a kiss squarely on her mouth. Luckily, the surprise didn't cause her to flinch for more than a second— that would've given everything away with the family watching.

He kept his mouth over hers, a firm hold of her waist, and felt the instant Jules began her own playacting. She slid her hands inside his suit coat, dug her nails into his back, making him wince, though not in pain.

Kissing her felt...different...awesome. Because it was more than kissing. Not only was his mouth into it, but his brain, and his heart was hammering against his rib cage, behind his ears, making his muscles weak, then flex with strength.

Enjoying it way more that he should've been, he shut his eyes tighter, just going with it, his head full of a sweet buzzing sound. Just as he fisted the back of her dress, Jules's hands slid down and grabbed his ass.

Actually grabbed it and squeezed.

This shook Dexter wildly awake enough to break their kiss and sway back half a step.

"Get a room!" Roxy called.

But he barely heard as he looked down into Jules's bright eyes. She was breathing as hard as he was while wearing a huge, gratified grin.

"That's the idea," Dexter called over his shoulder in a purposefully impatient voice, never taking his eyes off Jules. He wasn't sure what more he was supposed to say at a moment like this, so he grabbed her hand and dragged her into the house, saying good-night to people as he passed, heading toward the stairs.

"What was that?" he asked her out of the corner of his mouth. "Good to see you, Michael, 'night."

"The grand finale," Jules replied. "I knew what you were doing—I heard what Roxy said."

Dexter exhaled, wishing his pulse would slow down. An adrenaline rush, that was all—not the fact that that might've been the hottest kiss of his life. And it was nothing but an act.

For all he knew, he'd never feel that rush again, that teetering of the earth when she kissed him back, when he felt her breath on his cheek, imagined holding her in his arms for hours. Maybe forever.

"I think you succeeded," he said. "Though a little warning would've been appreciated. My mother was there."

"Like the warning *you* gave me before you kissed me in the middle of a party? And I know Eileen was there, that's why I did the butt thing. They need to assume we can't keep our hands off each other."

Dexter shut his eyes momentarily, feeling her warm palm against his as they climbed the stairs. "Mission accomplished," he muttered.

He steered her to their bedroom, waited until they were both inside, then locked the door, blowing out a long breath while loosening his tie.

"I consider the evening a bona fide success," Jules said, pulling off her bracelets in front of the mirror. "We talked to people, added backstory, and made out in public. No way there's doubt now."

Made out. With Jules. Just thinking it made Dexter's chest burn, his stomach spin like he was nervous. What the hell was the matter with him?

The answer was logically simple. It was no longer just physical. Jules was in his head, and he had no idea what to do about that.

He sat on the foot of the bed and tried to breathe slower, work out the kinks in his neck. "No—yes, right," he said. "I think we have that covered."

"And it wasn't so bad. Kind of fun."

He yanked at his collar. *Why the hell is it so damn hot in this bedroom?*

"Wait." Jules turned around, her hands at the back of her neck to unclasp a necklace. "Are you upset?"

"About…?"

"Me squeezing your cheeks?"

He focused on the floor while gritting his teeth. "Why would I be upset about that?"

"It's fine," Jules said. "You can grab my ass next time—if there's need."

"There won't be," he growled, walking to the other side of the room to his suitcase. "I have no intention of grabbing your...anything."

"Nice," Jules said, sarcasm coloring her voice. "What's wrong with you?"

What was *wrong* was that he needed her to stop talking, stop giving him ideas.

He removed his jacket so he wouldn't die of heatstroke. "Nothing," he said. "I'm tired."

"Same here." It was quiet as they both turned their attentions to that rectangular-shaped, duvet-covered elephant in the room.

The last thing Dexter needed at the moment was to imagine sharing a bed with Jules... Her elbow propped on a pillow, palm cradling her head as she talked to him about astrology, how she dreamed of making it as a painter—feared it, too—how they somehow shared the same worries about the future.

That nervous whirring in his stomach switched to high speed. Only it wasn't a bad feeling.

"I'm going to change," she said, "but I didn't bring pj's. I don't wear them unless it's cold." She glanced at his dresser. "Do you have something I can borrow?"

Scratch that. The *very* last thing Dexter needed was to think about Jules sleeping sans pajamas. So he pulled the second drawer open, grabbed the first shirt he touched, and tossed it to her without looking.

"Perfect. It's long enough that I won't need anything else."

"Good, good." He stared at the wall. "Do you want to"— he paused and motioned to the bathroom—"first?"

"Thanks." But she didn't go in right away. Instead, she sat on the bed and unlaced her sandals. It took forever because of the long laces that wrapped around her ankles.

Dexter turned a one-eighty to look out the window,

watching the parade of headlights disappear down the hill. A few minutes later, the bathroom door shut. He exhaled and unclenched his fists, unclenched everything.

Get a freaking grip.

He quickly took off the rest of his suit, hung it in the closet, then rummaged through a different dresser drawer until he found pajama bottoms. After a quick thought, he pulled out a T-shirt, too. His mother really should get rid of all the clothes he'd left here since he'd moved away after graduation.

Just as he'd tied the drawstring, the bathroom door opened and Jules came out wearing nothing but a hockey jersey—not the Philadelphia Flyers that he'd bought at a game, but the jersey with his name on the back, the one he'd worn when he'd played left wing on Hershey High's varsity team.

It was so big on her that it gaped at the neck and hit her midthigh.

"You were pretty big in high school." She tugged at the neck hole.

And the tension is back. "We wore pads."

Dexter grabbed his shaving kit and practically dived into the bathroom. He brushed and flossed and felt like going as far as taking a cold shower. Maybe that would get rid of the nervousness in his stomach that still hadn't gone away. How was he supposed to sleep tonight?

"Hey." Jules tapped the door. "Have you thought about the sleeping arrangements?"

That was all he'd been doing for the last five minutes. "Hadn't given it a single thought. Why?" he said, adding the appropriate amount of nonchalant swagger to his voice. When she didn't reply, he smiled, knowing a girl like Jules would demand a guy like Dexter sleep on the floor or out on the roof, even if it was raining.

"Well, I was just wondering…do you want the right or left side of the bed?"

His cocky smile dropped. Now what was he supposed to do?

Nothing, he thought, looking at himself in the mirror. *Not a damn thing. This is Jules, not a regular woman. Sweet Jules who loves her grandmother. Kindhearted, infectious, charming-as-hell Jules. The woman I can't get out of my head.*

After a steeling breath, he opened the door. "The right side," he said, tossing his shaving kit on top of his bag.

"Cool! I'm a lefty."

He lifted what he hoped was a brotherly-type smile. "And they say we're not compatible."

"What do *they* know?" Her hair was piled on top of her head, her face clean of the little makeup she'd worn, and yet her fair skin had an apple-cheeked glow.

"I'm keeping our door locked," he said. "Not that I expect anyone to burst in, but we might as well play it safe."

"Fine by me," she said, pulling back the covers on the left side of the bed.

Crap. He was really getting in there with her. Not that it was a big deal—it was just Jules. The mermaid girl with the loud voice and bare feet. No big deal at all.

Was he lying to himself now?

"Get the light," Jules added, punching her pillow. "Oh, unless first you want to…"

When she didn't go on, Dexter felt a band pull tight in his chest.

Unless I want to do what? What??

"I didn't ask," she continued. "Do you like to read in bed?"

"No. I'm good." He turned off the light. "I drift off fast." Clouds covered the moon and stars, allowing very little light in through the window. Now he just stared down at the sheets. Should he warn her that he was about to climb in? No, that was stupid. She was obviously fine with it, and he was, too. Totally, totally chill.

He got in bed and eased onto the pillow, sensing Jules's body right beside him…wearing nothing but a worn and frayed jersey from his glory days…and maybe nothing else. He rolled onto his side and scooted to the edge. Even though Jules was the size of a jockey, it was still only a double bed, and he felt every time she moved, breathed.

"Tonight was fun." Her whisper filled the silence.

"Yeah?"

"I miss hanging out with your family. Rox and Vince, especially."

"They miss you, too," he said, staring at his ancient 76ers poster on the wall.

"I just wish…"

When she didn't finish, he rolled onto his back, craning his head to look at her. "What do you wish?" His eyes traced her silhouette. She was on her back, too, chin lifted, eyes open, blinking slowly. The bed rocked when she rolled to her side and faced him.

"I wish I were here under different circumstances. I don't wish it wasn't Vince's wedding—I'm really happy about that. I just wish we weren't, you know. We're hurting your family and they don't even realize it. It breaks my heart."

Hearing her voice catch made the breath rush out of him, made his forehead tick with pain and an overwhelming desire to comfort her.

After that kiss on the lawn, Dexter had felt his first real twinge of guilt. Just like Jules, he hated lying to his family. They would find out the truth someday, and it certainly wouldn't strengthen familial bonds. If he thought he was estranged from Dad now, how would it be then?

"I know," he said. For a moment, they looked at each other, so close he could've reached out and drawn her to his chest, just held her until the remorse in both their hearts evaporated.

When he felt her foot move under the sheets, he threw back the covers and sat up. "I'm going to"—*climb out the window*—"sleep on the floor."

Jules sat up. "Am I hogging the covers?"

He snatched his pillow and the blanket at the foot of the bed. "No, it's this damn mattress. It's been too short for me ever since my growth spurt at fifteen. My feet hang off the end." He dropped to the floor, didn't bother using the blanket.

"Are you sure?"

"Totally. I'll be out like a light in two seconds."

"Do you need another pillow?"

"Nope, perfectly fine." He saw her lean over the side of the bed to look down at him, so he drew the blanket over his body. "See? All cozy. Now, let's get some sleep."

She sighed in the darkness. "Okay. Good night, then."

"Yeah, 'night." He rolled to face the wall, not relaxing until he heard her lie back down.

Despite what he'd said, Dexter had a hell of a time falling asleep. First, he thought about his father, how he had to talk to him before he flew back to New York tomorrow. Next, he tried to concentrate on his meeting with Three Jacker Media on Friday, on that one PowerPoint design that still wasn't right. Every time he got close to drifting off, he heard Jules move, heard her breathing in the dark. When he did manage to sleep, it was filled with restless dreams.

Correction—*one* dream, one fragment of one dream that cut off every time a petite woman in a Vegas limo turned to face him, fisting the front of his shirt until a single button popped off.

Sometime in the middle of the night, Jules had gotten up, because the next morning, he woke to find a mug next to his head, filled with room temperature water that flooded the air with the smell of mint.

Chapter Eight

The surroundings were unfamiliar, but at least Jules knew where she was when she yawned herself awake. She sat up and rubbed her eyes, blurry from the sunlight streaming through the sheer drapes. The clock radio read ten thirty.

The wedding was at noon. They'd better get a move on.

She crawled to the foot of the bed, but Dexter was gone, his spot on the floor empty. The pillow and blanket he'd used were back in place on the bed, making it look like they'd slept next to each other all night.

She'd never admit it, but she was grateful he'd moved to the floor. Playing it cool was one thing, but ever since that kiss on the patio, she's been more than a little shaky.

In fact, all of last night had left her shaky. She'd had a blast with Dex, trading get-to-know-you stories as they'd dressed for the party, sharing crazy-ass smiles meant to get out of sticky conversations, laughing every time they had a quiet moment together. How he'd been so protective and sweet about defending "his wife's" reputation. And lastly, how she'd wanted so badly to scoot over in bed just to be close to him.

They were friends; they had a foundation now. But there was also something else. Though the thought of what it might be wasn't exactly welcoming.

Would he ever want a relationship? Could a womanizer change his ways? Commit to one woman? Maybe in chick flicks, but in real life…? Probably not.

The smell of shampoo and aftershave filled the bathroom, and traces of steam still clung to the corners of the mirror.

Wow, she must've slept hard to have not heard him shower and shave. Had she been snoring? Did Dexter see her sleeping with her mouth wide open?

His laptop was gone, which meant he'd gotten up at the crack of dawn to make business calls or finalize a merger. Even on his brother's wedding day, he couldn't put work on the back burner. Yet another reason it was foolish to consider him as anything more than a friend…her partner in a business deal.

Jules took a long shower, swiping Dexter's razor to shave her legs while her deep conditioner did its thing. She'd left the bathroom door open a crack to hear if he came back, so it was a surprise when she found a note on the made bed.

I TOLD THEM WE HAD A LATE NIGHT, it said in tight block letters. I FIGURED THAT WAS A REASONABLE EXPLANATION. FOOD IS IN THE KITCHEN. ROXY'S BEEN ASKING FOR YOU. WEDDING'S IN AN HOUR. I'M A GROOMSMAN, SO IF I DON'T SEE YOU BEFORE, TRY NOT TO MAKE MATTERS WORSE.

Jules crumpled the note and hurled it across the room, missing the trash can. *Try not to make matters worse.* What the heck did that mean? She hadn't done anything to make it worse. Well, okay, she should've talked to him before spouting off about their fake sex life.

Fine. Whatever. I won't make it worse.

She blow-dried her hair, then fingered it into a loose

French twist. The dress she'd brought for the wedding had a high neck, so wearing her hair up would look more… presentable? She shouldn't care about that, either. The Elliotts knew darn well what she was like. Just because she'd married Dexter didn't mean she'd suddenly change. Good people like the Elliotts would never expect that.

She stepped into her long pink dress, zipped the side zipper, then fastened the clip at the back of her neck. It was vintage Halston from the '80s that reminded her of Molly Ringwald's prom dress in *Pretty in Pink*. At least the top half did. The bottom half was full and pleated and puffed out when she spun. It was one of her favorite outfits. With no jewelry besides one jingly charm bracelet, she slicked on lip gloss and headed downstairs.

Hunger pangs clawed her stomach the second she entered the kitchen. The room bustled with catering staff, and she jumped out of the way when one dashed between her and the coffeepot. She preferred tea in the morning, but since it was almost lunchtime and she wasn't about to riffle through Eileen's kitchen, she poured a tall helping.

After a few sips hit her bloodstream, she smiled and leaned against the counter. She'd forgotten that Eileen Elliott took it upon herself to keep the town's namesake afloat by infusing everything she could with their chocolate. Another deep, gratifying sip. It wasn't like café mocha you'd buy at Starbucks. Eileen's coffee had a taste all its own, and Jules felt sixteen again.

"Finally!"

Roxy entered the kitchen wearing a dress even shorter than the one last night. The girl had great legs, but did she need to show so much of them all the time? Jules laughed inside, feeling like the big sister Roxy never had. But maybe should have…

"Sorry, I slept late."

"Dex told us. They're all out back, it's about to start. Any coffee left?"

"Aren't you in the wedding?"

Roxy shook her head, her short hair bobbing around her chin. "Maddie has six girl cousins who expected to be in the wedding." She shrugged and poured coffee. "It's a Southern thing, I guess. But it's a load off. I hate weddings."

"Me, too." Which wasn't even true, but a knee-jerk reply.

"Is that why you eloped?"

Oh, snap. Had she and Dexter covered that? *Stay as close to the truth as possible.* "Dex knows that about me; he wanted to make it as low-key as possible."

"So you went to a Las Vegas wedding chapel at midnight?" Roxy eyed her over her mug.

"That might not seem low-key to you, but I'm from Vegas. A chapel on the Strip is the same as city hall." She glanced toward the patio door, longing to escape before she *made matters worse.*

Freaking Dexter getting in her head.

"It was romantic," she added. "Our whole relationship has been one leap of faith after another. Getting married was *my* big leap for him."

She must've been becoming a very convincing liar, because saying that felt completely true.

"Hey." Jules pointed outside. "Looks like Danny's telling the organist to start. Shouldn't you be with them?"

Roxy's mug landed on the counter with a thud. "Shoot, it's starting early. Want to sit with me in front? You're family."

"Thanks, but I'll hang in back and finish my cup, if that's cool."

"Sure." Roxy gave her a smile and squeezed her hand. "See you later."

Jules peered outside again. Wanting to see Dexter, but also not wanting to. Oh, her broken brain!

An unsupervised serving platter of pigs in a blanket made her mouth water. She swiped one, popped it in her mouth, and tried not to think what kind of nonmeat she was eating. It was delicious, so she swiped another and bit it in half. Mmm, as tasty as the first.

At the opening chords of the bridal march, Jules inhaled the other half, picked up the bottom of her dress, and dashed out the side door. Two hundred white chairs lined the large backyard; at the front was a tall white arch covered in clinging vines and pale gray roses. Everyone was on their feet as Maddie, in a long white dress, walked up the aisle, arm in arm with her father.

Feeling touched and emotional was a completely natural reaction. But Jules hadn't expected such a lump in her throat. She'd never have anything like this. Not that she'd want a traditional wedding ceremony, or a ceremony, or a wedding at all.

She found an open chair on the back row and sneaked in. It made her smile to see Vince beaming at his approaching bride. She was sincerely pleased for him. He'd been one of her best friends for years, and deserved love and happiness.

Doesn't everyone? Don't I?

The lump in her throat grew.

To the left of Vince stood his groomsmen—a line of Elliotts wearing pale gray suits, light pink ties and one small pink rose pinned to their lapels. Dexter was second in line between Luke and Danny, and damn it all, the man stood out like one of the royals.

Okay, fine, even if she hadn't realized it all these years, Dexter was by far the hottest Elliott. No use denying it. The knot in his tie was perfectly square, perfect side part in his dark hair, though his boutonniere was a bit off-kilter.

The tiny imperfection made her heart skip a beat, maybe even goo a little.

Through the two hundred people between them, Dexter caught her eye and gave a little nod. She was about to wave her fingers when a memory suddenly resurfaced. She saw them at *their* wedding, could feel the rented veil on her head. Dexter smiling at her, laughing together, hysterically laughing. At what?

"I do," he'd whispered. "I sure the hell do. You're exactly what I need, Jules—right now and forever."

Suddenly, her chest filled with so much heat and pressure, she could almost drown in it, while her eyes remained locked on Dexter across the yard. Her mouth was dry, but she tasted something on the back of her tongue. Last night's kiss. It was Dexter she tasted, recalled perfectly how his mouth had felt against hers.

You're exactly what I need, he'd said in front of that mutton-chopped Vegas minister. Had he meant it? Or was she recalling a false memory? Imagining what she wanted him to say?

Someone poked her side. She blinked and gasped when she realized with horror that the two hundred people had sat down, and she was the only one still standing, gazing across the empty space at Dexter.

Two hundred people were now turned and staring at her.

"Sorry!" she called out, waving in the general direction of the bride and groom. "Your turn. I'll sit now. Go ahead, Vince." She gave the thumbs-up, then quickly dropped to her seat.

Dexter's brow furrowed when he looked away from her, and she felt like an idiot. Yes, she wanted to remember what had happened that night, but her sporadically resurfacing memories sure had bad timing.

The rest of the ceremony was a blur, and before she knew it, the band was playing, and Vince and Maddie were having their first dance. Judging by the state of the chairs and tables, she'd totally zoned out through the toasts and the cutting of the cake.

"That was a nice touch." Dexter was at her side, holding a champagne flute out to her.

She took it automatically but put it on the table. This was bad, very, very bad. Her heart should not speed up when Dexter came near or when she thought about him. Why couldn't he start yammering on his Bluetooth or flirt with a trampy-looking guest? Wasn't that what the guy was all about?

"Nice touch?" she asked.

"Staying standing after everyone sat, looking gooey-eyed at me."

Jules felt a flush coming on. Bad, bad timing. "I'd never look gooey over you."

"I'm saying it was a good thing. People totally bought it."

"Oh." She reached for her glass, but it had already been cleared away by the über-efficient waiters. "That's why I did it. Obviously."

She glanced away, in case she was still blushing, while swinging the bottom of her skirt.

"We should dance now— Jules. What the hell? You're not wearing shoes." He was staring down at her feet, shock creasing his face.

"I told you I wasn't going to."

"Last night you said you weren't, but then you did."

"So?" She pulled up her dress a few more inches and showed her bare feet. What was so wrong with them? They were pretty.

"Has my mother seen you?"

"Yes. And who cares?"

Dexter groaned, and was very obviously trying not to look at her feet. "It's not proper."

"I'm not proper, either." She placed her hands on her

hips and tipped her chin to eye him, relieved to be engaging in something that pointed out their glaring differences. "You knew that when you married me. Didn't seem to bother you then."

"I was *drunk*," he said a bit too loudly, even though the music was blaring. He cleared his throat then took her hand, leading her away to the same semiprivate corner he'd dragged her to last night. "Neither of us can be held accountable for that night."

"Ah, so the only reason someone like you would ever possibly marry someone like me is if he was too smashed to think straight?" She turned away. "Nice. Thanks."

"Talking is a waste of energy."

"Let's dance, then. People expect it."

"Can you even dance"—he pointed his chin at her feet—"like that?"

"Really, Dexter. You've got issues. Among other things, you're way too concerned about what other people think."

He crossed his arms. "You knew *that* before, and married me anyway."

"I was obviously under some delusion that it didn't matter. If I was thinking *at all*."

"Shh," he said, getting in her face. "You need to learn to use your inside voice."

"We're *outside*. And never shush me again. Seriously. You know darn well this isn't about my feet. You think they're cute, you just can't admit it."

She caught the flicker of a smile in his eyes, and knew he was ready to loosen up. Had making one joke done that?

"Is there a problem?"

Jules glanced past Dexter's shoulder at Quent Sanders, dressed in a suit and tie.

"Why the hell are you here?" Dexter said through a clenched jaw, muscles working under his skin.

Quent held up a wineglass. "Your mother invited me."

"No, she didn't."

"Okay, so I invited myself. With my father away, I have an especially keen interest in his cases that I'm overseeing. Yours in particular." He eyed Jules. "Looks like you two aren't getting along. Seems strange that one day after you signed for the house as a married couple that your relationship is on the rocks. We call that *fraud*."

Dexter glared at him, the vein on his neck throbbing.

Okay, she'd had suspicions before, but now Jules was convinced there was bad blood between these two. It wasn't the right moment for her to ask, since—if they really had been together for six months—Dexter would've already told her.

"Who says we're not getting along?" Jules said.

"Looked like the beginnings of a full-blown fight from where I was standing."

"Looks are deceiving," Dexter said. "That wasn't a fight, it was foreplay."

Jules's eyes were probably as wide as Quent's, but she didn't have time to react further. Dexter wheeled around and slid a hand to the back of her neck. Her body didn't fight when he pulled her in.

From sheer force, their teeth hit together, but Dexter's strong grip wouldn't allow her to flinch. Not that her brain gave her that option. Both his hands held the sides of her head and she had to grab his elbows to hang on. Without breaking for air, his hands moved down her arms, taking each of her hands and leading them to clasp around his neck.

Even though it was hopelessly wrong—make-believe at its worst—Jules let herself fully sink into the kiss, felt its warmth and energy sing through her bloodstream, fill her head. She wanted to kiss him, to be as close to this man's beating heart as possible.

Next thing she knew, she was off her feet, Dexter carrying

her away.

"Had enough fighting, baby?" he said in a husky voice with enough volume that she knew it was meant for Quent to overhear, and thankfully snapping her out of fantasy land. "Time to get outta here?"

"Oh, yeahhh," she said, pulling back so she could bite his lip and thrust both hands through his hair. She knew Dex would hate that…messing up his perfect part. So she kept at it, opening her eyes a sliver to see he was taking her around the side of the house to another entrance.

"Oh, *baby*! Oh, my *husband*!" she cried theatrically. "Take me to our marriage bed before I burst with love for you!"

Dexter's face was at her neck, but she heard him chuckle, felt him shake with laughter. When she inhaled to call out something else, his lips crashed over hers, probably to stop whatever he thought she was about to say. The forceful pressure of the kiss was still there, but the intensity was different, softer, more lingering and deeper.

Like *he'd* slipped into fantasyland, too.

When she'd run out of air and was forced to break the kiss, she looked into his blue eyes, now dark and intense. For a split second, everything felt…real.

This realization, fear, and uncertainty made her want to squirm out of his arms.

"Don't leave me," he whispered. "Not yet." He glanced over his shoulder. "Let's get inside first."

Once they were in the mudroom, Dexter set her down. Her muscles were weak and strained, rubbery. She felt flushed, and her heart was galloping way out of control.

"A little warning would've been nice," she said.

"There wasn't time." He was having trouble breathing, too, and he stepped back, pressing a fist to his forehead. "What is that douche bag doing here, anyway?"

"Checking up on us."

"That's not part of his job. He's lucky I don't call the cops."

"Why do you hate him so much? What's with you two?"

Dexter opened his mouth to reply, but closed it and ran his hands through his hair, straightening it into place. "Nothing."

Oh, obviously it's nothing. You only look like you want to murder the guy every time you see him.

She wasn't supposed to care about Dexter, or his feelings, or what made him upset. Even if she already did.

"I gotta get out of here," she said, needing to put space between them. Lots of space.

"There's a wedding reception going on. We can't disappear."

"Oh, please. We just made the PDA exit of the century. No one will miss us for at least an hour. And I didn't say you had to leave."

Dexter eyed her and shifted his weight. "Where are you going?"

"Grams's cottage," she said, thinking fast. "It's why I'm here in the first place."

"You don't have the key yet."

"Don't need one. I know how to get in. Can I take your car?"

"Um, sure." He led the way as they walked through the busy kitchen, and Jules tried not to enjoy the feel of his warm, steady hand on her arm. "I'll get the keys for you."

"Keys?" Roxy was at the end of the hall. "To what?"

Suddenly, Eileen was there, too. And Natalie and Luke. Why did the Elliotts always travel in herds?

"My car," Dexter said.

Eileen arched her brows. "Juliet? You're leaving?"

Jules couldn't stand seeing the confusion in her eyes—all of their eyes. "Just to the cottage. I haven't been there yet, so…"

Eileen turned to Dexter. "Oh, you're *both* going." She

put a hand to her chest and laughed in relief. "For a second, I thought… But that's silly."

No reply was coming to mind, and Jules scrambled for a lie as a fresh wave of blush crept up her neck. *Please don't hiccup, please don't hiccup.* "Um, well, I was going first—"

"We're both going," Dexter cut in. "How odd would it be if I wasn't. Right, dumpling?" He cupped her cheek affectionately, all part of the act.

"The reception isn't over for another hour," Roxy said. "Are you coming back, or—*ouch!*"

Natalie elbowed her. "Of course they aren't coming back," she said out of the side of her mouth. "They've been married two days. I know I wouldn't spend my third married night under this roof." She took Eileen's hand. "No offense. You know what I mean."

"Of course I do." Eileen smiled, then turned to Jules. "Well then, don't let us keep you. Go upstairs for your things and we'll say a quick good-bye for now."

Jules couldn't move. Not until her loving husband's hand pressed into her back did she get her legs to work. Dex at her cottage was *not* part of their act.

• • •

"That was your fault," Jules hissed when they were alone.

"What was the alternative? You just *have* to see the cottage now." Right after Dexter said it, he felt like a jerk. It *was* kind of his fault. If he'd had two seconds to think, he would've come up with an excuse to tell his family, but they'd caught him off guard.

He hated being caught off guard. Hated pretending, lying. He'd been so off his game this weekend.

"I'm not even dignifying that with a reply," Jules said, pushing open their bedroom door and nearly slamming it in his face. "If you're in my house, you'll suck out the positive aura."

"The what?" he said, deadpan. Despite himself, it was cute when she got this way, all new-agey and prickly. No shoes.

"Let's just get it over with."

For the next few minutes, they packed their bags in silence.

"Farewell, all you ghosts of Dexter's past." She slapped a fake high five on Allen Iverson, then hung on to the doorknob. "Never grow up," she said to the room, "because if you do, you'll become a work-obsessed, washed-up playboy."

"Washed-up?" Dexter said.

"Wasn't talking to you."

He laughed and had another of those sensations to hug her.

They said a quick good-bye to Vince and Maddie, and a "sorry we can't stick around to see you off, but we really, really have to get going—if you know what I mean." For added effect, Dexter rested a hand on Jules's ass. The entire time. He felt her flinch but didn't move it even a centimeter. *Karma, babe.*

Jules smiled and waved as they pulled away from the house, but he knew from the way her knee bounced under her dress that she was ticked.

"Never do that again," she said as they headed down the hill.

He smirked and slid on his sunglasses. "Do what, exactly?"

"That was a violation."

Yep, she was ticked, and he didn't even mind. Maybe it made him an ass, but he kind of liked her like this, too. Emotion put color on her face, fire in her eyes, heat in her voice. When all of that passion was aimed at him… Hell yeah, he liked it.

"What you did to me last night wasn't a violation?"

She looked away and shaded her eyes. "Just don't talk.

The drive will be faster."

Honoring her wishes, he didn't reply, but he did laugh. Damn hard.

A few minutes later, his phone beeped. He was maneuvering a windy part of the hill, so he asked Jules to answer.

"Swipe your finger across the face," he instructed. "You don't know how to use a smartphone? Why don't you have one, anyway?"

"You wouldn't understand."

"Is it a Virgo thing? If so, you're right."

"*You're* Virgo," Jules said, that feisty kitten again. "I'm *Cancer*, and someone named Angela is waiting for you to answer."

"Oh." Dexter kept his eyes on the road. "Let it roll to voicemail," he said, making a tight left.

"Dear me." Jules hit a button and dropped the phone to her lap. "I hope you're not missing a date or booty call, or whatever she is."

"Booty call?"

"I *said* 'or *whatever*.'" Her voice was so loud, a flock of birds flew off the telephone wire they drove past. "I'm not down with today's man-whore vernacular. You should've taken the call and told ever-faithful Angela that you can't hook up at the moment because you're with your wife." She gave him a big, bright, too-toothy smile.

He narrowed his eyes at her, but seeing that smile aimed at him—full of sarcasm and sass—made him want to kiss her, then let her keep talking, then kiss her again.

Instead he adjusted his shades and stepped on the gas.

Jules didn't have to direct him. Even though he hadn't been to her grandmother's place since high school, he knew where it was.

"Oh, my grrrrshhh," she said in her highest high-pitched

voice, her fingers covering her grinning mouth. "We're here."

Dexter had barely put on the brakes when Jules was out of the car, skipping toward the cottage. That's right, skipping, in bare feet, her mermaid dress and hair streaming behind her like a comet's tail. He couldn't help smiling at how excited she was. Until he saw the house.

Ten thousand dollars won't put a dent in this.

Wearily, he got out of the car and removed his sunglasses. His memory might've recalled the address, but not how tiny the place was. "Cottage" was not a misnomer. It was so small, it reminded him of a beach bungalow or a hunting cabin. Nice view of the lake, though, and the paint job and landscaping looked relatively maintained.

Jules was having a hard time opening the front door, until she punched the wood right under the knocker, and the door magically opened. It might've been his imagination, but Dexter smelled incense wafting out of the house.

The living room was something out of the '60s. Light wood paneling, canary-yellow walls, and an orange shag rug were just the beginning of this hodgepodge of a room. Sheer curtains every color of the rainbow hung beside the windows, none of the end tables matched, and a red velvet couch was the focal point of the room. The walls were covered in blindingly bright paintings. Some framed, some on bare canvas, and some on paper, even just scraps of paper.

The whole room was so jarring that Dexter wondered if he should close his eyes for fear of triggering an overstimulation coma.

The sound of Jules's bare feet skidding across the hardwood floors in another room reached him, along with her non-stifled squeals of delight. Obviously, the house wasn't jarring to her. She'd told him a million times how much she loved it.

Hoping for something he could relate to, he walked

through the kitchen. Besides a carved-up butcher block table, it consisted of little more than appliances tinier than what you'd find at Ikea, one long, narrow butcher block counter, and a shower rod mounted to the wall with hanging pots and pans. From the look of it, everything in the kitchen was old enough to have been gifts to Grandma Rosy when she'd graduated from high school.

The room did have something pretty kick-ass going for it. The windows. Practically the entire wall was either a window or a sliding glass door that went out to the back deck.

"Are you dying?" Jules said, flying into the kitchen. "Without Grams, I thought it might feel different, but it still has the same energy." She drew in a deep breath, then twirled into the living room. "Same vibe and vibrant chakras. Can't you feel it on your skin?"

Dexter stared at her. Was she speaking English?

"It's, uh, well... That's a nice painting over there," he said, pointing to an unframed canvas covered with a bunch of squiggly lines in various shades of blue. Something a three-year-old might've done with his fingers.

"You like it?" Jules beamed. "It's mine."

"Oh." He looked at it again and rubbed his chin. "How old were you?"

Her grin quirked. "That's a random question. Nineteen, I guess. Maybe twenty. Few years ago."

Dexter tried really hard not to burst out laughing as he replied, "Oh. Nice. Um, I should check out the rest."

It wasn't an actual hallway since the house was too small for such a necessity. It led to the guest bedroom. Or maybe it was a graveyard where pillows with tassels came to die. The master bedroom was connected to the first bedroom by a bathroom with walls the color of the Caribbean Sea.

"What do you think?" Jules said, floating in from around the corner, bright-eyed and smiley. "Is it what you remembered?"

"Not at all. I mean, I don't remember it being so"—while backing up, he knocked against a tall, rickety bookshelf lined with empty wine bottles—"cluttered."

"Grams is a collector," Jules said. "She loves beautiful things." She picked up one of the bottles, but then her hand froze. "Loved," she corrected, her voice weakening as she set it back down. "Grams *loved* beautiful things." She walked out of the room. No more free-spirited spring in her barefoot step.

Sensing her mood change made Dexter frown and follow after her. He wished there were something he could do to make the loss of her grandmother easier. Maybe just being with her, giving her someone to talk to, would help. She'd opened the glass door off the kitchen and was out on the deck.

"Whoa," Dexter said, shading his eyes from the sun. "This is awesome."

"You've been here."

"I don't think I ever came out back this way…" He trailed off as he stepped onto the wood-planked deck. The size of it was easily more square footage than the entire house. Wicker chairs and tables, wooden seats, benches, plastic lawn chairs, and a few beach loungers were spread around the deck. Dozens of plants in ceramic pots, hanging plants, ivy and natural vegetation, all coming back to life under the spring sun.

What Dexter couldn't keep his eyes off was the lake. No other house was built so close to the water. It was probably less than a two-minute walk, or forty-five seconds if he followed his impulse and ran straight for it to take a swim.

"This is impressive," he said, walking past a family of faded ceramic garden trolls in the corner. "Does the house have its original floors and beams?"

"I'm sure it does. Probably original plumbing, too."

He moved to the middle of the deck, slid his hands in his

pockets and turned to stare at the house. "It'd have more curb appeal if you could see more of this yard from the front of the house. A place like this, if the integrity is sound, is worth a lot."

"Five hundred thousand. Maybe more after the renovations."

"Renovations? I thought you said it's all original."

"It is. Now. *I'm* renovating. Grams and I planned to do it together, but…" She tucked some hair behind an ear. "We ran out of time."

"You cannot renovate this house. That's insane." When she didn't reply, he had to laugh. She was wise about many things, but maybe real estate wasn't one of them. "Jules, listen. This house is a classic. If you upgrade anything, that'll make it less historic. People are into retro these days."

"I don't care what people are into, I'm building an art studio—screened in."

"Where?"

She stomped a foot. "Right where we're standing."

Dexter felt the blood actually drain from his face. "No, you can't. Are you nuts? This…" He spread his arms. "This is the focal point of the house. This is what sells it. And you want to take away half of it to add a screened-in porch?"

"Not a porch. A *studio—my* art studio. Right here has incredible natural light year-round. It's perfect. Grams was all for it."

"That's ridiculous."

Jules folded her arms. "Why do you care? It's not like you're going to live here."

Okay, she had a point, and maybe he'd gotten a bit carried away. "I'm just thinking of your…your future. The value of the house will depreciate."

"I'm never selling. It's where I'm going to live."

This was news to Dexter. Didn't she live in Vegas? "I thought it was just a property you'd use in the summer."

She chuckled a bit sarcastically. "Some of us can't afford a summer house. Some of us only have one primary residence. And this is mine."

"Let's just drop it," he said, knowing that arguing right now was pointless. He'd never considered the difference in their bank accounts to be a big deal, but apparently it was to Jules. He pulled his cell from his pocket and checked the time. "I suppose it's useless for me to fly out today. I'll change my flight to first thing tomorrow morning."

"Fine."

"I need you to promise you'll lay low once I'm gone. My family will think we're together in Manhattan."

"We already told them we're living here."

"I'll fix that, and it's not like you'll run into them." He looked her squarely in the eyes. "Promise me, Jules, promise you won't go into Hershey for at least a month."

"A month?"

"You can go to Lancaster or Bethlehem when you need food or whatever."

"Gee, thanks for your permission."

"You know it's how it has to be. Not counting Roxy and maybe my mom, I think the rest of the family would be okay with the truth now. But do you really want to take that chance? The news will shoot straight to Quent Sanders."

For a moment, she stared at him in terror, then pursed her lips as her shoulders dropped. She'd done the mental math just like he had. "No, I can't risk it. I supposed you'll tell me when it's safe to show my face in public again?"

"Sure." The return of her sass made him smile. Sass was almost as appealing as her sweet side. Which did he prefer?

Definitely the sweet—the real Jules.

"I'm assuming there's no landline here," he said. "So I'll need your cell number."

"Why?"

"For one thing, to let you know when…how did you put it? When it's safe to show your face. Also, in case my lawyer has any questions."

She twisted her lips. "I don't give it out to just anyone."

"Not even to your husband?"

"Well…"

He shook his head and sighed. This adorable, free-spirited girl needed so much taking care of. For a second, Dexter wondered if he'd be the perfect guy for the job.

And just like that, another whirlpool of nervousness hit his stomach. Though he knew by now it wasn't nerves, even if his mind still didn't know what to call it.

"Here. Hold on," he said, going into the house for a pen and paper. "This is my number. Call me and I'll program yours in."

"My phone's dead."

"Recharge it."

"Ugh. That's such a pain."

So many muddled feelings were zapping through his brain and body that he didn't know if he wanted to kiss her or spank her.

Instead of either, he suggested they walk to the lake. It was a pleasant afternoon for April, and he hadn't been to Conewago in years. They didn't talk much, mostly because Dexter found a spot with good reception and spent a bulk of the time on the phone. If he wasn't getting back to the office for another day, plans needed to be adjusted.

After office hours, he was supposed to meet with his team to talk about Friday's meeting with the investors. If he screwed up this golden chance, he might never get another. And also, at the end of the month, he'd officially be an ex-employee of Elliott Technology. Jobless.

It was definitely a twinge of nerves that hit this time. He'd been in Hershey two days, and still hadn't explained to his father. Their once-close relationship was getting more and more strained. If he left in the morning without clearing the air, it might never be repaired.

Dad hated talking socially on the phone, so Dexter knew he shouldn't just give him a call. At this, he had to chuckle. Jules obviously didn't like cell chatting either. Maybe her adverseness to technology wasn't strange after all.

While he sat on a boulder, Jules skipped stones across the lake, the afternoon sun glowing orange across its smooth surface. As he spoke with his assistant, Jules waded up to her calves, kicking water while holding up her long skirt. She had the bottom of it tossed over her shoulder, giving Dexter a very nice, though very distracting, view all the way to her midthighs.

"I'm assuming there's no food in the house," he said, ending his call. "Nothing fresh."

"Doubtful," Jules said, her cheeks flushed and rosy.

"What's the name of that restaurant on the other side of the lake?"

"Jigger Shop?"

"Yeah." He smiled, reeling in a youthful memory. "They had the best sundaes."

"Totally." Jules was smiling, too. "But they're only open from Memorial Day through Labor Day. There're a few other places in town."

"Great. I'll wait while you…" He was about to say for her to put on shoes, but didn't bother. "I'll run to the house and grab the keys."

"Okay," Jules said, playing with the ends of her tangled hair, the golden sun shining behind her. She was in the car when he came outside; the bottom of her dress was soaked, but she either didn't notice or didn't care.

He couldn't figure her out.

But wanted to.

They ate dinner across the street from a small art gallery. Dexter would've been blind to not notice how often Jules glanced that way, a wistful look in her eyes. It was cool when she talked about art, and he was about to ask her about it, but stopped. What if she brought up that painting of hers with the squiggly blue lines? What if she asked him what he liked about it?

It's very…blue. And quite…squiggly.

No, he'd better keep replying to emails.

The sun was nearly setting by the time they made it back to the house. Dexter was about to accept an incoming call when Jules frowned.

"Do you mind?" she said.

"What?"

"Having that annoying technology constantly running along with your one-sided conversation isn't the vibe I want in my house."

Dexter could've given a dozen reasons why her argument was beyond mere quirky, but simply stayed where he was. "I'll take it on the back porch."

"If you don't mind," she said with an angelic smile. "Thank you."

Jeez, this woman. Talking crazy but with the sweetest countenance. With the right guy, she'd be lethal.

Dexter walked across the deck toward the lake. His call took forty-five minutes, and since he'd gotten only a few hours of sleep the night before, thanks to crashing out on the floor, he was pretty beat.

They hadn't yet discussed sleeping arrangements for tonight. Obviously they didn't need to share a bedroom let alone a bed this time. And he was more than ready to hunker down anywhere, then catch his 10:00 a.m. flight.

When he got to the house, Jules was curled in one of the wicker patio chairs. The porch light was on; she had a blanket tossed over her and was flipping through a book. She looked so comfortably at home, he felt envious.

"I'm gonna sack out," he said. "Which bedroom should I take?"

"There's only one."

"Not two?"

"The second isn't really usable. There's a bed. Kind of. But it's buried under pillows and art supplies. Grams was getting ready for me." She bit her thumbnail and looked past him, doing that zoning-out thing. "I put your bags in the master. We can share, I don't mind, whatever."

Dex had never been one to turn down an invitation like that, even if it was platonic. "Okay. I'll just...then..." He pointed to the house, and when Jules smiled casually and flipped a page in her book, he walked inside.

Instead of the dust and old incense he'd sensed before, the house now smelled like citrus. All the windows were open and Jules had set up a few standing fans. It made a huge difference, and Dexter felt much more at home. Until he stepped into the master.

At least this bed was bigger than the one back in his old room, but a dark pink canopy hung from its wrought iron frame, heart-shaped pillows lined the foot of the bed, and the entire room looked like it had been decorated by a '60s love guru.

He had no idea how long he stood in the doorway before Jules came up behind him. "Thought you wanted to sleep. You like the right side, yes? Grams always kept a spotless house, but I changed the bedding."

He hadn't noticed this earlier when Jules had been sitting on the deck, but she'd changed into a tank top and tiny sleep shorts.

"Um." No, dammit. The whole room practically screamed sex.

Abstaining from that was mind over matter. But suddenly, that same image from last night flashed through his mind: Jules propped on a pillow, chatting away like the adorable, addictive little chatterbox she was. Smiling at him from one pillow over.

Ignoring an emotion-tugging image like that was *not* mind over matter for Dexter. He had no idea how to fight it. Therefore, no way could he share a bed with her.

"I'll, um…" He grabbed his bag. "I'm just gonna sleep on the couch."

"Why?"

"I snore."

She put her hands on her hips. "Since when?"

Since never. "It's been years. Probably sleep apnea—I should get tested." He began backing out of the room, running into that same shelf with the wine bottles. "Got an extra blanket?"

Jules tossed him a quilt from the cedar chest. "You sure?"

"Yep. I'll be fine. S-sleep tight now." He closed the door, shutting her inside the bedroom, even though she'd said nothing about going to bed now.

In the living room, he took possession of the red velvet couch, grabbed a green pillow with bright orange suns embroidered on the front, turned off the light, and settled in.

For just one night, he thought as he tried not to hear the water running in the bathroom, tried not to wonder what his wife was doing in there.

Chapter Nine

Jules was pulling the whistling kettle off the flame when she heard a tap at the back door. Grinning Roxy was waving through the glass. What was she doing here? It was barely 7:00 a.m. After making her heart stop racing from surprise, Jules smiled and opened the door.

"Good morning."

"Morning!" Roxy gave her a one-armed hug, because her other arm was carrying a rolled-up yoga mat. "You ready?"

"For…?"

"Sunrise yoga. We talked about it yesterday before you left the wedding. Remember?"

Jules had a vague recollection of it, but couldn't remember actually inviting her curious sister-in-law to the cottage. Though she must have. There were so many lies flying around, she couldn't remember all of them.

"Am I too early?" Roxy frowned. "Is Dex still in bed asleep?"

Jules's Lemon Zinger shook in her hands, splashing over the sides of the cup. "Um, no, he's…" Casually glancing past

Roxy, she peered into the living room. The back of the red velvet couch faced the kitchen and two sets of fingers curled around its top. Between them was the upper half of Dexter's head, wide-eyed, staring at her over the couch like Kilroy.

Crappity-crap. Roxy could not discover that Dexter had slept on the couch. She'd blab it all over town, and Quent would sue Jules for false…something or other, then take her house.

"Hey," she said to Roxy, "would you bring me another tea bag? They're in the ceramic Elvis on the counter." While Roxy's back was turned, Jules pantomimed wildly at Dexter to stay down and sneak out of the room. He understood her gestures because a second later, Kilroy was gone and on all fours, crawling across the shag rug.

"Do you have coffee?" Roxy asked.

Jules bolted to her side and threw an arm around her, making sure she kept turned the other way. "Coffee? Sure, yeah. Grams didn't drink it, but she always kept a can of freeze-dried on hand for guests. Um…" She tapped her chin in deep thought. "Let me think a minute where it might be. Hmmm. Why don't you check the pantry—*no, wait!*" She jerked Roxy in the other direction when she saw Dexter's reflection in the window, crawling toward the bedroom. "I think we're out. Right, yeah, sorry. No coffee, but tea galore. Have a cup?"

"Sure," Roxy said, stepping back and stretching her neck to the side like Jules had given her whiplash. "Dex? What are you doing down there?"

Quel busted.

"He's, um, stretching! Aren't you, baby?" Jules shot him a look that said to follow her lead. "It's the child's pose, see?" Why wasn't he moving into position? How could he not know the child's pose?

"Right," Dexter said, kind of twisting his back while

lifting one hand off the floor.

"That's not child's," Roxy said.

"He likes to combine poses—he's very advanced." Jules smiled dotingly. "You can get off the floor now, sweetie pie. Enough stretching."

Dexter dropped his chin and stared at the floor for a minute, then exhaled and stood, brushing off his knees. His hair was sticking straight up and sleep lines from the pillow striped his cheek. Jules's heart did a full backflip at how doggone adorable he was.

"Think I'll hit the shower now," he said, hooking a thumb toward the bathroom.

"You're not doing sunrise yoga with us?" Roxy asked.

"Um." Dexter rubbed the back of his head.

"Isn't that why you were just stretching? Warming up? I want to see the master in action. Jules told us how good you are."

"I did say that," Jules said, trying not to giggle.

"Well…"

"Oh, please. Don't make me beg, big brother."

Jules did giggle now, even harder when Dexter's face drained of color. "Of course he's joining us." She moved to his side and patted his arm. "You wouldn't miss it, would you, honey bunny?"

He looked into her eyes while wrapping a huge, strong hand around her arm. Jules could feel the heat of his annoyance, but wasn't letting him off the hook. "Not for the world, pooh bear."

"I'll wait outside on the deck," Roxy said. "I can tell you guys want to kiss or whatever, so take your time." A second later, the back door closed.

"Thanks a lot," Dexter growled in a low voice, squeezing her arm.

She smiled up at him. "You're welcome, dearest."

His eyes narrowed as he dropped her arm, muttering under his breath. "Tell her I went for a run."

"Big guy like you can't handle a little yoga?" She crossed her arms, offering him something she knew he couldn't resist. "I'll *bet* you."

He gave her a long, appraising look. "Stakes?"

"If you complete an hour of sun salutation, then I'll…"

"You'll?"

"Not sure. What do you want?"

He rubbed his scruffy jaw and shot her an up/down scan that made her heart backflip again. "I want you to not add on to the house."

She rolled her eyes—no more heart gymnastics. "Get off that, please. It has nothing to do with you."

"It's a really bad idea. Trust me."

"Ha! Said the spider to the fly. How about I give you a massage after yoga, so you'll be relaxed for your flight. Massage is my day job, and I charge big time."

"Are you any good?"

She tried not to be insulted by the question. "I make the highest tips every week."

"Okay, you're on."

Won't matter, Jules thought with an inner smirk. *Sunrise salutation might be ideal for beginners, but he's so tied in knots, he'll snap in half.*

Dexter went to the living room for his bag. "But I have to be at the airport by nine thirty."

"Plenty of time. Pooh bear."

• • •

An hour later, Dexter couldn't feel his legs. Or his arms. Or most of his head. But he'd stuck with it, dammit! It might've severed his spinal cord, but he completed a solid hour of yoga.

The first few times through the sunrise salutation were a piece of cake, though did Jules have to keep explaining to Roxy—so apologetically—why his poses looked different?

Was it his fault a normal man wasn't supposed to bend like that?

Now he was flat on his back, staring bleary-eyed at the morning sky, "listening to his breathing." If Jules said that one more time, and in that annoyingly calm yoga voice, he'd punch a wall.

If only he could lift his arms.

"Dex? Sugar lips?" Jules nudged his shoulder with her foot. "Time to shower. You have a *lot* to do today. *Remember?*"

Dexter closed his eyes and groaned.

"I think he's dead," Roxy said. "Did you hear his back crack during the last upward dog? It registered on the Richter scale."

"He's fine," Jules said, leaning over to gaze down at him, blocking the sun. "He overdid it, showing off for you. Right, my excellent strong man?"

"Yeah," Dexter said, somehow finding the strength to roll over and push himself off the deck to stand. Every muscle in his body shook with the effort. "I should've warmed up more. Won't make *that* mistake again." He sent Jules—who was grinning like the cat who'd swallowed the canary—a glare as he walked to the back door. If she hadn't looked so damn cute in her tie-dyed yoga tank top getup, he might've done more than glare.

But even his eyelids hurt.

When he stood still for a moment, he felt a humming through his body, like his blood was alive. The "nala" Jules had described. Despite the muscle pain, he felt…great. Energized. Maybe yoga and the other stuff Jules was into wasn't all that odd.

"Can I have some water?" Roxy asked, stretching out on

a vinyl beach chair. "Mmm. I could chill on this deck forever. Maybe I will. Such an amazing view."

Jules shot Dexter a look he easily interpreted. Dammit. If his sister planned on hanging out here, he couldn't exactly pack his bags and leave for the airport—which he was supposed to do in an hour.

"Hey, sexy lady." He whistled a low catcall at Jules. "You know that special clause in your wedding vow. When *I* shower, *you* shower." He nodded toward the house. "You have two seconds to take off those clothes before I do it for you."

After the initial look of alarm left her face, Jules played right along. "You talk a good game, Mr. Yoga Master, but you don't scare me."

"I scared you last night, didn't I? Three times, if we're keeping score." When Roxy still didn't offer to leave, he added, "This time I won't be nearly as gentle. And your two seconds are up."

"Okay, you win," Jules said, then peeled off her tank top and threw it over a chair, leaving her in nothing but tight yoga shorts and a purple sports bra.

Dexter froze. Yes, the woman had looked sexy as hell in his hockey jersey, and that towel, but he'd never seen so much of her skin at one time—not that he could remember, that is.

Freakin' wedding night amnesia.

For a moment, his muscles strained, torn between moving forward to take her in his arms and holding himself back from doing just that. Maybe he needed another hour of yoga to clear his head.

"I won't be as gentle this time, either," Jules said, walking past him and slapping his butt...which didn't help the argument going on in his brain. "Now *you* have two seconds. Lose the clothes, sweet cheeks."

What if he did take off his shirt and kept going? And what if Jules kept going, too? What if there was a pile of workout clothes on the deck and —

"You guys are equal parts cute and disgusting," Roxy said. "Dex, you know I'm still traumatized from watching that YouTube video of Luke and Natalie making out at Hersheypark. Please don't strip naked. I might never have a healthy relationship again."

"Better scram, little sis," Dexter said. "I'm about to do more than strip my wife naked."

Jules's mossy green eyes grew wide and her lips peeled apart. Was she forcing herself to remember this was make-believe, too?

"Disgusting — again," Roxy said. "Mom and Dad will be here any minute, so there isn't time for kinky newlywed shenanigans."

"Your parents?" Jules stared at her. "Coming over?"

"Didn't I tell you? Sorry, I meant to when I first got here."

Dexter was now fully shocked into the present. "What are you talking about?" He looked at Jules. "Did you invite them?"

Jules had a hand on her cheek while she squinted off to the side. "Mmmaybe?"

"No one invited them," Roxy said. "They wanted to surprise you, but since no one likes the parental pop-in, I meant to warn you."

Dexter scanned the patio for his cell to call his parents and feed them a story about wanting to be alone with Jules. A story that wasn't at all untrue.

Too late. A car was turning onto their street.

He and Jules shared a quick and silent look. She made a fist and opened it while subtly shaking her head. She didn't know what to do, either.

"Better put on your shirt," he said.

"Why?"

He sighed. "Please."

"Okay." Jules rolled her eyes and pulled her tank top over her head. "You're so conservative."

"So is my dad."

Oh. Perhaps his parents' popping in was a good thing. Dexter desperately needed to talk to his father.

There isn't much time if I'm going to catch my flight, he thought. *Some things, though, are more important.* He'd meant that in regard to Dad, and yet his eyes slid to Jules.

"Like Dad cares," Roxy said.

"Jules, darling, may I have a brief word with you in private?" He nodded at the back door.

"Certainly, darling dear." She smiled and trotted inside, but rounded on him the second they were alone. "I adore your parents, Dex, but—"

"Sorry. They do this."

"How are you gonna make your flight?"

"I'll tell them something—an emergency at the New York office." Then he thought for a quick moment, a bit stunned by what he was about to propose. "Unless…"

"Unless…?"

"Unless I stay another day."

Jules's jaw went a little slack, but that was the only alteration in her expression. For someone who prided herself on keeping her independence, no entanglements, she didn't look as aghast as he'd expected.

Why? Did she want him to stay?

Since he currently sucked at reading women's nonverbal communication, he'd have to just come out and ask—

"Dexter? Juliet?"

He'd have to ask later.

Mom's voice coming from the living room was singsong cheerful. "Knock knock."

"In here," Dexter said in a monotone voice, eyes locked on Jules. "Don't panic. We'll figure it out."

She looked at the ceiling. "Comforting."

More of that dead-sexy sass he loved.

Loved? Wait, not—

"Hi, you two," Mom said as she and Dad came into the kitchen.

Jules immediately went to them, giving each a big hug and kiss. "Welcome," she said with a bright smile. "We're so glad you dropped by."

"Well now," Dad said, looking around the room, keeping his hands in his pockets, "this is quite an unusual house, isn't it? Unique."

"Thanks," he and Jules said at the same time.

"We're happy here." He put an arm around Jules and gave the top of her head a peck.

"We sure are, honey bear," Jules said, though it was clear to him she wasn't comfortable.

Was it because his parents were here? Or his impromptu suggestion about staying?

Obviously, another day away from New York wasn't the best solution for him. He had two weeks to get his ET life in order before he left the company. Additionally, each day this week had a built-in after-hours meeting with the small tech team he'd formed over the last few months. The team that would hopefully become the employees, cofounders of his own company.

But first, they desperately needed this one last investor.

"I was just putting on some coffee," Jules said, filling the kettle at the sink while closing a drawer with her hip. "Would you like some?"

"We'd love a cup," Mom said.

"Me, too!" Roxy exclaimed, sliding the screen door shut.

Dexter caught his mother giving Dad a sharp look.

"Ahem." His father shifted his weight and coughed under his breath.

"Dad," Dexter said, grabbing the moment. "Can we talk a minute?"

After a beat, Dad nodded, and Dexter gestured to the back door. As he crossed the room, he saw the way Jules was looking at him. He might not be an expert at reading expressions, but the openhearted concern on her face was unmistakable.

Although she couldn't have known the reason, somehow, she knew he was troubled. The pressure on his chest, along with the mixture of unnamed emotions swirling in his stomach, made him want to take her hand, squeeze it tight, and then tell her everything, his entire life story.

Once outside, Dexter led his father to a pair of straight-backed padded lawn chairs at the end of the deck. For a long moment, they sat in heavy silence. Dexter knew full well this was his conversation to initiate, so he finally launched in.

"I want to explain why," he began.

Dad only looked at him.

"First, I apologize for springing it on you last week that I'm leaving ET. I've been thinking about it for a long time, not seeking reasons to quit, per se, but knowing it would happen someday."

"Okay." Dad nodded. "Do you have a plan?"

"I do." Dexter took a deep inhale. "At first, it was just an idea. Overseeing product management keeps me in the loop about what's hot out there and how to market it. Lately, I've been spending more time with the design team. After a while, the idea I had grew into something tangible." He paused and rubbed his palms together. "What the product is isn't important. But it's something I'm very passionate about."

"You should've brought it to me first."

"I did. You blew it off."

The moment Dexter said it, he regretted it. Sometimes, he could be blunter than was necessary. A trait he'd picked up from the man sitting across from him.

Dad sat up straight. "That isn't fair."

"A big part of me was glad you did. I've worked with you for nine years, but even before that, I knew what made you tick as a businessman. You built Elliott Tech from the ground up. Creating something completely your own." He looked toward the lake. "I want that, too. I have for years."

"Why the rush? The technology boom has miles before it hits the ceiling." Dad leaned forward and gave him that steady, paternal blue-eyed gaze. "This product of yours, do you have capital behind it?"

"Not yet."

"Any investors?"

"A few, but I'm meeting with a big one on Friday. That signature on the line will seal the deal."

"Dexter." Dad shook his head, his voice grim, disapproving. "Do you understand what you're walking away from? Salary, insurance, benefits, stability. You're risking everything on an idea and one *big meeting*. That's reckless."

"Maybe. But it's my risk to take."

"Not anymore." Dad turned toward the house. "You have a wife now. A family. Juliet's a wonderful girl, and we're happy you're together, settled down. But let's not pretend she can bring in even a quarter of what you're giving up."

"Jules supports me," he shot back. "Maybe not monetarily, but in every other way."

Right that second, he wanted to tell his dad the truth. And then—despite how Dad still didn't get why Dexter was quitting ET—he wanted to ask for advice, answers to questions, such as: Why did his chest hurt and then fill with warm, soothing air when Jules was around? What did the nervous whirlpool in his stomach mean?

"Well, I've said my piece." Dad rose to his feet.

Discussion over. Dexter dropped his chin, shoulders

slumping in disappointment.

"And I'm sorry, but I just don't approve. I can't."

"Okay," Dexter replied. They were at an impasse. And even though it might be juvenile, at that moment, Dexter wanted more than ever to make his father proud. This meeting, yes, this one meeting had everything riding on it. If it went south, he'd have nothing and no one to fall back on.

In silence, father and son returned to the house. When Dexter opened the door, there was a loud, lively conversation going on in the kitchen. Hearing Jules's voice made his stomach do that…thing. Then another voice rang out, one he recognized but didn't expect to hear in a million years.

The blood in his veins turned to sharp shards of ice when he saw Quent Sanders cradling a mug of coffee in *his* kitchen—*his* house.

"What's going on?" he said, trying to keep his voice at a composed level.

"Look who stopped in," Roxy said with a great big smile.

The guy must've had a death wish to stand so close to his sister. Among the other secrets, the shit Quent had done five years ago to seventeen-year-old Roxy was the worse secret Dexter was keeping. He'd always thought hiding the truth from Roxy—and everyone—was the right thing to do, but that was when she'd been away at college and had no contact with Quent.

"Nice place," Quent said, extending his hand to shake. Dexter didn't want to be a dick in front of his mother, so he kept his mouth shut and shook Quent's hand. "I didn't actually plan on coming in, but I was driving through the neighborhood and saw all the cars." He shrugged. "Thought I'd say hello, check to see how you're settling in."

"Thanks again," Jules said, but her voice sounded guarded, distrusting. His wife had excellent intuition.

"I'm sure you're always welcome," Roxy said, beaming

at him.

Dexter did not like that. It was a good thing she'd be back at Rutgers in a few days. But even New Jersey didn't seem far enough away.

"Did you get everything worked out, hon?" Jules asked, handing Dexter a cup of coffee while giving him a subtle glance through her long lashes. The moment their eyes locked, he felt the connection they shared. Though it was new and unfamiliar to him, it was strong.

"Yes," he said, wanting the connection to last. "Thanks."

"Um, so, babe," she added, lifting a smile so bright that he knew instantly it was fake. "Y-you'll never guess what."

Dexter had an eerie feeling he didn't want to know. "What?"

Jules visibly swallowed and blinked rapidly. "Your mother's throwing us our very own wedding party."

"Just the family," Mom inserted.

"Quent, too!" Roxy chirped.

Over my dead body.

"Nothing fancy," Mom continued. "Jules even offered to have it right here."

Dex glanced at Jules. "She did, huh?"

"We feel awful that we didn't get to celebrate with you properly." Mom added.

Dexter lifted both hands, palms out. "That isn't necessary—we understand. No party is needed."

"Nonsense," Mom said, waving him off. "We're doing it and that's final."

He looked at Jules, and once again, they exchanged a panicked look disguised as happy smiles. "Well, thanks, then," he said. "When?"

If it was in a couple of weeks, he'd just have to fly back to Hershey. It would be a pain but he'd do it.

"Tomorrow night," Jules said, doing that toothy smile

thing that meant she was about to start flushing like hell. "Isn't that just…just great, sweetie?"

At the news, Dexter's stomach hit the floor. How could this get any more complicated? "Mom, seriously, you don't have to—"

"Dex," Dad said in a stern voice, "your mother wants to give you this gift. Don't insult her."

After all these years of working together, and even with the current tension between them, until now, Dad had never made Dexter feel like he was under his thumb, given him a direct order.

"I know you have an important meeting in New York on Friday," his father added. "And that you have other loose ends to tie up at the ET office, but I"—he cleared his throat—"I'd very much like it if you took the next two weeks off."

Dexter could only stare at him, openmouthed. When they'd talked outside, Dexter must not have expressed how vital the next month was—the next few days, particularly. How was he supposed to stay in Hershey for two weeks?

"It's not that I'm keeping you away from work," Dad continued before Dexter could form a reply. "Every marriage needs to start with a proper honeymoon—if your marriage is important to you. Alone time is vital, er, or so your mother says, and I…I need you to accept this as a gift from me. To both of us, for your new life together."

Dexter was so touched by the uncharacteristic gesture, he didn't know what to say. Two weeks alone in this house with Jules. His brain spun at how that might be—hypothetically. Before his imagination could take him too far, he figuratively held his head in his hands to stop the spinning.

There was no way it could happen. But how could he break it to his father?

Telling him the whole truth was the only way. But if he did so in front of sleaze bucket Quent Sanders, Jules would lose everything.

Maybe, though, he could tweak his plan of flying out today and leave directly after the party. If his parents were serious about giving them alone time, they'd never know.

In his head, he was calling colleagues to plan a conference call for this afternoon to discuss the adjustments and Friday's meeting. It wasn't close to being as sufficient as face-to-face, but it would have to do.

Hold up. When he'd mentioned to Jules earlier that he'd thought about maybe staying, she'd seemed less than thrilled. This whole thing was still an act to her, and he'd misinterpreted everything—even his own feelings. What a damn fool.

"Well then," he said, sliding an arm around her, making himself feel nothing. "Thanks, Mom. We're honored." He hadn't realized he'd pulled her so close to his side until he heard her breath rush out.

By simply looking into her eyes, he knew her mind was whirring, trying to figure out why he'd agreed to the party. He had a new plan now—emotion-free—and he'd share it with her soon enough.

Trust me, he said, sending his thoughts her way. *Please, trust me.*

Surprisingly, her shoulders relaxed as she leaned in. Trusting him.

Chapter Ten

Jules wasn't exactly honored, but Eileen Elliott was so darn sweet, Jules couldn't help agreeing to the party. Besides, it would take a soul completely lacking of feelings to not sense tension between Dexter and his dad. Was there a disagreement they hadn't settled?

It was a little heartbreaking to think that. The whole Elliott family was so close. Maybe this party would be a good thing for Dexter.

If that was the case, she'd willingly go along with it—even the two weeks of fake honeymoon if need be. She knew how much she owed Dex for not spilling the beans about their non-marriage when the truth would've made his life so much easier.

Still, how could she possibly survive with him in her cottage for two weeks? She wasn't so emotionally stunted that she didn't realize she had feelings for him. Feelings that Dexter wouldn't understand—because he'd never felt them. He was never with one woman long enough to feel anything but physically gratified.

Didn't he know there could be so much more?

"Thank you," she said, once the family was gone.

"No need," he replied as he picked up his phone and headed for the back door.

While washing the rest of the dishes and wiping up the kitchen, Jules kept an eye on him. First he was sitting, then pacing, then sitting again, then he walked toward the lake, phone pressed to his ear the entire time.

Was he talking to a woman? One of those other women in New York? How many were there? And could she ever compete?

No. Because that was what Dexter wanted. No strings, no commitments, total freedom from entanglement. She used to think she wanted the same thing. Now she wasn't sure.

Taking her time, she wiped off the counter and hung up the dish towel, all the while feeling the spare bedroom staring at her as if it had eyes…each tube of oil color and every paintbrush called to her like voices from the dust, asking why she hadn't come to see them in the three days since she'd been in Hershey.

She'd been dreading this moment…longing for it, and dreading it.

The time had come, though, even if made her stomach twist.

After running her palms over her shorts, Jules went to the spare room. Behind the dresser and in the closet were her art supplies.

She dragged out the paint-splattered and well-used heavy wooden easel, and then chose a brush, holding it to her nose. Sweet memories of Grams came flooding back. So many happy times.

Normally, she'd spend the next few hours going through all her paintings and drawings, playing the remember game. For the past week, she'd been dying to paint—fearing to paint.

There was no room for fear. The first-time-entries submission deadline for this year's Mount Gretna Outdoor Art Show was at the end of the month.

Butterflies fluttered in her stomach whenever she thought about entering. Grams was never in favor of arbitrary people or panels judging her art. Jules agreed vocally, but inside, she needed to know if she had what it took. For her whole life, she'd dreamed about being a professional artist. She'd even taken a huge leap of faith and quit her job, canceled her lease in Vegas, to move to Hershey full time in hopes of making it as a painter.

The savings she'd been socking away would support her for maybe a year, even with the money from the bet, now earmarked for the renovation. That made her think of Dexter. How dare he tell her she was making a mistake by adding on to the house? She'd never dream of selling, so it didn't matter if an art studio lowered its value.

Feeling cross with him again made her feel good. It was how their relationship had started—except for the getting married part—and it was how it should remain.

A heartbeat later, though, she found herself smiling at how hard he'd tried to hold those yoga poses this morning. She had to give him credit—he'd lasted a lot longer than she'd expected. If he'd do a few more sessions with her, he'd get better. More in tune. More flexible. More...

Jules broke off her thoughts when she started biting her lip, imagining how an experienced guy like Dexter might use his flexibility.

As she wandered into the living room, she shut her eyes and mentally thwapped the back of her head. No, he was an "experienced" guy for a reason, and may never be willing to change.

A stack of old albums was stored between the wall and the bookcase. Jules pulled out the four on top—the ones she always went for first—carefully removed them from their ancient covers, then stacked them in order on the record player.

The living room filled with music that brought back so many memories, for an instant, she almost couldn't breathe. She wrapped her arms around herself until the sadness from loss was replaced by happiness.

Before she knew it, she was swaying around the room, doing the waltz step Grams had taught her. Joy filled her heart, but sadness clung to the edges. It might never go away completely, and she'd have to find a way to live with it. After all, she'd lived her whole life feeling some kind of loss—this was nothing new. Not even with Dexter.

"Is this Basie?" His voice made her nearly jump out of her chair.

"Sammy Davis Jr.," Jules said, looking up from her sketch pad when Dexter came in.

He filled a glass of water at the sink. "I know who's singing, but is it with Basie's orchestra?"

"Oh. Yes." Jules tilted her head. "You know Count Basie?"

"I do." He took a long drink. "My parents' country club was my day care. When I was a kid, I used to sneak into the ballroom during classes."

"You liked big bands?"

"It was more that I liked when the women's dresses flared out."

"Started out early, did ya?" She was trying to play it off like she didn't care what he did with his life, but the dig was forced and made her feel hollow.

Not replying to her comments, he moved to where she'd dragged a chair close to the window. "Why didn't you come outside to…" He dipped his head to see what she was doing. "Thought you were a painter."

Jules flipped to a blank page, self-consciously. No, not

self-consciously. She'd never been insecure about her art, but Dexter would probably stare at it and call it a mess. His expression earlier hadn't been hard to read.

He knelt behind her, his body warm, as he studied the various brushes and pencils over her shoulder.

"I'm both," she replied, standing up, needing space. "I do both. *Can* do both." *Crap, stop being so floopy!* "I'm a painter, but before I start a new piece, I like to free-sketch, to get the creativity flowing."

Or to avoid the fact that I haven't been inspired to paint in months. If she wasn't inspired, how could she move forward?

"While playing Basie?" Dexter said.

"Grams has records I've listened to forever."

"His version of 'April in Paris' from the *Live in Sweden* album is my favorite."

"That's…" Jules put down her pencil. "That's my favorite of his songs. But I prefer it on the Brunswick studio album."

Dexter leaned against the table. "No way. Live versions are always superior. No mixing, nothing overproduced. Just the count's piano, the orchestra, and heart."

Heart? The things she learned about Dexter when they weren't even trying… Did he discuss his love of big band music with anyone else? Those *other* women?

"What about the studio version of 'I've Got You Under My Skin'?" she asked as she walked to the fridge.

"I'll give you that one, but you've got Sinatra on vocals. Nothing touches that." He grinned and swayed back, gaze drifting into the middle distance, like he was hearing the song in his head. "I've always wanted to dance to it," he said. "But it was a rare album, never made it to CD or digital."

"I have the record."

"Really?" Dexter smiled out the window, then looked at Jules. "Want to—"

The words stopped dead in his mouth as he scanned her

outfit. While he'd been outside on the phone, she'd changed out of her yoga clothes. Okay, some of her friends *had* referred to the flesh-colored material that barely reached midthigh as her "naked" dress, but she hadn't worn it on purpose. And yes, she'd taken an extra second to pull her hair back on one side and pin in a flower. But that wasn't because of Dexter.

"It's on the shelf over there." Jules pointed to the stack of albums.

"Oh, um, cool." He looked away and cleared his throat. "Think I'll go for a run instead." Without another word, he left, wearing the same clothes he'd been in all day.

Puzzled, Jules returned to the table and sat before her sketch pad. But her gaze found Dexter as he trotted across the deck, then onto the path toward the lake. His movements were smooth and elegant. It took less than a minute for him to reach the shore. He bent, touched a bolder, then turned to run back the way he'd come, only to stop at the far end of the deck, touch it, then turn again, like he was running wind sprints.

For a while, she just watched, mesmerized by his movements, concentration, the line of sweat spreading down the back of his T-shirt. Without thinking, she pushed her sketch pad aside and reached for a paintbrush.

It wasn't the literal re-creation of an athlete framed by a blue lake that she painted, but the abstract images representing how she felt as she watched that tireless athlete. Reds and bright blues, swirls of green, happy yellows. She couldn't stop until she filled the entire canvass.

Sitting back, she exhaled a long, stale breath that seemed as though she'd been holding it for months. Only then did she notice it was dark outside; one light came from the living room.

"Dexter?"

"Who else would it be?"

Jules stood, feeling achy from sitting in the same position for so long, but happy and relieved—inspired, finally inspired after all this time. As she turned on the stove and filled the kettle, she also felt light-headed. When was the last time she'd eaten? While the Elliotts were here? She looked at the pig clock on the wall. It was seven o'clock.

Dexter lounged on the couch, his feet propped on the coffee table under a stack of hot pink pillows, computer open on his lap, head resting on one of Grams's hideous crocheted blankets. Her fingers twitched for a paintbrush and miles of canvass.

"Want some dinner?" she asked.

"I already ate." He was wearing glasses, and looked quite comparable to one of those sexy nerds in a magazine. "There's some for you, too, in the fridge."

"Some what?"

"Sushi. I went into town. Decent food for being in the sticks. Hope you like California rolls. I figured they're safe."

The desire to paint, to cling to her new inspiration, was momentarily replaced by need of sustenance. "Wow, thanks." She might've broken the sound barrier by how fast she bolted to the fridge. A little brown bag sat on the empty top shelf. She really did need to go on a proper grocery run soon. Which reminded her of something.

"So, the party tomorrow?" she said as she unloaded the bag. Two California rolls were untouched in individual clear wrap. Her mouth watered, and she wanted to thank him again for being considerate. "Have you thought how to get out of it? I'm assuming by how late it is, that you're not flying out tonight, but you will tomorrow?"

"I've been thinking about that." Dexter walked to the kitchen and refilled his mug. It had faded cartoons of the Flintstones on it. Jules had given it to Grams about a million Christmases ago.

A silly thing like seeing Dexter with it made her heart swell.

"I have a new plan," he said. "The party is the perfect opportunity to get out of our situation completely."

Like a dummy, Jules's silly, silly heart sank.

"Oh yeah?" she said, biting the inside of her cheek. "How?"

He took off his glasses, pinched the bridge of his nose, then put them back on. "We'll have an argument in front of them."

"They see us bicker all the time. Thanks to you, Quent thinks it's foreplay."

"This will be different. We'll make it a real fight — I'll storm out and...can you cry on cue?"

"I don't think so. And why would I cry?"

"Because our marriage is over. We'll stage a big fight and everyone will know we're on the rocks — maybe we have been for a long time and thought getting married would fix it, but it didn't and now we're tired of pretending we're not miserable."

Just keep on sinking, silly little heart.

"You've thought a lot about this." She went to the record player, putting the albums back in their cases. "I hate fighting. I hate lying. I hate everything about this." She put the last album away, then looked at Dexter wearing glasses and drinking from her Flintstones mug. *Well, maybe not everything...* "But it'll probably work. If that's what you want."

"It's what we both want. Right?"

Jules nodded, but inside she felt like crying.

"I'll complain that you're a workaholic and your job always comes first, even after you promised you'd changed. It's true, you know — the work thing."

"I'll complain how you never take anything seriously. You're always floating around, doing your own thing, and that you can't even focus enough to paint — your big dream, right?—the first thing about you that I fell in love with. I mean, the fake me and the fake you."

How could he be so cold? Apparently, to Dexter, everything they'd been through really had been make-believe.

It was a fake fight over fake feelings, but still, his comment about her not painting stung. Up until a few hours ago, it was true.

"Fine," she said. "I'm a free spirit and you can't handle it. That'll sell itself."

"Totally. If we stage the fight early enough in the evening, I'll be able to catch the red-eye."

"Hallelujah," Jules said, picking up a coffee table book about horses and flipping through it without seeing the pages. "The sooner the better."

• • •

Dexter was coming in from the deck after finishing a quick call when he found Jules in the kitchen. At least she'd pulled an oversize sweater over that non-dress. It'd been difficult to concentrate on work earlier with her sitting there, lounging on a pile of pillows, eating sushi, while looking all chill and half naked.

"Are you a late-night coffee drinker?" she asked.

"I am."

"Thought so." She passed him a steaming mug, then slid over the half-gallon carton of chocolate milk. He took it and splashed some in.

"How did you know I take it with chocolate milk?"

She took a sip from her own mug. "I'm very observant. Plus, I know your mother."

"This is true." He picked up a spoon. "Although I would rather have some of that peppermint drink of yours."

"I showed you how to make it."

"I know, but—"

"Dexter Elliott." She shut the fridge. "Do not give me the line that it tastes better when *I* make it."

He couldn't not grin. "Isn't a line if it's true."

Jules laughed indulgently and shook her head, handing him her bottle of peppermint oil. "Three drops, babe. You can do it. I'm pulling for you." She winked before disappearing into the living room.

Dexter made a fist and pressed it over his chest, unable to remove the smile from his face.

He liked this girl. A lot.

After concocting his new beverage, he went to the couch, sighing on his way to sit as he eyed his computer.

"You've been working on the same thing all evening," Jules said as she perched on the other end of the couch.

"Yeah," he said, trying to banish unhealthy thoughts by squeezing the bridge of his nose. "I've got this meeting on Friday and—"

"So you've mentioned."

When she winked over her mug, he smiled and eyed her soft sweater, wondering how it and she would feel in his arms.

"What's the big deal about this meeting? You have a million of them."

He waited a beat, but felt Jules's gaze, so curious and open. "This isn't a meeting with or about Elliott Technology."

After a moment, she set down her mug. "You're thinking of leaving your job?"

The question made him exhale a dark chuckle. "I'd be a colossal moron to do something like that, wouldn't I? Just ask my father." He shook his head and stared across the room. "A *colossal moron*."

"That's what your meeting's about? Something else."

Dexter looked at her, at her head tilted to one side, her sweet eyes. "Yes. Something else."

Jules adjusted her position on the couch to face him, pulling in her knees. "Do you want to talk about it?"

Luke and Vince were his usual go-tos. But other than his father, he hadn't breathed a single detail to anyone about leaving the family business, or his meeting with Three Jacker Media.

Yes, he wanted to talk about it. But not with his parents or brothers or therapist. He wanted to talk to Jules.

He removed his glasses and set them on the coffee table. "A while ago, I had an idea that I took to ET's R-and-D team to see if something like it already existed in the marketplace. Which it did—in a way, so I came up with a unique twist, which doesn't exist. I ran the idea by my father." He paused and rubbed the back of his neck, feeling knots of stress. "I don't think Dad really got it. Maybe it's too out there, I don't know. The idea wouldn't go away, I couldn't stop thinking about it, and since it's not in competition with anything at ET, it wasn't a conflict of interest if I worked on more developing."

"And you did?"

He nodded. "It got bigger, took on a life of its own. Without realizing it, I'd built a team of software developers, engineers, graphic art techs—all from outside ET, though my assistant moonlights a bit for me, keeps me organized. After a business lunch a few weeks ago, I hung back with one of the guys who's involved in start-ups. I pitched him the idea over beers and pretzels, and..."

"He's interested."

"Very. But I didn't agree to move forward with it—not right then. I couldn't."

"Because you're loyal," Jules said. "You love your father and you're respectful. I'm not a businessperson, but even I know that kind of loyalty is rare, impressive. Desirable. Probably makes your start-up guy want to work with you even more."

Like a dam being released, Dexter felt a tidal wave of gratitude toward Jules, the woman on the other end of the couch who didn't wear shoes. The woman who got him, understood, held his hand when he needed it.

"Thank you," he said, feeling choked up and lame. "That means a lot."

Their gazes held, and once more, his head and mouth filled with words he wanted to tell her. Words his tongue couldn't form. Before he could do anything, Jules slid over next to him, their shoulders bumping.

"Tell me about it."

For a second, he couldn't move. Couldn't swallow.

"On your computer," she prompted. "You've been glaring at the same page for hours. Show me or talk through your idea. Since technology is my archenemy, I probably won't understand much, but if it'll help you…"

Dexter might have zero personal experiences with relationships, but he also wasn't dense. Jules couldn't care less about his new business. But she would sit and listen because she thought it might help. Because she was caring. Because she was Jules. The most caring person he knew.

Besides his family and close friends, Dexter couldn't think of a woman in his life who wanted nothing from him. Not an expensive dinner, or a ride down Fifth Avenue in a flashy car, or a night with him at the Plaza.

Their relationship—he didn't even stumble over the word—might've begun as a Vegas mistake that turned into a business arrangement, but it was different now. He felt it, and he knew she did, too.

Taking a moment to let that sink in, run through his brain and his bloodstream, Dexter opened his laptop. "We're past the idea phase now, still developing the final software, but we have an introductory prototype." He stopped and looked at her. "You know what, now that I think about it, you might be the perfect person to run this by."

"Really?" She sat up straight and flashed a proud little smile. "That's so cool."

"Can't believe I didn't think of it before." He removed the screen from his computer, turning it into a tablet, handing it to Jules. "For frame of reference, you've used Corel Painter, right?"

"Don't think so."

"You've heard of it, though?"

She frowned. "Is it something to use in the ocean? Painting coral or rocks? I think that might be illegal."

"It's a computer program, kind of like ArtRage."

"Haven't heard of that, either."

After realizing he was barking up the wrong tree, he smiled. Why would she know of computer programs about making art? She was charmingly old-school. "Okay, well, the concept is making pictures on the screen—on the computer. Tracing, drawing freehand with anything you can think of, lead, chalk, crayons, pens, and painting in all mediums, oil, acrylics, watercolor, even a mixture. Our technology is advanced and specializes in combinations, collages, and framings."

"Making art on a computer," Jules said, drawing out the words.

"Exactly. It's just one of the applications—there're dozens." He flipped to a screen showing the PowerPoint presentation, then to the example of what their program's operating system will look like. "Touch the screen," he said. When she didn't, he drew a line down the center, then clicked an icon, making the line look like a brushstroke of thick red oil paint. "Now you try."

Hesitantly, she made a zigzag over his line, touched an icon, and turned her line into light blue acrylic.

"Awesome, right?" he said. "And this is nothing. Practically every artistic tool is right here. Any size or type of brush, any color combination. You can save your work on one device then reopen it from anywhere. Completely mobile. After you've done all the editing you want—and those tools are in the thousands—you print it. It can go on any type of paper, even canvas. It's literally virtual art."

"Virtual art," she repeated.

"I thought you'd like it."

"*Like* it?" She stared at him. "It's awful."

The comment made him flinch. "Why?"

"This"—she tossed the screen on his lap—"is exactly what's wrong with the world. You want to take art, something that requires open space and time and air movement and freedom, and confine it in a computer? You turned it into technology, cold science." She stood from the couch and paced to the other end of the room. "You're clipping its wings, putting it in a cage."

"I'm making it accessible."

"Are people too busy these days to carry a sketch pad if they feel like drawing? Instead they just pull out their baby computer thing, draw a tree with one finger, press a button, then print it out and call it art. No, sorry, *virtual* art—because it's not real."

Normally, he liked it when she got kitten-feisty, but this was all wrong.

"Jules, calm down."

"You don't know what real art is," she said, wringing the bottom of her sweater. New stains of paint on her fingers stood out. "When's the last time you were in a gallery? I'm not talking about some opening in Chelsea where you're there to have a business meeting and not actually look at the art. A real gallery, like the ones here in Mount Gretna that feature local artists. They're beautiful and moving—emotional, and that can't be created on a computer."

Seeing the genuine injury in her eyes made his world

stop. And once again when it came to Juliet Bloom, he was an idiot. If he'd considered for two seconds, he would've known. She didn't wear shoes or own a smartphone, why would she be in favor of virtual art?

"I offended you," he said humbly. "And I'm sorry."

When she looked at him, her cheeks were red. "Okay."

"But I'm not sorry about the idea," he added. "I see it through your eyes, though, and I get what you're saying."

"Thank you."

Dexter pushed his computer away, wanting to make amends. "You were sketching earlier and I know that's your painting on the wall." He pointed at the squiggly lines. "What else have you done?"

She peered at him kind of funny, then extended her arms out to her sides. "These."

It took a moment before he realized what she meant. "All of these? There's got to be a hundred," he said, gazing at the walls, every square inch covered with some kind of drawing or painting.

"Eighty-nine. Grams counted last year."

"And you did them all?"

"I'm an artist—it's what I do."

"Right." Okay, so he didn't get the meaning of bright pink sunflowers that morphed into blue ocean waves and orange sun rays, and he knew nothing about technique, but he had to be impressed with the sheer volume of work. No one spent so much time at something if they didn't love it, if passion didn't surge through their veins like bolts of lightning.

"Do you have more at home in Vegas?"

"Not nearly as many," she admitted, slowly walking back to the couch. "Real life was there. I had a job and responsibilities—bills to pay. But when I'm here…" Her voice trailed out as she gazed into space. "It's like I'm completely free. I've always felt that way—it changes people, I swear. I feel no weight on my shoulders, no responsibility other than to create. I have a lot of artistic friends in Vegas. Some have never found their muse. I have, and it's always been here in Hershey, Mount Gretna, this cottage facing the lake."

Finally, Dexter understood why this place was so important to Jules. It wasn't just her grandmother's memory, it was the house itself. For a minute, he felt jealous. Besides the weekends he'd spent at home during college, sleeping late and eating his mom's cooking, Dexter had never felt free and weightless like how Jules had described.

But man, did it sound appealing; *she* sounded appealing. He wanted it—what she'd described.

But would it work for him without her?

"I'll, um, take the couch again," he said. "We'd better call it a night."

Chapter Eleven

Dexter was in the middle of the recurring dream of getting ready to bungee jump from his office window. His father was always in the dream, behind him, watching, but this time, his corner office was full of his family, Quent, Rosemary Granger, and Jules.

He was jumping, though. No matter who was watching. It was time. Something suddenly broke his concentration. A knock at his office door. A pounding so loud it sounded like a wrecking ball.

"*Ouch.* Holy mother of…"

The voice shook him awake, and at first he just stared across the room. Streams of morning sunlight touched its edges and corners, illuminating tiny whirlpools of swirling dust coming off the antique furniture. He grabbed his phone. It was after nine o'clock. Since when had he been a late sleeper? He yawned and stretched, wondering if he could find that "nala" from yesterday.

More pounding made it impossible.

Dexter was on his feet, storming bleary-eyed toward the

sound. "Stop! What in holy hell are you doing?"

Jules peered at him through the most ridiculous pair of safety goggles while lowering a freaking sledgehammer. "Did I wake you?"

"Did you *wake* me?" He stepped back and looked around. The breakfast nook table and chairs were moved away from the wall and covered in a tarp. The wall between the window and back door had a hole in it the size of a basketball. "What are you trying to do?"

"Knock down this wall, so you better move, it's not safe."

"Safe?"

He noted her perpetually bare feet. At least she was wearing steel-toed boots, which looked five sizes too big.

"I know what I'm doing." She swung the sledgehammer and hit the wall, causing Sheetrock to fly and the windows to rattle.

"You're supposed to remove the glass first. Did you shut off the circuit breaker?"

Ignoring him, she took another swing. Wires and beams inside the wall showed through. This focused, eccentric girl was going to seriously hurt herself if she kept going. When she wound up to swing, he grabbed the tool out of her hands.

"Whoa. Hold on."

"I told you I know what I'm doing."

"You're acting crazy."

"It's perfectly sane to do home construction on my own home. And yes, the power is off. I'm not daft."

He rubbed his eyes, then his stubbly chin. He hadn't shaved since Sunday. "Jules. You can't knock down this wall until the glass is out."

"I tried." She ran the back of a hand across her forehead, smearing a line of white drywall chalk. "I'll have someone come out later this week and help me with that part."

"Nope. No way."

She stepped up to him, hands on hips. "We've been over this. *You* don't have a vote."

"I realize that." Had he ever met a more stubborn woman? "Will you at least let me hire a contractor?"

"No." She took off her goggles and tossed them on the tarp. "I'm doing it myself. I don't need a professional."

He could only imagine what would happen if she continued on her own. "Look, I know you're totally, totally capable, but the guy who lives across from Mom and Dad has a construction company, a small one—*indie*. I think he builds houses for Habitat for Humanity." He paused for Jules to roll her eyes on cue. "Let's have him come here before you go further. These old houses can be tricky. I know you'd hate to mess anything up."

If she went along with it, that might buy him time to talk her out of renovating. Give him ten minutes and he'd patch the hole in the wall she'd made.

"I suppose it wouldn't hurt to have a second opinion, just in case. Think he can come out today—this morning?"

"Why don't we wait until later? Family's coming over tonight for the wedding party and we don't want a bunch of broken glass and loose wires hanging around, right?"

She shifted her stance, wobbling in her big boots. "Okay, I'll wait a day. Then you won't be here to bug me about it." She smiled and fluttered her eyelashes, but the usual sass wasn't there. Maybe the thought of him leaving made her feel weirdly anxious, too. "But will you call your guy today? I don't want to put it off."

He swallowed and tried not to ogle the slice of skin showing between the top of her shorts and the oversize white T-shirt tied at the waist. She had dust on her arms and face. And was she sweaty? *Damn...*

"S-sure, sure," he said. "I'll set it up for tomorrow."

"Great." She exhaled contently and stared out the

windows toward the lake.

Dexter wouldn't admit it to Jules, but this part of the house, and the hundred square feet of the deck, *was* the perfect place for an art studio. So much light and warmth and space. He understood why she was determined, though he was too practical to be in favor of it.

"I'm dirty and hot," Jules said, pulling back his attention. "I need to clean up."

"You shower, *I* shower," he said automatically.

"Yeah, right—not!" She swatted his arm. "I think I'll go for a swim. The water's pretty cold, but I like it that way. Wakes up my mind and my body."

It wasn't hard for Dexter to envision what that might look like. "What do you need for tonight?" he asked, to have something to do. "I can clear out some of the furniture so there's more room. I'll run to the store, too."

"Already did that," she said. "I used your car. Hope you don't mind, but you were dead to the world. You're a really heavy sleeper."

"I never used to be," he said. "And it's fine that you took the car. Feel free whenever you need."

"You're not moving the furniture, though."

"But I was thinking—"

"Not one piece, Dexter." She pointed at him with playful scorn. "There's plenty of room, and since it's casual, we'll be sitting most of the time, either inside or on the deck. The weather's supposed to be beautiful."

If he persisted in the argument about furniture, he'd never win. "Is there anything else I can do?"

She pushed out her lips and combed her fingers through her hair. "I made bread this morning. It's rising in the fridge. I picked up jam and cheese from the farmers' market, and these cute little avocado-bacon wraps. They'll take twenty minutes for me to put together. I bought all the ingredients for lemon bars with Hershey's chocolate chips—Natalie and Luke will love those. You can pick up some wine if you think your family will expect it."

"I'm sure they'll each bring a bottle," he said, a bit taken aback. "You did all that this morning?"

"I'm an early riser and you snore."

He laughed, enjoying—more than he'd ever expect—the simple couple-type conversation that flowed so easily between them. When he was back in New York tonight, he would miss it. Immensely.

"Well, thanks," he said. "I didn't expect you to take care of everything. I was prepared to have it catered."

"Why? I love entertaining. Besides…" She rubbed her nose. "I'd like your family to have one last good impression of me before they hate my guts. It's important to me—I've known them forever. It'll suck to lose them." Before he could reply, she added, "I'm going for that swim."

And she was out the door, kicking off her boots, walking across the deck in her bare feet, not bothering to take a towel. Dexter watched her the whole three minutes it took her to get to the lake, not even trying to fight back the warm feeling moving from his chest to his stomach.

He set up shop on the deck, knowing Jules didn't like him conducting business inside. Even though she was away, he respected her quirky wishes. He made a few phone calls, replied to a hundred emails, then when he was done with the red-hot issues concerning ET, he opened the PowerPoint file.

Despite his opposite views on the subject, Dexter couldn't help replaying Jules's words. To someone as gifted as her, his program wasn't real art.

Maybe it wasn't. Perhaps the opinion of a true artist he trusted was the exact kind of feedback he needed. The benefits of having Jules in his life—for even these few days—still hadn't ceased to surprise him.

At the sound of voices, he glanced toward the lake. Jules's form was in the water, splashing around, but there was also a figure on the shore. Dexter squinted and sat forward, then he was striding across the deck, trying not to break into a run.

"Leave, now," he said, slightly out of breath.

"I brought the house papers," Quent Sanders replied, leaving the shore and walking over. "Signed and notarized."

"You were supposed to fax them to me."

"Why do that when I can hand deliver?" He grinned and passed Dexter a sealed, legal-sized folder. "I'm all about giving that *personal* touch to everyone. Amazing view here, anyway." He turned in the direction of Jules in the water. "Can't take my eyes off it."

She was close to shore, but must've been on her knees or sitting, because the water was up to her shoulders, strawberry hair floating around her. Dexter didn't have to account for each item of clothing on the rocks to know she wasn't wearing anything.

"*Amazing* view," sleaze bucket Quent repeated in a lower voice, a sleazy, sleaze bucket voice. "Must run in the family— and I'd know. I was just about to take a closer look—"

With no time to analyze the white-hot rage blurring his vision, Dexter reacted by cocking back and cold-clocking Quent right on his sleazy mouth.

• • •

Jules tried to yell *stop*, but nothing came out. And she wasn't exactly in a position to get out of the water to make him stop. Letting Dexter see her was one thing, but Quent?

"Dexter!" she shouted. "Don't!"

Too late. Dex was staring down at where he'd knocked Quent flat on the ground, holding his fist inside his other hand, face dark as thunder.

"Don't hit him again," she called. "Walk away."

"I won't touch him," Dexter replied in a disgusted voice.

"Is he breathing?"

"Of course."

"Bleeding?"

He paused. "A little."

She needed to get out of the water and help, but when she tried, Dexter shot her a steely look. "Babe—stay where you are."

She nodded and stumbled back, swimming out a little farther. She'd never seen him so pissed, not enough to punch a guy. "Get me a towel, then. We need to call 911."

"I'm fine." Quent's voice was hoarse as he sat up. "It's nothing."

Dexter scoffed. "I broke your nose, man. Be thankful that's all the damage."

When Quent wiped his face, Jules saw the blood. "Dexter," she called. "Help him."

"He doesn't need help, do ya, Quentin?"

"No," Quent said, bringing his shirt to his nose. More blood.

Dexter extended his hand to help him up. Quent glared at it, but finally allowed Dexter to pull him to his feet. "Never speak of my wife like that again," he said in a low, menacing voice, thunder back on his face. "Never speak to her again, or to any member of my family. And if I hear even a whisper of a rumor that you've contacted Roxy, you'll be very, very sorry. Do you understand?"

Quent nodded, and without giving her even a split-second glance, walked toward his car parked on the lane. Dexter stared after him, hands on his hips. He didn't move a muscle until Quent's car was gone.

"Did he touch you?" he said, whipping around to Jules. "Did he hurt you in any way?"

"No," she said, but her voice trembled. "He surprised me. I didn't hear his car, but suddenly he was here."

"He'd probably been watching you from the trees."

"*What?*" Jules gasped and threw her arms around herself to cover up.

He stared down at the ground, not looking at her. "He won't be back. I promise."

"What happened between you two? Did he hurt Roxy?"

The laugh Dexter exhaled was dark and laced with anger. "It was a long time ago. He seems to have a short memory about it because he still thinks he's allowed around my family. That'll stop now. He must get off on causing trouble, pain."

She wanted to ask him, wanted to help him through it, if she could. But he seemed in no mood to calmly discuss.

"Do you want me to bring you a towel from the house?" he asked. "I'm sure you're cold."

Jules looked down at herself, at the upper half of her body submerged in water. Uh, yeah, Dexter might not've been able to see it crystal clearly, but she was certainly displaying evidence of being cold.

"Thanks, but I'm okay. If you could maybe just head to the house now, I'll grab my clothes and be a minute behind you."

He nodded, squinting up at the sky nonchalantly. "Okay."

After he'd taken about three steps, Jules swam until she touched the bottom. But the action made her wince and cry out.

Dexter swung around. "What's the matter?"

"I don't…" She took another step. When her right foot burned, she stumbled forward.

"Jules." Dexter was at the shoreline, stripes of worry across his forehead. "You're hurt."

"No, well, yeah." She floated back and reach for her foot. The second it made contact with air, it stung like hell.

"You're bleeding."

"I must've cut it on a rock. I tripped when Quent was here, but didn't feel it until now."

"Can you walk?"

"Yes." But when she tried, she winced again and grabbed her foot protectively.

"How bad is it? Let me see."

Was he seriously expecting her to crawl out of the water buck naked so he could examine her foot?

"Here. Wear this." He pulled off his black T-shirt and tossed it to her. It landed on the water right at her face.

"Thanks." She definitely didn't make a point to breathe in the lovely, manly scent of Dexter before the whole thing was wet. Once the shirt was on—and so long it was practically a minidress—she swam to shore, rotating so she drifted in feet first.

"It isn't bad," he said, down on one knee while holding her injured foot. "Multiple cuts all along the bottom. You need to stay off it."

"Easier said than—*whoa*!"

In the blink of an eye, Dexter waded into the water, took her around the waist, and hoisted her out, not a single stumble as he treaded to shore. He held her in his arms like a baby as he silently carried her toward the house. Yes, his shirt she was wearing was long, but not long enough that it covered the underneath parts of her body, making Jules keenly aware that his hands were touching bare skin.

She shut her eyes, and to block out feelings of embarrassment, she concentrated on his hands, how they felt, their warmth and strength. Next, she concentrated on his skin, his chest, the side of his neck, how he smelled the same every time she was near him. When she thought about his heart, his humor and bravery, and how he made her feel warm and protected, she couldn't think of anything else.

"Do you have Band-Aids? A first aid kit?" he asked as he stepped onto the deck.

"Above the bathroom sink."

"I'll bring you a towel. Will you be okay out here for a minute?"

"F-fine," she said. Her teeth chattered as Dexter gently set her down on the chaise longue, making sure her foot was elevated.

"Use the end of the shirt to keep pressure on it," he added. "Be right back."

As he walked away, his back muscles flexed when he opened and closed the door. His jeans were wet, too, and clinging to that body in the most perfect way jeans could cling to a guy. It was so beautiful, she wanted to whimper.

He was back a minute later, carrying supplies. Lucky for her, he was still shirtless. Or was it *un*lucky, because she couldn't keep her eyes off him?

"First thing's first," he said. "You need out of that before you freeze. It's sunny enough on the porch that you'll warm up quickly, but…" He placed one of her cotton dresses on the table beside her, then opened the towel, holding it up like a curtain between them.

Without speaking, she pulled the wet shirt over her head, momentarily struggling with it when it got tangled in her hair. She threw it across another chair, then pulled on the dress, leaning back to tug it all the way on over her legs.

"Done!" she said in a bright voice.

Dexter slowly lowered the towel. "Ahem. Right. Okay." He dragged a chair to her feet and sat. "Let me take a look. Hmm." He ran a finger across the arch of her foot. Tingles started at the point of contact then sizzled north.

"Do you want to tell me about Quent?"

His initial reply was a mere clenching of the jaw, but then he said, "I haven't told anyone."

Translation: he didn't want to talk about it.

"Okay, but you seem to carry unnecessary baggage. Aren't we good enough friends now that we can share the bad stuff?" She touched his arm. "I'm here to listen, if that's all you need."

"I'm going to slide this up a little." he said, as if she hadn't spoken. He pushed her dress up to her knee, then gently lifted her foot and held the heel in one hand.

"We met in high school," he said without preamble. "I was a senior, Quent was a sophomore."

Jules didn't say a word.

"We got along fine, but Quent picked up some habits— drugs, bragging about going bareback, every douchey guy cliché out there. I played hockey and basketball, pretty clean living comparatively. Couple months into fall semester, the school did a campus-wide drug sweep. I was with Quent when the officer was leading the dog through the locker room. A second later, Quent was gone and the dog was heading straight toward me, barking like the devil. Long story short, I got busted for a bag of weed in my backpack, but several witnesses came forward saying they saw Quent slip it in there when I wasn't looking."

"What happened?" Jules asked, hanging on his every word.

"In the end, nothing happened to me, but the next day, Quent got expelled. I never said anything to anyone. I'm no narc, but Quent blamed me, used to trash my car, egg our house, pretty much made senior year a living hell." He paused and stared into the middle distance for a moment. "Anyway, a few years later, he and Roxy started hanging out. I didn't know about it for a while because I was working in Manhattan, and thought Quent was in college out west."

As he spoke, his head was lowered, and he dabbed medicated cream on the bottom of her foot. "Does it sting?"

he asked.

"No," Jules whispered.

"Even back then, Roxy's never been able to keep secrets, and she told me they were dating. Quentin Sanders doesn't date. He manipulates and hurts for the hell of it." It was quiet for a moment as he began wrapping her foot in gauze.

"I hadn't talked to him in almost five years, but he hadn't changed—he was making it a point to mess with my sister on purpose. I contacted him and told him to end it, but…"

He broke off, and Jules touched his arm again, gazed at his lowered head, wishing so much that she could help.

"Quent just laughed," he finally said. "To paraphrase, he said my sister was…too good to stop playing with."

Jules couldn't speak, so she slid her hand down his arm and wrapped it around his hand.

"A few days later," he continued, still not looking up, "he did break it off. But Quent's a pathological liar, and instead of cutting her loose, he said he was spending the summer overseas with the Peace Corps, which of course Roxy loved."

"But he wasn't?"

Dexter shook his head. "He was living with a woman— one of his mother's divorced friends, actually. She was paying for his college and law school because evidently Quent lost his tuition at a casino in North Dakota. The guy had major issues, and I could've almost felt sorry for him had he not reached out to Roxy again, told her he'd joined the military and was being deployed."

"Roxy told you that?"

"No." He pulled her hand toward him and squeezed. "Quent did. He made it a point to tell me everything he'd said and done to her, and he…threatened to do worse if I told her the truth."

"Blackmail?"

"There was no money involved, just my sister. He was

hurting Rox, but she didn't know. He was doing it to mess with me, and I couldn't do anything about it."

"Dex." She cupped her other hand over his, pressing them together.

"At the end of that summer, right before Roxy was leaving for college, they ran into each other. She thought he'd been deployed. Quent told her he'd been wounded in action." He scoffed darkly. "A war hero. He just wouldn't let her go no matter what I offered, so I had to ride it out from two hundred miles away. He bragged that he'd gotten into Puget Sound, and Rox would be in New Jersey soon, and I was sure it was finally over."

When he didn't finish, a cold, black, heavy cloak of understanding wrapped around Jules.

"Until this weekend," she said, feeling sick. "Until I brought him back into your lives."

Dexter finally lifted his chin to look at her, but she could barely see from the tears flooding her eyes.

"Dex, I'm sorry. I didn't know. I'd never hurt Roxy...or you. I'm so sorry." Her voice shook, her throat was thick, and when she tried to pull her hands away, Dexter wouldn't let go.

"Hey." His voice was soft, close. "Jules, hey. I know that. Trust me." He touched her chin. "I know."

For a moment, they just sat, holding hands, staring into each other's eyes, and Jules's heart hadn't felt this full since the last time she'd been in love.

When everything had gone wrong.

"My"—she cleared her throat—"my foot hurts a little."

"It'll stop soon," he said, sitting back and releasing his grip on her hands. The sudden coldness of his absence made her shiver. "But you have to stay off it for the rest of the day," he added, "otherwise the cuts won't heal."

"I can't," she said. "Your entire family's coming over tonight."

Dexter packed up the first aid kit. "I'll take care of that."

"You're canceling?"

"No. I mean, I'll take care of it. Get the house ready."

She lifted an eyebrow. "The food?"

"You tell me what to do. I'll even let you help if your foot is elevated at all times."

She exhaled a sound of amazement. "You'll do all that, host and everything?"

His eyes drifted from her face to her foot, and he tucked in a frayed piece of gauze. "I know tonight's important to you."

For about the tenth time in an hour, Jules's heart filled with warmth. Despite everything she thought she once knew, there was so much more to type-A Dexter.

She looked at him, at his dark hair and blue eyes, the muscles of his chest, his arms and hands. Then she thought about all his wonderful qualities, too many to list. Suddenly, her heart was beating so fast it felt like it was trying to burst out and fly.

Then wrap around Dexter Elliott.

Chapter Twelve

"'Night." Dexter waved. "Thanks again." As soon as the last taillight disappeared, he shut the door.

"Well."

From across the room, he shared a tired smile with Jules. "Well."

"Your mom loved the bacon wraps. Who knew?"

Dexter chuckled and leaned against the couch, feeling worn out but energized. "I've never seen her eat with her hands like that."

"It's the cottage," Jules said. "It does something to people. Think about it." She stood and hobbled across the room.

Dexter's instinct was to rush over, put an arm around her, and let her use him as a crutch, like he'd been doing all evening. Now that his family was gone, it didn't seem…proper. No more need to play the doting husband. How many times had she told him in the last five days that she was independent and didn't need anyone? Least of all a husband.

It was nice when she needed him — or at least *acted* like she did. He loved when she'd look across the room and without asking, he knew she needed to lean on him. He'd never felt more like a man than when he was making life easier for her. His wife.

A part of him felt like he owed her. Even though nothing could change the past, an enormous weight had been lifted off his shoulders after he'd told her about Quent. She'd sat there and listened as he'd gone on and on, sharing with her what he'd never shared with another soul.

Yes, he owed her. But that wasn't why he'd played host tonight, it was because he'd wanted to.

He swallowed and looked the other way. "Think about what?"

"The cottage," Jules replied. "Today, for example. Only once did I have to kick you out to the deck when you were on the phone. And tonight, your cell was on the dresser the whole time and you didn't talk about work once."

Dexter could've explained that he hadn't talked work because he didn't want to get into it with Dad. But his cell? Huh. Not once had he even thought about it. There were probably a hundred messages and missed calls, but he didn't care.

Tonight, he'd been Jules's husband, and that had taken top priority.

"Do you want to keep the living room this way?" she asked.

It had been totally Jules's idea, but Dexter had heartily approved when she'd suggested they move one of the chairs and two of the end tables (along with all their knickknacks) into the spare bedroom before the party.

"Only if you like it."

"Ha!" That loud, cheerful voice echoed from the kitchen. Hearing it made him smile, made him want to go to her right then. Just to see her.

"With the furniture spread out like this, it gives the room

a better…" He paused to search for the right word. "Feel… flow."

Jules was in the middle of a snort-laugh when he entered the kitchen. "I hate to tell you this, but you just described feng shui."

Dexter laughed too, and took the mug she was holding out, the smell of peppermint warming him all over.

"And you're saying my magic cottage can't change lives."

He chuckled under his breath and took a sip, allowing his eyes to linger on the long black skirt she was wearing, its thick lines of off-white paisleys around the waist. Her black shirt, low neckline, rolled-up sleeves, short enough to show a slice of toned stomach whenever she moved her arms.

It had been a relentless challenge, but he'd managed to keep his hands off that skin all evening.

"Hey," Jules said, bringing him back to the present. "What about the fight?"

"What fight?"

"We were supposed to fight in front of your family. That was the whole point of tonight—the exit strategy." She set her mug on the table. "You're supposed to be catching the red-eye."

"Oh. Right." He rubbed his chin. That fake argument had completely slipped his mind. He'd been too caught up in… being a husband.

A knot formed in his chest, clenching tightly. It was a new kind of pain, though not actually painful. He didn't know if it was a good feeling or a bad one. Bad, of course. Jules was right; he was supposed to have laid the groundwork for their divorce and been on his way to New York.

"I kept trying to bring it up, but then I'd get sidetracked."

"Thinking about your virtual art meeting?" she said with an exaggerated eye roll.

"Exactly." No reason for her to think it was anything else.

"Speaking of, Natalie really loves your paintings."

"No." Jules shook her head. "She was just being polite."

"Trust me, I doubt Nat says anything she doesn't mean."

"You think?"

"The one over there, with the big daisies." He pointed at the wall. "You called it *Urban Blossoms*. She wants it. I heard her talking to Luke about it before they left."

"She can have it."

"How much?"

"I'd never sell a painting to a friend, let alone *family*."

"Natalie isn't really your family, though."

Jules frowned at him and blinked, processing the comment he wished he could take back. Before she turned away, Dexter saw the sadness in her eyes, the same misplaced anguish as when she'd blamed herself for Quent. He'd do anything to take that away, by putting a friendly arm around her, a squeeze of her hand, just like she'd done for him.

"Well, she feels like family—they all do," Jules snapped as she poured the rest of her tea down the sink. "Could you get all your stuff out of my room now? I want to go to bed."

He stared at her screwed-up expression that he didn't understand. The moment to comfort was gone. Too slow, Dex had let it pass. "Sure," he finally said.

For a while, he tried to work, but couldn't keep his mind on his project. With the couch turned the opposite way now, he kept finding himself staring across the room at the bedroom door. The light had been out for hours, he hadn't heard a sound, but he knew she wasn't asleep.

Something was wrong with Jules, though he didn't know what. And his damn brain wouldn't let him think of anything else. Could her foot be bothering her? Knowing how hard-ass-determined she could be, a little foot pain wasn't enough to put her in a bad mood.

What could it be?

He shut off his computer and lounged back on the couch, eyes drifting from the door to the wall. Jules's paintings. Maybe because he'd listened to her explain some of them to his family tonight, he was seeing them through different eyes. As a group, they had an underlying energy. Chaotic, yes, but her brand of chaos was addictive, and it weaved its way through his brain all night.

No sledgehammer or annoying sister waiting to do yoga woke him the next morning. He'd done it all on his own. He knew Jules was already up because he smelled her mint tea in the air, so he sat up, looked straight through to the kitchen and out the window.

As expected, Jules was on the deck, feet curled up, mug in her hands. Morning sunlight made her hair look almost red. When she tipped her chin, laughed, then spoke, a cold chill hit Dexter's spine.

She wasn't out there alone. Someone was with her. Someone like Quent.

Feet tangled in the blanket, Dexter tripped over himself as he pushed from the couch and sped toward the deck. "What are you—" he began the moment he flung open the door. There was no one on the deck but Jules.

She stared up at him. "Hold on a sec."

Dexter almost fell through the floor. "Are you talking on the phone?"

"It's Roxy," Jules said, displaying his cell. "My phone isn't charged and yours wasn't password protected and I figured you'd have her number saved. Hope you don't mind."

"*Of course he doesn't mind!*" came Roxy's voice through the phone.

Dexter chuckled, pulse slowing to non-attack mode. "I don't mind, but I am mildly shocked—so out of context."

She held up a finger. "Rox, sorry. Dexter's awake and, um, *up* now. Gotta go!" She snickered and held out the phone.

"Your sister thinks we have sex every five seconds, but I swear it's the only thing that makes her go away. Oh, not that I…"

"No need to explain. I know you like Roxanne as well as anyone, but she can be a little much. She grew up in a mansion with only my parents for her last formative years. Never taught personal space."

When Jules smiled, it felt like he hadn't seen it in ages.

"If your phone is dead, or you need a number, or whatever, you can always use mine," he added. "My car, my computer, my…well, anything else I have that you want, it's yours."

Hell, man. Calm down. Talk about smothering.

"Thanks. Rox is heading back to Jersey on Friday. I don't know if I'll see her again, so I wanted to say good-bye. She didn't know it was good-bye, but…"

Seemed a good night's sleep hadn't done much to lift Jules's mood. He tried to remember when it was last night that she'd started sounding sad. It might've been when they were talking about her painting, the one Natalie liked. Maybe he'd insulted Jules without realizing it.

"Have you got a lot going on today?"

"Not much," she said, gazing toward the water. "My foot's better so I might go for a hike. The trails at Governor Dick park should be dry enough now. Is your contractor friend coming to look at the house?"

Dexter nodded. "Tomorrow afternoon, it's all set."

"Great. What about you? Did you rebook a flight?"

Why did it seem like she was trying to get rid of him? Of course he needed to get back to the city ASAP, but did she have to push him out the door?

"Not yet. I wanted to talk to you first." He pulled up a sea-foam-green chair and sat across from her. "I'm stuck and need your opinion. Probably more than just your opinion."

"About what?"

He waited a moment. "Art."

"Yeah?" As expected, her face lit up, but then she narrowed her eyes.

"I'm well aware you're not in favor of what I'm doing, the software program. But I think you can help me, if you're willing."

She pressed her lips together disapprovingly, but after a moment, her expression softened. Jules was selfless. If a friend asked for something, she would give it.

"What kind of help?"

"Well, I didn't like your reaction—how you said virtual art isn't real art."

"It's not."

"Okay, I know your thoughts on the matter, but I'm thinking, maybe if I understand art a little better, or maybe an artist's mind—like yours—the art part of the app will feel more authentic. Believe it or not, I don't want to turn the world into robots. Computers are useful, and more available to kids who'll never be able to take an art class."

"Kids?" Jules said, leaning forward.

"Didn't I mention this is a program for schools?"

The brightness in Jules's eyes nearly took his breath away. "No, I didn't know that."

"I've already earmarked the first version to go to a district in Queens. I've done a lot of volunteering there, and—"

"You volunteer at schools?"

"When I can," Dexter said, wondering why she kept interrupting. At least she hadn't flat-out refused. "I've been unusually busy this year, but I think about them all the time. Which is why I want them to get the program first. It'll have to go to the after-school program initially, because of all the red tape to get added to the curriculum, but it's a start."

"No, that's...that's really wonderful. Kids in after-school programs need it the most." She paused and bit a nail. "Dex, I'm so impressed."

He wondered why, but didn't want to derail when she wasn't hating the idea, just happy she was on board. "So, will you help me?"

"Of course! Anything you need. Have you eaten breakfast?"

"Um, no, but—" He stepped back as she sprang to her feet.

"Me neither. We have that case of Hershey's bars from Natalie. Oh! And all those apples your mother brought over last night. I can chop them up and make French toast."

"Sounds great. Want me to start chopping?"

"You shower first, then we'll switch and you can do all the apple chopping you want."

Dexter was about to remind her of the "I shower, you shower" joke, but he already wanted to act on it more than he should. "Okay," he said instead. "I'll be back."

Even though his muscles still ached from death-by-yoga, plus floor/couch sleeping, and he'd love to stand under the hot water for a solid hour, he was out of the shower, shaved, and dressed in ten minutes.

"Your turn," he said.

"That was fast." Jules looked up from a pile of half-peeled apples. "You're in that big a hurry to chop and discuss art?"

Honestly, he'd been in a hurry to get back to her. He wanted to be with Jules—wherever she was. Admitting that was a little unsettling, and it wasn't just that he wanted to see her face, that amazing body…most of all, he wanted to talk to her, about art or anything. He wanted to hear her voice, that loud, contagious laugh that bounced off the lake.

"Chopping apples is my life's ambition." He took her knife.

"Okay, just cut those there into one-inch squares. I kept the skin on half to add texture and color."

"You're even an artist in the kitchen," he said with a smile.

Jules smiled back and blushed at him in a way he hadn't seen since waking up in Vegas. It made his heart full stop.

"If you finish before I'm done, you can start the syrup. Recipe's right there." She pointed at an index card on the table, then twirled and disappeared.

You shower, I shower, he thought as he heard the water turn on. He was lucky to not slice off a finger as his mind drifted to the gorgeous creature one wall away, separated from him by a see-through shower curtain covered in orange seahorses.

"How you doing?" she called from the bedroom a few minutes later.

Dexter looked up from the pot of cubed apples, water and sugar he was stirring. "Coming along."

Jules wandered out wearing a denim skirt and gray T-shirt with a faded cartoon of Wonder Woman on the front. "Hmm," she said, inspecting his work over his shoulder. "Looks good. Can you keep it up for another few? I want to dry my hair."

By the time she returned to the kitchen, Dexter was already straining the apples. They were covered in a thick glaze of sugar, brown sugar, and their own natural sugars. He hadn't had apple-covered French toast since high school. Mom used to make it for him on every birthday. A smile broke out on his face as he thought of that, widening when he thought of Jules suggesting the same meal.

"You're good at this."

"Just followed the recipe," he said. "It was three steps."

Jules flipped her wavy hair over one shoulder, sending her scent everywhere. "Yeah, but most guys I know don't have the patience. I'm learning so much about you. What else goes on in that brain of yours, huh?" Grinning, she knocked a fist against the side of his head.

If she knew what was currently going on in his head, she'd run and hide, lock the bedroom door, then block it with a dresser.

In private, she'd shared with him about not wanting a long-term relationship, not wanting to lose her independence by falling in love. Dexter's reasons against the same thing were different, but even his commitment-phobic mind was beginning to see the benefits…screwing with his mind just enough that he still hadn't booked his flight to JFK, hadn't answered his phone all morning, and instead was making homemade apple syrup in the kitchen of a sexy bohemian artist he couldn't get out of his head.

"Plate. Here's your plate. Dex?" Jules was holding out a platter of steaming French toast, smiling at him.

"What?" he asked when her smile quirked.

"You were zoned out."

He took the plate from her. "You wish."

She tipped her chin and laughed. "I know a thing or two about zoning out, and you totally were."

"Whatever."

They moved their plates to the table by the windows. It was after ten, and the sun was bright and warm through the glass.

"I can't get over this view," he said, and before he could drive home his next point, Jules cut him off.

"I'm knocking down this wall. Maybe tomorrow, if your contractor friend gives the okay."

"What did I say?" He gave the innocent eyes. "You're paranoid, ya know that?"

She laughed, took a bite, and looked out the window. Dexter took his own first bite, chewing slowly. Jules's French toast was perfect, but his syrup on top of it tasted a little burned. Maybe it was just that bite. Nope, his next was even worse. He glanced across the table at Jules. She was eating like nothing was wrong, but there was no way she hadn't noticed.

"So, I have a few questions," he said, trying not to gag as

he took a long swig of coffee, extra heavy on the chocolate milk. "How long have you been painting? I remember when we were teenagers. You were what—fifteen when you went out with Vince?"

"Uh-huh." Her voice sounded nasally, as if trying not to breathe through her nose while she ate. Then she took a sip of mint tea. "I've always been an artist. I had the aptitude for it when I was really little. My mom saved drawings from before I could even talk."

"But you didn't go to art school?"

"Too expensive." She pushed the food around her plate. "A lot of artists are never trained professionally. That's probably why I painted so much when I was younger. I knew I needed experience over education. I don't regret it, though. I've developed my own style that I'm really happy with." Her expression brightened. "I have Grams to thank for that. I don't know what path my life would've taken if not for her."

Dexter moved his plate to the side. "Kind of funny how we don't realize we're being influenced until it's too late. Not in a negative way. Like how Rosy influenced you and my father influenced me, yet we didn't even know it at first—at least I didn't."

"You're stressing again," Jules pointed out. "You were relaxed last night and this morning, but now, your jaw's clenching." She reached across the table and pushed the front of his hair off his forehead. "The little vein right here pops whenever you're stressed. It's your tell." She kept her hand on his face for a moment, then let it drop.

He wanted her to touch him again. He'd give anything for it.

"I am stressed," he admitted. "Stressed and sore as hell." He cracked his neck, then groaned. "Your yoga really kicked my ass. The stress, though, goes with the territory of being an Elliott."

"We all need a break sometimes — to recharge. A day or even a few hours, if you can."

He laughed under his breath and began stacking their dishes. "Where can I get some of that?"

"From me." Jules was smiling and gazing off to the side. "I never renege on a bet. You did an hour of yoga, which means I owe you one full body massage."

• • •

When Dexter came out of the bedroom, Jules had drawn all the shades so the house was dim and shadowy, even at high noon.

He'd had plenty of massages at the club after golf or hockey. Never from a woman he knew, however, let alone was crazy-ass attracted to on every level.

It was probably a very bad idea to get naked, lie on a table, and allow Jules to rub oil all over him.

But she was right. He was stressed and needed professional relaxation help. Especially now that so much was at stake with his meeting on Friday. Two dozen people were trusting him to change their lives, to be part of something new and great... Risky.

His shoulder muscles tensed again by just thinking about it.

"Are you ready for me?" he asked, holding the towel around his waist.

"I am," Jules said, using that calming yoga voice that used to drive him bats. "Come in."

The living room was just as dark, with the exception of one lamp in the corner, casting a soft red glow from the scarf draped over the shade. Jules stood in the middle of the room. Her hair was pulled back in a knot on top of her head, and she wore all white, a short-sleeved top and long pants that flared over her feet.

"Is that your uniform? Cute." Nervousness made him jokey.

"Shhh." She placed a finger over her lips and waved him forward.

She'd set up a table that looked like every other massage therapist's table he'd ever seen. A white sheet lay over the top and another was folded at the foot.

This is for your health. Mental and physical. Just forget it's Jules.

"Would you like music?"

"Um, no. I don't know. On second thought—yes. Music would be great."

She nodded and kind of floated to the record player. A few albums were stacked, ready to be played. He expected pan flutes or Gregorian chants, and was surprised when Count Basie at the piano came on. Light, mellow strings in the background.

He wasn't sure if he was supposed to say "namaste," so he kept his mouth shut.

"We'll start facedown, if that's okay?" she said. "You'll lie here, your face there so your neck will relax. The table is heated. You'll only need a sheet, which is on the end. After you lie down, pull it up as high as you'd like. I'm turning around while you get ready. Keep the towel on or not. Whatever you're comfortable with."

Honestly, Dexter was about as comfortable as when he got his first physical in the seventh grade. But Jules was being extremely professional, and he knew he was safe in her hands.

Her hands…

Right before unknotting the towel, he gave it one last thought. Then dropped it, got on the table, pulled the sheet to his waist, and positioned his face in the padded rest.

"Ready?"

"Uh-huh," he replied, his voice muffled as he stared down

at the rug. He heard the floorboards creak as Jules walked over.

"I scented the oil with cinnamon. Men seem to like that, plus it gives the oil extra heat. Tell me if your skin is sensitive to it."

The second she touched him, he flinched.

"Are you okay?"

"Yeah, sorry."

"Are my hands cold?"

"No—no." He wanted to sit up and tell her everything was all right. That it was him, not her, who was freaking out like a nervous kid. "You just…surprised me."

"I understand." Jules's voice was soft and flowy, drifting around the room like all those skirts she wore. "I'm going to touch your hand first. Is that okay?"

He chuckled. "Yes."

"Just checking. Don't want you jumping out of your skin again." He heard the smile in her voice, then felt her touch his hand, slide it across his arm until it reached his shoulder. "What kind of pressure do you like?"

He thought about saying something smart-ass, but didn't. "Firm."

"Like this?"

Dexter closed his eyes as Jules kneaded his shoulders, pressing in on the left side where she felt a knot. "Yes, that's good—*ow*."

"You're a little tender there. Sports injury?"

"You could call it that," he said, purposefully monotone. "I'm on my honeymoon."

Jules pinched that tender spot again, making Dexter suck in a sharp breath. "Oops, so sorry."

She was kneading again, focusing on that knot and the matching one on the other side. She was stronger than she looked, because she was really working him over. It felt great, really relaxing, until he'd remember it was Jules's hands sliding across his body.

Chill, dude…chill, he chanted inside his head. *It's just a massage. She's a professional.*

"My flight's in the morning," he said, needing to make conversation.

Jules's hands stopped moving. "Oh, yeah?"

"There were a few messages I needed to check on my phone before I came out. My overworked assistant booked my flight and set up a conference call with my group for three o'clock this afternoon. It's our final crunch before we meet with the investors. I've missed our last three calls." He paused to chuckle. "If I miss this one, I might as well call off the whole thing."

It was a joke, of course. Everything his team has worked for was riding on this final conference call to make their pitch extra perfect, then to kill it at Friday's meeting.

"I know it's important. You won't miss it," Jules said, her fingers manipulating his neck muscles, the base of his skull. Damn, it felt amazing. "I won't let you."

"Thank you," he said, the words coming out in a relaxed exhale. The woman really did have magic fingers, magic hands that worked down his spine. The heated massage bed coupled with the cinnamon oil was suddenly way too hot; so was the damn sheet over him. Her hands? Yes, they were definitely hot, the hottest thing to ever touch him.

Think of Charles Barkley, his first season with the Sixers. Picture, in detail, that epic dunk over Jordan.

"Can I tell you something?" Jules's voice was so quiet, Dexter wondered if he'd imagined it.

"Sure." He swallowed and tried to breathe normally. "I'm kind of at your mercy."

In more ways than one.

She laughed, and her hands stopped moving. "It's something I've never told anyone."

Chapter Thirteen

Jules didn't know why now was the time she felt like sharing. Or why Dexter was the only person she could share with.

That was a lie. She did know. It was because she knew him, trusted him—with everything. Plus, she wanted him to know.

"Are you still there?" he asked, his voice muffled.

After a nervous laugh, she unclenched her fists, which were tucked under her chin. "Still here." She gazed down at his back, each spot that she'd touched now glistening with oil. If she didn't move to his feet and legs, she'd start on his back again—his lower back—and just keep on moving down...

Professionally, she'd given plenty of glute massages, and it was never, ever sexual. But this was Dexter, and she could not touch his butt. She felt flushy and giggly just thinking about it.

"You were going to tell me something?" he prompted.

She blew out a quiet breath and swiped a wrist across her dewy forehead. *Be professional, Jules. If Dexter was actually paying for this, what you're thinking right now is grounds to lose your license.*

"I sold a painting to a private collector."

Dexter didn't say anything at first, then he pulled his head off the face rest and looked at her. "My instinct says to tell you congratulations, but my instincts are always wrong when it comes to you. Should I just say great, or lose all respect for you for selling out?" He leaned on an elbow. "Is it a good thing to sell to a private collector or not? I need context."

"It's a good thing," she said, still not having the guts to touch him after all her dirty-minded thoughts. "Sort of." He gave her an eyebrow arch requesting information. "Lie down. It'll be easier for me if I don't have to look at you."

He laughed but then went quiet. "Really?" After she nodded, he shrugged and lay back down. The sheet had shifted, uncovering the dent at the top of his…

She pulled her eyes away and moved to his feet, picking one up and kneading it like it was a batch of the toughest sourdough. "Some artists consider adding to private collections a sellout, particularly if the money is good."

"Was your money good?"

"Yeah."

"Awesome, Jules. Stickin' it to the man."

"Yeah well, like I said, no one knows about it."

"Except me?"

She stared down at his back, rising and falling with deep breaths. "Yes," she said. "Except you."

"Why? Are you sensitive to what your artist friends think? That doesn't sound like you."

She moved up to his calf, working the muscle on autopilot. "Truthfully, I'm insecure about it. It was good money and he wants three more, maybe a portrait commission—which is kind of a sellout. But what sort of painter am I if I don't paint?" Unexpected tears clogged her throat and it was hard to swallow. "The goal of every artist I know is to be in an important gallery. I know that'll never happen to me, and I should be happy with my one painting that is in a gallery."

"Which gallery?"

"The one here in town. The owner is good friends with Grams. I'm sure he was just doing me a favor, I don't know. There's an art show in Mount Gretna every year. It's prestigious for this area, and a lot of the pieces get shows in Philadelphia. Some in Boston and New York. I've wanted to enter for years, but this is the first time I feel ready."

"Then go for it," Dexter said. "To hell with what anyone else thinks. No one's opinion should matter but yours, Jules. If you love what you do, then screw it. Sell a painting to the Republican National Committee if that's what it takes to live your dream. Never give up on that."

"Dexter, that's really sweet," she choked out, blinking back more tears. Who would've thought Dex would be the one person whose pep talk she'd actually appreciate? "It is my dream, but like I told you a few days ago, it's hard and scary, and…I haven't painted seriously in a while."

"Not true," he said, rolling to his side and scooping up one of her hands. She froze at the unexpected touch, wanting more. "You painted the other day. See? New color stains on your fingers."

For a moment, she looked at him through the darkness, preparing for what she knew she had to say next—something else no one else knew. "The last few months, I've been blocked, like I was missing something important I couldn't find. At first I thought it was Grams, but even when I got here to the cottage, I still couldn't do it." She paused and closed her eyes in a long blink. "Until you."

Having zero follow-up, she could only let the words hang in the air and land where they may.

Slowly, Dexter sat up, his face a blank canvas.

"Uh-uh, back down you go," she said.

"No." He moved to sit on the edge of the table, the sheet

over his lower half. Well, at least the room was semi-dark so he wouldn't see how badly she was blushing. "I'd like to know, what changed because of me?"

"Everything," she said without thinking. "I can't explain, it's like I'm…open. Being with you opened me. I don't know how or why, but I can't express how grateful—"

"I don't want gratitude," he said, cutting her off midsentence. "Listen to me. You'll do whatever you want, and it won't matter what I say, but you *have* to keep painting. You love it, I know you do, because you light up when you talk about it. You fill the room with energy and warmth." He took her shoulders so they were face-to-face. "Jules, it's your dream. You're going to paint every day until you have the perfect piece to enter that contest. You'll win it, because you're amazing. And then I'll take you to the gallery in New York where it will hang. Awing the world forever."

If not for his grip on her shoulders, she wouldn't be able to sit up straight anymore. Those words… She'd never felt such support, even from Grams. Because this came from a man with no strings, no reason to say what he did. Except that he wanted more for her. He cared.

Though there was no way he cared for her on the same level she cared for him.

"Dex," she whispered. "That means…"

"Jules."

"…so much…"

"Juliet." He cupped her cheek, his thumb moving across her skin.

Before she slipped away, she closed her eyes, trying desperately to drum up all the fears from before, how she swore she'd never love again or lose her identity over a man.

With Dexter, though, those fears didn't exist. He knew her, all her quirks and needs to stay her own person. With him, she'd never have to worry about that.

His thumb traced across her lips, making her tremble. A heartbeat later, his thumb was replaced by his mouth, in the sweetest, deepest kiss.

Finally, she did slip away.

His other hand moved to her waist and in one swift motion, he pulled her onto his lap. "I've wanted to do this for days," he said, his breath against her neck.

Jules took his face between her hands and tilted it to meet her eyes. "Really?"

He raised a wicked grin, then kissed her again, causing white dots to explode behind her eyes. Red dots. Rainbow dots.

"Your lips," he said, running a finger across them. "Last night when the family was here, it took everything in me to not kiss you."

"No." She laughed.

He hugged her tight. "I almost jumped in the lake to cool off."

Jules kissed him hard, combing her fingers through his hair. "My superhero," she whispered. His hand slid inside the back of her shirt, making her shiver with pleasure, making her remember they were on a massage table, and she was one toga costume away from his body. The thought made her pull away, take a breath.

But Dexter unleashed a sexy growl and drew her back to him. "I'm not letting you go."

He kissed her mouth, her collarbone, the notch at her throat. Everywhere he touched turned to fire, causing giddiness and relief like morphine to flood her bloodstream.

"I've never wanted"—he paused to kiss her forehead— "so much."

"Dex," she whispered, her breathing jagged. "You're leaving tomorrow."

"Am I?"

"Dex." She curled her fingers around his shoulders, feeling hard muscles flex. "I'm not one of those other girls."

"I know you're not," he said, tugging a strand of her hair that had fallen loose. "That's exactly why I…" He didn't finish but just stared into her eyes—his were dark with desire. "Juliet, you're nothing like any of those other women." Her eyes fluttered closed when he kissed her slowly until her body arched. "You're my wife."

Not a shred of doubt remained in her mind. Her last fear of Dexter not changing his womanizing ways was now gone, causing another burst of giddiness to zip through her veins.

"I understand, though," he said, "if you don't want to, if you don't trust—"

"I do," she said, cutting him off with a kiss. Afterward, she pulled back, looking him in the eyes first; then she glanced over his shoulder at the bedroom.

Dexter grinned, then kissed her squarely on the mouth. Next thing she knew, he was on his feet, whisking her away in his arms.

Chapter Fourteen

Dexter opened his eyes to see a pile of pillows beside him. It wasn't a shock this time when they moved and yawned. "Hey," he whispered.

The pile of pillows sprang limbs as two feet curled around his leg, and then hands found his chest. "Hey, you."

He sighed contentedly as he pulled the whole pile of pillows over to him. Jules's body was soft and warm, the underside of her hair still damp with sweat. She tucked her chin and Dexter ran a hand from her neck all the way down her spine. When he felt her body shudder against him, he wasn't contented anymore.

"What time is it?" she asked. Her wild mermaid hair was curtaining one side of her face. He pushed his hands through it, never wanting to stop touching it. She rolled to her side, and his hand found her hip bone. Okay, so there were many, many places on Jules he never wanted to stop touching.

"After six," he replied, skimming his fingers along the curve of her waist, up her arm. "At least I think so. The sun looks ready to set."

"Six? Dex, you missed your three o'clock conference call."

"Indeed."

Dexter stared up at the ceiling, remembering back a couple of hours when he'd realized he was going to have to make a decision about that. This was around the same time Jules was demonstrating how flexible yoga made her, and in his brain, there was no decision to be made. But now—

Jules kissed his neck, and he closed his eyes, taking it in, the feeling of her soft lips, her breath, her little tongue. *Damn... No decision at all.*

"Did you sleep?" she whispered.

He rolled his head to face her, their noses touching. "A little."

"Yeah, right." She laughed and snuggled close, wrapping an arm around him. "You snore—not loudly, but you sleep like the dead."

"You must be right about this house." He kissed her nose. "It changes people."

"Told ya." She smiled. "Because believe me, I tried to wake you a few times."

Dexter propped an arm under his head. "What did you plan on doing if you succeeded?"

Her big green eyes looked off to the side. "Well, I think I'd rather show you than tell—*eep!*"

All in favor of show over tell, Dexter pulled her on top of him, feeling her curves and softest places. "Baby, I do like the sound of that."

"We have to eat first," she said, her hair falling past her shoulders, landing on his face. "You especially. I know you didn't eat much breakfast."

"The apples were burned," he whispered.

Her body shook with silent laughter. "They were perfect, pooh bear." She ran a finger across his jaw, over his mouth.

His muscles flexed, then relaxed at her touch, like they had for the last five hours. Not only his body, but his mind and heart came alive when she was near. It was a new reaction, one he was just beginning to understand, but definitely loved.

"I'll get us something," she said. And before he could stop her, she was literally rolling off the bed.

"Jules?" He sat up after he heard a thud. "You okay?"

A second later, her head popped into view. "Fine." She smiled and blew the hair out of her face. "Landed on pillows. Did you notice Grams loves pillows?"

He laughed and leaned against the headboard. "You don't say." When she stood up, she was wearing one of his T-shirts. "Plan on going somewhere?"

"No," she said over her shoulder, framed in the doorway. "But you've also noticed how people tend to drop in any time of day without an invitation."

"Now *that* I have noticed." He also noticed that his shirt, though long on her, wasn't quite covering everything it should in the back. Which made Dexter want to spring from the bed and drag her back with him.

"Coffee?" she called from the kitchen.

"Don't think I need it. Just bring me a PowerBar—maybe two. Better make it three."

"Trying to beat your own record?" she said, coming back with apple slices, some of the bread she'd made yesterday, one Hershey's bar, and a bottle of water. "You really will need protein for that."

"This time, I'll remember all three." He relished the feeling when Jules looked at him, then away, that irresistible blush marbling her throat.

"Then I guess we both better eat." She sat cross-legged on the bed, the food between them like a picnic. "Open up," she said, holding an apple slice.

Dexter bit it in half, then sucked the rest of it in, along with her fingers. "Delicious," he said. "Best meal I've had all day."

"May I have my hand back?"

"Oh." He opened his mouth, releasing her fingers. "So sorry. I thought they were for me to keep."

Jules leaned back and laughed, making the bed shake.

That laugh, he thought. *That big, scrumptious mouth. All that joy.*

She hand-fed him a piece of her homemade bread, slathered with butter and jam. Then he did the same for her. After they'd each had a few drinks of water, Dexter was so done eating.

"Hey," he said, sliding a finger down her throat, then hooking it on the neck hole of her shirt. "Afraid I'm going to need this back now…"

It was the middle of the night when Dexter left the bedroom. He paused in the doorway to look at Jules, hair strewn across the pillows, moonlight making her fair skin glow. A volcano burned in his chest when he looked at her, thought about her.

But for now, he'd let her sleep.

His own mind wouldn't let him do the same. It had been racing for the last hour until he finally couldn't keep lying there.

He filled a glass at the sink—adding three drops of peppermint oil out of habit—pushed back the curtains from when Jules had drawn them for his massage, then gazed out the window. He smiled and shook his head. There was no way he was going to let her ruin this view.

The woman had plenty of charmingly screwball ideas, but he could talk her out of this one if he worked hard enough. His smile twisted as he thought of some creative ways he might convince her. They all required never leaving their bed.

Their bed. The pronoun had popped in his head without a thought. His wife. Their bed. It felt as natural as breathing.

The living room was striped with moonlight, and he nearly

walked straight into the massage table. Both sheets were on the floor. He remembered the way she'd looked right before he'd kissed her. She'd never been so stunning.

His computer was plugged in but on the floor out of the way. Automatically, he stepped toward it, but then stopped. There were emails waiting, and probably even more missed calls on his cell since he'd blown off the conference call. Were they so important that he needed to deal with them in the middle of the night?

Maybe. Probably. Definitely.

Damn. He ran a hand through his hair. *Jules is right. I really am a workaholic. What would she advise me to do right now? Repeat yoga mantras, then "breathe through it."* He laughed under his breath. *Or maybe she'd tell me to zone out, or get lost in a painting until I found my Zen place.*

At the thought, his eyes moved to one of her paintings on the wall. Even though the room was dark, the bright colors practically leaped from the canvass. This one was watercolor, and the red circles—which might've been abstract roses— blended halfway down, then bled together along the rest of the canvas. Wasn't abstract art supposed to represent something?

What did bleeding roses symbolize? Death? Rain? A funeral during a monsoon?

He was supposed to have picked Jules's brain about it yesterday, but he'd made a sharp left turn instead.

Another painting was wavy, vertical lines in orange and yellow that curled into waves in bright blue. One corner had two green dots. Dexter stared at it, concentrating, but couldn't figure out what it was supposed to be. Sun rays? Why were they up and down? Were the green dots clouds? Airplanes? Two rendezvousing spaceships about to crash?

He shut his eyes, seeing waves, orange lines, bleeding roses, and a fiery crash.

His exhausted mind spun from lack of sleep and lack

of order. Even his nonartistic brain understood that his subconscious was trying to tell him something—something he'd been pushing away, ignoring for hours.

Barely a second ticked by before he realized what it was.

He shouldn't have missed the conference call. It was irresponsible, unprofessional, inexcusable, and even with the past week being so chaotic, there'd been no excuse to have dropped the ball, not when so many people were counting on him.

The team wasn't prepared because he'd disappeared on them, and it would be entirely his fault when Friday's meeting blew up in his face.

He had to fix this. Now.

There was nothing to do but ask the team to pull an all-nighter. Burning through an income he didn't have anymore, but suddenly grateful for his bet winnings, he would book connecting suites at the Ritz-Carlton, and they'd push through. It was the only way; no time for anything else.

He gritted his teeth as he practically lunged for his laptop, powering it up impatiently. How the hell had he gotten so distracted?

For a split second, he wanted to blame Jules. If she would've reminded him about the meeting, maybe he wouldn't have missed it. If he hadn't been so thrown off schedule by being in this house with her, he wouldn't have been distracted from work at all.

But that wasn't fair. Even if it might've been partially her fault, Dexter couldn't place the blame on her, even if that made it easier. Nothing to do now but try to fix the mess.

Jules knew what he was trying to do, and surely she'd understand why he had to leave. This was important, very important. In Dexter's racing mind, it was the *most* important—it was everything.

If Jules didn't understand that… Well, then he'd be forced to do whatever he had to to make her.

Chapter Fifteen

Jules stretched out one leg, investigatively, but that side of the bed was empty. She sat up, alone.

"Dex?" There was no answer, but she heard movement in the kitchen. Smiling, she pulled on the same shirt that he'd sexily removed from her last night, painfully slowly, kissing each inch of her skin as he exposed it.

Holy maithuna. She might never wear another piece of clothing ever again.

Dexter wasn't in the kitchen, but on the couch, typing on his computer faster than lightning. "Hey, you. Good morning."

He typed for another few seconds, then lifted his chin. "Hey."

"Whatcha doing?"

"Working. I should've sent this out yesterday."

She sat on the arm of the couch. "Tell them it's late because you were all tied up."

"Yeah," he said, typing again. "That won't fly with the board of directors."

She slid off the arm and landed beside him. "Hi there,"

she whispered, then kissed his cheek. It took a second, but Dexter finally turned his face and kissed her.

"Hi." He looked at her for a moment, but his expression wasn't right, not like before. Well, actually it was exactly the same as before…exactly like the morning they woke up in Vegas. He blinked his blue eyes, wearily.

"How long have you been up?" she asked.

"Since three."

"Working the whole time?"

He nodded while reading his computer screen.

Jules opened her mouth to say something else, but the words stalled. Dexter was completely dressed. No tie or jacket yet, but black pants, black belt, pressed white button-down. He was even wearing his shiny shoes.

"Dex," she said, feeling a slight stir of discomfort in her stomach, "do you—"

"Would you hand me my cell?" he said, talking over her. "It's plugged in over there."

"Um, sure. You weren't talking on it, were you?" she said, trying to make a joke. "You know that's not allowed."

"I was—sorry. It was important."

"I'm kidding. You're allowed to do anything here." She was about to add "it's your home, too," but didn't. He had a lot of responsibilities, especially if his computer program took off. Dex's being busy was something she'd have to get used to.

"Want coffee and eggs? We're out of apples." She smiled, but he didn't look up.

"I don't have time. Speaking of, if you need to use my car, better make it soon. I changed my flight to a few hours earlier."

That knot of discomfort in her stomach tightened. "Thought you hadn't booked your return flight yet."

"I took care of it this morning. You knew I was leaving today."

"Yes, but…" She trailed off when his phone in her hand vibrated. "You're getting a call."

Finally, he looked interested. "From who?"

"Angela."

"Oh." He shrugged. "Let it go to voicemail."

The face of his cell went black, then lit up. "You have six missed calls from her. Six voicemails, too."

"Yeah, I'm sure."

His short answers made discomfort turn to full-on unease, with maybe a tiny bit of distrust. "Is she a friend?"

"I guess you'd call her that."

"From Manhattan?"

After a good five seconds, he nodded.

Who was this maybe-friend of his from Manhattan calling six times?

Of course the answer was so obvious, it shouldn't have hit her over the head with such force. Angela was one of *those* women. One of those hundreds whom Dexter had spent a night with, then disappeared.

The swirling swell of emotions inside her twisted and wrung tight.

"You going to see her again?"

"Really wish I didn't have to."

Jules closed her eyes. Well, she couldn't expect his past life to just evaporate. She was falling for a man who had baggage and flaws. She'd known that all along.

"Are you okay?"

When she opened her eyes, Dexter's were on her. It wasn't the same expression of compassion he'd worn when she'd hurt her foot, but at least *something* was there, and at least he wasn't still typing on that wretched computer.

"I'm surprised, that's all."

"About…?"

She took in a deep breath, held it in her lungs, then blew

it out. "I thought… I thought you were staying."

"Why?"

Enough of this. It was time for a leap of faith—a big one. And if he wouldn't take it, she'd take it for the both of them. "Because you should. Because I want you to stay."

"Why?" he repeated.

Was the man dense? "For *us*. Aren't we an us?"

"I suppose, in a way."

"Dexter," she snapped. "Why are you being like this? And don't you *dare* say, Like what?"

He sighed and walked over, but it was as if he wasn't really seeing her. "I can't do this now. There's no time. I have to get back."

"And you'll get together with Angela, too?"

Dexter took a beat before tilting his head. "I already told you I was."

"Huh. Guess that shouldn't surprise me." Jules was shocked at how much sarcasm was in her snort of reply.

"What shouldn't?"

"How eager you are to get to New York—back to her and your old life."

He put his hands on his hips. "Are you accusing me of something specific or speaking in generalities?"

"Oh!" she growled at the ceiling. "I hate when you talk like this. You're a robot."

Dexter opened his mouth, but didn't speak at first. "I have no clue why you're behaving so irrationally, but I told you two seconds ago that I don't have time." Irritation and impatience wrapped around every word, but Jules didn't care.

"Time for what? You missed your conference call." She bit her lip and waited. When she got nothing but his blank robot stare, she went on. "Yesterday, you said if you missed it, you might as well cancel Friday's meeting with the investors. So I thought…"

"You thought…" He lifted his eyebrows. "You thought I was going to call it off. Abandon everything? Then, what? Move to Hershey? Work for my father again? Now *that's* playacting, Jules. Just like how we started this whole thing."

Despite how she knew she'd started it—caused his annoyed and stressed-out attitude—each of his words was an arrow to her heart.

"I'd never cancel the meeting with Three Jacker Media," he continued. "They don't reschedule." He shook his head, and for a flash of a moment, he looked regretful. "I thought this might happen, I worried… You and I—we hardly know each other. We're talking about my work, my number one priority. If you don't get that—"

"I get it," she snapped, taking on another arrow. Because what he was actually saying was work was more important than her—than them. She would never be his first priority.

"Believe me." She crossed her arms, anger leaping to the front of her emotional queue. "You've made your feelings crystal clear."

"Good."

"Stop it!" She stomped her foot, furious now—at him, at herself. "Why are you being such a giant ass?"

"I didn't realize I was. But if I am, it's because you *say* you understand why this is important to me, when you obviously don't. You're forcing my hand."

"So let's talk about it. No, sorry, I forgot you don't have time for that, and I don't want to right now, either. I want you out of here, and I want this shirt off of me." She tried to yank his stupid, smelly tee over her head, but her arm caught in the sleeve and her hair got tangled.

"Juliet? Dex?"

She froze, then quickly pulled the shirt back in place over her body. When she could see again, Eileen, Braxton, Luke, and Roxy stood at the front door.

Of course we have an audience.

"We heard loud voices," Eileen said.

Roxy grinned. "Were you about to—"

"*No!*" Jules and Dexter said together.

"He was just leaving," Jules said, pointing at Dexter. "Wouldn't want to miss your flight."

If he spent another hour in her presence in this mood, she's show him how *irrationally* she could behave. This trip to New York was perfect timing. It'd give them both a moment to cool off. She'd miss him, but even though she cared about him more than anyone, *wanted* him more than anyone, she obviously still had full possession of her independence.

If she hadn't been so heated, the thought would've made her ecstatic.

Dexter was pacing the room, the troubled look on his face making her irritation take a backseat. He stopped walking, looked at her with a furrowed brow, rubbed his chin, then dropped his arms to his side. "It's over."

"Over?" Eileen asked. "What is?"

"Our marriage," he said, not looking at Jules. "The relationship. Everything."

The words didn't make sense to her brain, but when her heart took on a dozen more arrows—poisoned-tipped this time—Jules slowly realized the truth…

Instigated by Dexter, unknowingly fueled by Jules, they were having that public breakup they'd planned. Their exit strategy. But she wasn't prepared for it—a breakup wasn't part of the new plan.

To her, this wasn't playacting.

"We're getting divorced," he added in a tone so matter-of-fact that she had no grounds to argue. They'd never talked about a real future together. Not really.

"Dex," his mom said. "Don't make impulsive decisions in the heat of the moment."

"I'm not. There's a lot more to this than anyone knows. Reasons no one else knows. Jules is in total agreement. This isn't one-sided."

"He's right," she said, keeping up her part of the act, while feeling tacks in her throat and an almost unbearable sadness. With the anger gone, overwhelming misery hung over her. This was really happening.

"What reasons?" Roxy asked.

Jules didn't know how to reply, but Dexter did—like a true pro, his part was preplanned.

"Forgot to give you this," he said in a quiet voice, still not meeting Jules's eyes as he handed her a small piece of paper. "You've earned every penny. And I should know."

. . .

Dexter felt like absolute shit saying that, but it was necessary. When he realized he had to end the limbo and confusion, the best he could do was end the whole damn thing by giving Jules her share of the money that he'd been carrying around for days.

The check was the final termination of their business deal.

He might as well have said "for services rendered." That couldn't have finished things more completely. It hadn't been his initial intention, but ultimately, there seemed no other way.

Not even Jules would want to stay married to someone like him.

Still…the look in her eyes—anger, sadness, devastating disappointment. He'd gone too far when the color had drained from her face. The window glass was still rattling from when she'd slammed the bedroom door. Locking herself inside.

He hated himself, and might for a long time, but he needed out. Work came first—it always had. He thought Jules understood that, but it was evident she didn't, which forced him to make a clear-cut decision. Yes, it was made in the heat of the moment, but once he put serious distance between them, Dexter knew he'd feel less guilt.

This was his fault, because he'd slipped up when he'd started to believe the lies, believe his feelings could be real.

"You can't split up," Roxy said, the family still standing at the open front door. "You're prefect together."

"Quiet," Luke snapped, glaring at her. "It's none of our business. Dex, I'm so sorry." He walked over to him and put a hand on his shoulder. It was probably supposed to make him feel better, but Dexter was so pissed at himself that he wanted to knock it away. "Do you need anything?"

He shook his head and stared at the floor. "Ride to the airport. I think I should leave the car."

"That's the *least* you can do for your *wife*," Roxy snarled, sounding so much like Jules that Dexter had to lock his jaw, shut off all feelings.

"My Jeep's out front," Luke said. "Now?"

Dexter exhaled and bit down hard until it hurt. "That'd be great." He glanced toward the bedroom. "I've got my computer, phone, and wallet. That's all I need."

"Dex?" Mom touched his arm.

"I'm sorry you had to witness that," Dexter said. "You should go now. I doubt she'll want to see any of you for a while."

He ushered them out then closed the door. It stuck, of course, which caused a pain to throb in his chest that he forced away. He gave his mother a quick kiss good-bye but didn't say a word more to the others. He couldn't look at them, couldn't look at the lake, the house. He just got in Luke's Jeep, fastened his seat belt, and stared straight ahead.

"Do you want to talk about it?"

"Not even a little."

"It's another fifteen minutes to the airport." Luke said, pointing at the car's GPS. "Long trip if we're both silent."

"Silence is golden after the week I've had, let me tell ya." Saying that made him feel like a dick, but whatever. Maybe he was a bigger dick than everyone thought. A giant ass, like Jules had said. He could live with that.

When they stopped at a red light, Luke kept looking at him, then away. It drove Dex effing mad. "Say what you need to." He heard the edge in his voice, but didn't care. "Get it off your chest, dude. Just stop staring at me—shit."

"I do have something to say." Luke's tone was calm, like Jules's yoga voice. Thinking that made Dexter want to jump out of the moving car.

"Not too long ago," Luke continued, "I went through hell to be with Natalie. I loved her that much, but didn't know it because I was too busy being an idiot. Not that I asked for it, but you gave me some good advice back then. Now I owe you. Plus, I'm your older brother."

Dexter was in no mood to argue, so he let Luke go on.

"Did Jules do something? Break a trust?"

"No."

"Does she have a secret identity in Russia?"

Dexter almost laughed, but it hurt his chest. "No."

Luke fell silent, but Dexter knew he wasn't finished. Good hell. He wanted this to be over so he could concentrate solely on what was important.

"You have a rep, man," Luke finally added.

"Yeah?" A pile of rocks sat in his stomach.

Luke's fingers gripped the steering wheel, white-knuckling the thing. "Did you cheat on her?"

"No." He looked Luke dead in the eyes. "I'd never do that."

"So what is it? You suddenly don't love her?"

Dexter stared out the passenger window, kneading the red-hot pain in his forehead. "Maybe I never did." It was the only answer he could give. But saying it felt like a lie.

"I'm no expert," Luke continued, "but I've been through a divorce. It was the worst kind of pain, but it was the right thing to do. You need to do the right thing for you, just think it through. Be honest with yourself. Ask the right questions."

"Like what?"

"Do you miss her? Right now, do you miss her?"

Dexter wanted to nod, but refused to move. So what if he missed her. That didn't change anything.

"Were you happier with her than without her? Don't bother answering because I know you were. We've seen you this week. You've changed."

"If I did, it was temporary."

"You're an idiot." Luke swerved to run over a pothole on Dexter's side of the car. "Truth hurts, doesn't it, bro?"

Something hurt, that was for damn sure. Was it the truth burning a hole in his gut? Truthfully, he couldn't think of the last time he'd been completely honest with anybody. Or completely himself.

No, he did know. The last time was when he'd been on that massage table with Jules…the hours that followed when it was just him and just her.

"I told her we barely know each other."

"What?"

"That was one of the last things I said to her." *Along with so many things I can't take back.* He closed his eyes, wanting to picture her but *not* wanting to. "Just like you, though, I know this is for the best. We don't belong together. It was an accident."

"Accident?" Luke slowed down as they neared the passenger drop-off curb. "What do you mean?"

Maybe he should tell his brother the truth. It might be cause for banishment from all future Elliott family betting, but at least he'd come clean.

It was no longer Dexter's secret, though. Telling anyone might jeopardize Jules's house. No matter what other crap he did, it'd have to be practically life-or-death for him to risk that.

"Nothing." Dexter shook his head. "It's over. Few months from now, it'll be like it never happened. I'm not a relationship guy. You know that, everyone in the whole damn world knows. I don't know why I thought this could be different, even for a second. I was stupid."

"Dex." Luke's forehead was lined with concern. "Want me to park? I'll come in, we'll grab a beer."

He shook his head again. "I gotta go. Thanks for the ride."

"Look, you've got a problem. Let's talk about it. I know it's none of my business, but we can figure it out."

Dexter was beyond talking, beyond thinking of Jules or any of it. He couldn't get out of there fast enough.

"You know what, Luke," he said, climbing out of the Jeep, "you're right, this is none of your business. I'm not some scientific problem you can solve with logic. So don't worry. Go back to your comfy life in Hershey. I've got more important things to do."

If he'd allowed himself to have any feelings, the way his brother was now looking at him would've made Dexter double over in pain. But as it was, he felt nothing.

"And here, take this." He tossed the check with his half of the bet winnings on the dashboard. "I don't want it. It's all bullshit."

Luke sat back in his seat. "Have a safe trip," he said, then pulled away from the curb.

The flight was on time, so that was one less headache he had to deal with. And the American Airlines Executive Club lounge wasn't crowded. Thank goodness for small miracles. Dexter plugged in his laptop and opened the presentation for tomorrow's meeting. He had the notes app open, which showed the comments beneath the slides.

Almost every one of the slides that had to do with the graphic interface had "ask Jules" in the notes.

He forced his fists to relax when he realized he was clenching them.

I'm doing the right thing, he told himself. *Long-term relationships aren't for me. Never will be. Luckily, I stopped this before I really did start to care. No caring—no drama. That's reality.*

When the other side of his brain tried to argue, Dexter gagged it.

With the notes app closed, he started at the beginning of the presentation. Maybe because he was upset with how he'd left things with Luke, but he was having a hard time concentrating.

In through the nose, hold, expand the belly and chest, out through the nose. Listen to your breathing, feel each breath as it leaves your lungs...

"Sir? Mr. Elliott?" Someone nudged him. "Your flight is boarding."

"Oh." Dexter sat up and blinked the cobwebs from his brain. "Thanks." As he shut his laptop, he noticed he was still on slide one. Where had the hour gone? No time to wonder. He rushed to the gate, the last passenger to board and strap in. He glanced at the empty seat beside him. Less than a week ago, Jules would've been right here, curled in a ball, no shoes, hair in her face, making sweet noises he now knew came from what he did to her when they were alone.

He swallowed the lump in his throat and looked away,

throwing the SkyMall magazine and two barf bags over that seat.

Seat belt sign is off. Time to get busy. He opened his laptop and settled in for the ninety-minute flight to JFK. Being on a plane, no distractions, was when he did his best work. The first slide was still bothersome. Was it something aesthetic? The logo? What was it about the color that bugged him? Or was it the placement in the corner of the slide?

Jules would say it was boring. Not enough flair or chi or too Virgo-y or one of her other phrases. She'd probably want to add a big sun to it, or flowers…with polka-dot rainbows. Something to make it beautiful and unique.

When a corner of his mouth twitched to smile, Dexter held his breath and made it stop. He shut his eyes, trying to drum up the cold, panicked feeling from this morning when he'd straight-up chosen work over her. Not from turbulence, his stomach lurched and he eyed a barf bag on the next seat.

When he closed his eyes again, what he saw was wavy orange lines, tall blue waves, brilliant red roses. All of Jules's painting were bright and alive, not jarring, though they sure the hell stimulated something in him. They came alive in his head like living things. Vivid and vibrant, full of energy, reaching out and wrapping around his mind, his heart.

Just like their creator.

Time had flown again, and the plane was taxiing to the gate. He hadn't gotten one thing done. He shut everything down and left the plane, jaw locked as he headed for the exit. Angela had texted that a car would be waiting at the curb.

Angela. Why had he made those comments about her to Jules? He knew exactly what she'd infer. *Giant ass.* Pain and heat punished his every moment; he was a total tool bag for doing that to her, making her feel like she was just another woman.

That she wasn't special.

The most special woman who had ever danced barefoot into his cold, colorless, pathetic, robot-like life.

If he was choosing not to be with her, it should've been for a real reason, not another lie. Yes, he'd never been in a healthy relationship. Neither had Jules. It would be the blind leading the blind. But was there anyone else on the planet Dexter would do a blind leap with?

Hell no.

He was almost to the security exit when he walked past a restaurant, the same chain he'd sat at with Jules when their flight was canceled in Vegas. One week ago tomorrow. They'd shared a pitcher of Vegas Sunrise, she'd made him laugh. She was different. So different—in all the best ways. She was exciting and sweet with long hair and a loud mouth that told him her moon was in his Saturn, or something. She'd made him feel warm and alive in ways he still didn't comprehend.

That stormy Vegas night, he'd wanted that feeling to last, he remembered that now. In a flood of memories, he was remembering everything about that night—the bet, the stakes, what exactly he would lose…and win. He'd wanted that feeling to last so badly that he'd summoned all his willpower to not kiss her a second time in the limo.

Because there'd been another bet. Between him and Jules.

Not kissing her would win that bet.

And he'd wanted to win the bet.

Not because of the money or the pride of beating his brothers. But because those ridiculously high, drunkenly irrational stakes created from too much Vegas Sunrise and zero inhibitions were if Jules couldn't get him to kiss her again, if she lost the bet, then she'd have to do the worst thing she could think of.

Get married.

Dexter stopped moving as full memories opened like petals of a flower after a long, dark night. *It was me. I started it—everything.* Never once had he wanted to get married, yet somehow—after an hour with Juliet Bloom—he knew he wanted to keep her with him for the rest of their lives.

One screwed-up bet had sealed the deal. Then Dexter had managed to screw that all up.

A passerby bumped him, causing his laptop case strap to slide off his shoulder. Something broke inside. Probably the screen, or the whole damn thing. For a moment, all he could do was stare straight ahead, a black hole in his chest growing larger and larger. A black hole that needed color and swirls, bright flowers and a great big pink sun.

Suddenly, he wasn't standing still anymore, but running through the airport, back to the gate he'd just come from. It was a commuter flight. Unless it was full, he'd be back in Hershey in a few hours.

If it wasn't already too late.

The shortest line at the ticket desk was five people deep. Dammit. *Dammit!* He pulled out his phone, ready to make a reservation online. No. Before that, he needed to talk to her. Right now. He touched a finger to his cell, but then froze.

Jules—beautiful, free-spirited, he-loved-her-so-much-he-could-strangle-her Jules—had never given him her number. He thought fast. Who was she most likely to be with if she was pissed to high heaven at him?

His fingers moved to speed dial. It rang so long, he was expecting voicemail.

"Hey, jerkface."

"Rox." Dexter panted, moving one person closer in line. "Is she with you?"

There was a heavy, long, meaningful pause. "Who?"

"Dammit, Rox. I need to talk to her."

Another pause, muffled voices in the background. His heart pounded so hard it hurt. *Please get on the phone. Please get on the phone.*

"She's not here. I don't know where she is, or who you're talking about. Even if I did—shh, wait, hold on— Even if I did, she doesn't want to talk to you."

"Roxanne." He pounded the phone against his forehead. "I know she's with you." He wanted to add that he could "feel it," but, even though it was dead true, it was too woo-woo to admit to anyone but Jules.

She'd get it. Because she got him.

He'd told her they barely knew each other. Ha! That might've been the biggest lie of all. Jules Bloom knew him better than anyone. She wanted better things for him, bigger things that he hadn't understood before he knew her. Balance, genuine stability, friendship, love... Love with your best friend.

In his heart, he knew...he hoped...that she loved him, too.

"Please hand her the phone," he said. "I need to talk—"

"Sorry, Dex, I gotta go. I'm...low on minutes."

"You've had an unlimited plan forever."

"Huh? Sorry, you're breaking up. I think I'm driving into a tunnel. See ya."

"Rox? Roxanne!"

But she'd disconnected. He swore under his breath and was about to hit her number again, but knew she wouldn't take his call.

Someone else would, though. Someone who was pissed at him for being a colossal douche bag, but would answer the phone anyway. Dexter swallowed, nodded a few times, then hit the number.

It rang once before the ringing sound was trumped by a calendar event popping up, reminding him of the meeting with Three Jacker Media tomorrow.

Chapter Sixteen

"You did what?"

Jules nodded, sitting across from Roxy at the Elliotts' kitchen table. She couldn't stay at the lake cottage with Dexter's stuff everywhere. It made her want to burn the place down.

"The whole thing, all of it since the elopement, was an act?"

Jules nodded again, feeling miserable. And then mad. And then miserable again. She had to tell someone the truth, though. Otherwise she was liable to jump in the lake and freeze just so her thoughts would stop festering.

It was a big risk telling Roxy, but it was a bigger risk to lose faith in all humanity.

"Girl, you're like a Drew Barrymore movie. Which one am I thinking of?"

Jules sighed. "I have no idea, and you're not helping."

"Should I be helping?" Roxy crossed her arms. "Honestly, if I'd known the whole story when he called, I would've made you talk to him."

"Rox." Jules pushed her mug away. "Please don't make this harder. It's bad enough."

"Yeah, it's bad—*your* bad. He was trying to apologize."

"No. He was trying to clear his conscience. He's got this big, all-important meeting tomorrow that his life depends on." She stared down at the table. "I shouldn't say that. His meeting *is* important. It's for an amazing idea." *An idea I wish I was helping him with.* "Bottom line, he doesn't want any guilt hanging over his head. That's what his phone call was about."

Her heart sank deeper. She didn't want those words to be true. Dexter didn't suddenly want her back. It was all about work—like it always was. No matter how she'd tried to bring something sunnier and brighter to his life, she'd failed.

She hadn't realized until right then, how much seeing him happy and cut loose had meant to her. Even though it had been for only a few days, she'd seen the subtle changes in him, the softening of his sharp edges, the way he slept better, ate better, held a downward-facing dog pose like a damn boss, punched out a creepy creeper one minute, then carried her to the bedroom the next.

Yes, she'd seen him change, but she'd changed, too. Because of Dexter, she learned how to be calmer, to take care of someone and allow them to take care of her, because that came naturally when you really, truly cared. And she was painting again—he'd brought that back to her, too. Even if she never saw him again, his words of support about living her dream were cemented in her mind.

Most of all, though, for the first time in years, he made her want to commit to a man so entirely that she'd gladly entwine herself with him, with no fear that she'd lose anything. She would gain.

Because workaholic, *non*-dating machine Dexter Elliott would've never let her lose.

Jules didn't know elation and wretchedness could live in

her brain at the same time. But they were. Judging by their final conversation, she was in love with a man who didn't have the capacity to love her back.

"Apparently," Jules said, talking so she wouldn't break out in primal sobs, "he'll be just fine — going back to his old ways." She propped her elbows on the table, holding her head in her hands. "He had a million calls from some hottie named Angela. He told me he's seeing her when he gets back to the city. Whatever. I don't care."

Saying it was like sand pouring down her throat from a dark and gloomy cloud overhead.

"Angela's his personal assistant. She's, like, fifty."

Jules looked up. "What?"

"Yeah."

"He *knew* I assumed she was someone he non-dated. So he was just being a jerk?"

Roxy nodded. "He does that because he's a child."

"He *is* a child." Jules pursed her lips, furious. But that didn't hang on long enough to help when the woe returned.

Only he's not a child. He's a big strong man with a beautiful spirit full of passion and kindness, and with eyes so blue that my bones melt when he looks at me.

"Why do you care?" Roxy asked. "If you're not right for each other and he's a big-time player and a child, why do you care?"

She shrugged. "Who said I care?"

"Aw. So you *do* care?"

"Stop." Jules pounded a fist on the table. "I know you really want us to be together, but you don't know everything. He said things to me." She pressed her lips together so the gloomy gray cloud wouldn't take her over completely. "Hurtful things. He meant them. He…he said he doesn't know me."

"Those are just words."

"Words are all he has. When I thought we had more, I was

playacting, daydreaming us into something we're not. I was painting the picture I wanted to see. It wasn't real."

"I'm sorry, Jules. What can I do?"

She shook her head. "Nothing."

Jules felt overwhelming skeeviness when she walked through the office door. Why didn't she sense it the first time she'd been here?

Quent Sanders had a swollen nose and a black eye. It was way immature, but she couldn't help smiling when she saw him. "Ouch," she said with an exaggerated cringe. "Are you okay?"

"What? Oh—yeah, I don't feel it anymore."

Liar. Skeevy creeper.

She wasn't there to chitchat, and wouldn't be there at all if she'd had the guts to ask the Elliotts the same question she was going to ask him. They'd only try to talk her out of it. The decision was hard enough, and it was probably a bad idea to be there, but her decision-making synapses weren't firing efficiently.

She hadn't slept at all last night. First, the bed still smelled like Dexter, even after she'd washed the bedding at midnight. The couch smelled like him, too. It was probably her imagination, but even when she'd wrapped up in a blanket and sat on the deck, she could smell him in the air.

The damn man was everywhere. Haunting her once-happy place with painful memories of what could've been. What almost was. What was so close to being hers but gone forever. Because she'd allowed herself to believe the make-believe.

The next morning, she'd sat at her favorite spot by the window, facing the deck and the lake. The blank page of her sketch pad remained blank. She hauled out her easel but had no idea what to paint. Her mind had become that dark cloud, stifling everything out of her. After her mother died, she'd felt the same, and couldn't do anything artistic until she was safe at Grams's cottage.

Where was she supposed to go now?

The third time she'd tripped over Dexter's stupid carry-on bag that he'd left behind, she knew she had to take steps to protect herself. Despite how he'd helped her finally break through her wall of fear, she knew her limits. If her heart was broken now, how much worse would it feel the next time he came into town?

Seeing him would shatter her into a million pieces.

No way would she let herself shatter again. This next move was all about self-preservation, no matter the cost.

"I'm wondering if you can put me in contact with a good real estate agent in Mount Gretna," she said to Quent, inwardly disgusted at being anywhere near him.

"I have a lot of contacts, sure. May I ask why?"

She took a beat, squelching the pain in her stomach at what she was about to say. "I want to sell my house."

. . .

Dexter slammed the car door shut and pounded the dashboard. "Come on, come on. Let's *move*."

"You don't have anything to say to me first?"

He looked at Luke impatiently. "Yes, sorry, I was a dickhead to you, now drive." He ignored his brother's chuckle as they sped from the airport, the Jeep's headlights cutting the darkness. Dexter bounced his knees and drummed his fingers on the sides of his seat.

"Dude, chill. It'll be okay."

"You don't know that. I really screwed up—can't you pass

this car? You're driving like a geezer."

Luke shifted gears and floored it, but it still wasn't fast enough. Nothing was fast enough to send Dexter back in time and undo what he'd done to Jules. His damn heart felt like it was caving in whenever he thought about it. Which was every two seconds.

Though Roxy still wouldn't talk to him, Dexter ascertained enough from Luke about what was going on. Jules wasn't staying at the lake house. The fact that she was too upset to be there was tragically his only bright spot of hope. If she was sad—maybe he had a chance. Even if he didn't deserve it, he'd damn well take it.

"Say something normal," Luke urged. "Your heavy breathing and twitching is wigging me out, man."

"Um." Dexter rubbed his palms together. "Who won tonight's game?"

"What game?"

"I don't know, dude. I'm trying to make conversation. But since we're on the subject, we should hook up for more sporting events."

Luke glanced at him. "Yeah?"

"Definitely. I'll fly out for the 76ers, and you should come for a Yankees game. Let's meet at a couple of bowl games next season. I really miss that."

"Me, too. But I follow the Mets now."

"Dude." Dexter laughed. "Since when?"

"Since all the A-Rod crap. Who needs that?"

They chatted for a while, Luke catching him up on sports news that Dexter hadn't had time to read about. It was like old times, and Dexter knew full well it was because of Jules. Her words when she'd first seen his childhood bedroom hadn't left him. Why had he given up something that had made him so happy?

No more of that. Family, love, relationships. He'd never

again sacrifice what was truly important.

"Did you pick up everything I asked for?" he said.

"No." Luke looked at Dexter. "Pops did."

"Dad?" He couldn't wrap his brain around that. After all the disappointment and strain, his father was actually... helping. "Did he tell you about my job?"

Luke nodded.

"Everything?"

"Yyyyep."

Luke put a hand on Dexter's shoulder and shook it, steering one-handed. Maybe he should've kept both hands on the wheel while driving like a bat out of hell. After all, this would all be for nothing if they didn't make it to their destination.

"You need to trust a little more, bro. Give people credit."

"Yeah," Dexter said, allowing that caved-in feeling to overcome him again. "In that case, I have something else to tell you."

• • •

It took a lot of groveling, especially when she'd given her notice so triumphantly, but Jules was able to get her job back at the spa. As non–dream jobs went, it wasn't a terrible gig, though it definitely wasn't how she'd expected the end of this week to go.

"Are you sure about this?" Roxy asked. "I think you're being rash."

"Maybe," Jules said, tossing her bag in the backseat of the BMW. "But rash is how I roll." She leaned on the car and pushed out an exhale. "I just can't stay."

"I get that. You won't wait to say good-bye to Mom?" Tears stung behind her eyes. She'd gone two days without crying and wasn't about to start now. Though what would

Grams say about holding in emotions? Leaving probably wasn't the best way to deal with this. But she didn't know what else to do.

She hadn't slept last night. Too many ghosts, even though she was three hallways and one flight away from Dexter's old bedroom with all the sports posters on the walls, and his hockey jersey that she'd worn. The jersey that was now secretly tucked in her bag. He'd never notice it was gone. It didn't mean to him what it meant to her.

"I can't," Jules said, speaking around the lump in her throat that was trying to choke her. "You tell her good-bye for me, and your dad, too." She almost couldn't breathe now. "Everyone."

Roxy frowned sympathetically and gave her a tight hug. Jules closed her eyes and hugged her back. She'd been the closest thing to a sister Jules had ever had—which wasn't saying much. Attachments weren't really her thing.

Now she was attached to the whole Elliott family.

"You'll come back to town though, right? When the house sells, at least?"

"Yeah." Jules nodded, needing to get out of there, pronto. "I'll leave his car at long-term parking and mail him the key." She was trying to sound detached, even though she heard the misery in her voice.

"I wish you weren't—"

"I gotta go," Jules cut in. "My flight's soon." She slid in the car and fired up the ignition, trying not to see Roxy waving good-bye as she drove away.

Another very bad, unhealthy idea, but since Jules was on a roll, why not?

There was plenty of time before her flight, but she hadn't

planned on making one last stop. It was a beautiful day, and the second she turned onto the narrow road, she slowed way down, taking in the view of the lake. Grinding the gear into park, she sat in the car in the middle of the road and just stared at it for a moment.

The flood of memories swimming in her head was almost overwhelming. Memories of Grams and all the wonderful times they'd spent together. The memories trying to drown her were of Dexter…

Him sitting on the deck because he knew she didn't like him on the phone in the house. His bed-head hair from sleeping on that old velvet couch he probably hated. Watching him play host when she couldn't use her foot. Being her crutch that night, physically and on another level she hadn't known existed. The look in his eyes right before he kissed her the first time…the same look she'd seen on him over and over, because every kiss was like their first.

Even though it hurt, she had to smile when she thought of all the good he'd brought into her life. She'd had a huger blast with him in six days than she ever dreamed was possible. But now that was marked as "experience," memories to chase the rest of her life.

From the spot where she sat, when she leaned forward, she could see the front corner of the cottage. Should she stop in one last time, or firmly cut her losses?

Her attention was pulled when a figure walked around the corner of the house. And was that the tail end of a work truck in the driveway? She started the motor and drove forward. What the heck? She'd specifically told skeevy Quent to not send any Realtors to the cottage until Monday.

After angrily shutting off the car, she held up the bottom of her long dress and charged to the back of the house, only to skid to a stop.

Pairs of sawhorses covered the deck, at least the far

section of what was left of it. And lumber, Sheetrock, tools. Someone was building on to the back, in the exact space she'd envisioned her art studio would be.

Someone who was hammering. Then not hammering. Then cussing up a storm.

"Hello?"

The string of profanity stopped, and Dexter came into view, covered in sawdust, with chunks of Sheetrock chalk in his dark hair, holding a hammer. "Hi."

She stared like she was seeing a ghost, afraid to move in case he vanished into thin air. Again. "You left."

"I came back."

The words didn't compute, and she stayed where she was, fisting the bottom of her dress. Seeing him made her want to cry—and then scream bloody murder, because she was so done with sadness, and dark clouds, and falling for a man who crushed her.

"If you're here because you want your check back, I tore it up. I don't want your money."

"I don't care about that."

"You shouldn't be here," she said, trying like mad to not let him see she was broken.

"Yes, I should. This is exactly where I should be. And you know it."

The part of her brain used for comprehending and deliberating was too drained for double-talk. "I don't know anything. I thought I did, but…"

"Jules, I'm sorry." He placed the hammer on a stack of two-by-fours. "I said terrible things to you. Terrible lies I didn't even believe. For one, Angela's not who you think."

"It's fine," she said, firming her stance, feeling the stabilizing earth beneath her feet. "If you're here to clear your conscience, you're good to go." She placed her palms together and gave a little nod. "Namaste."

"Don't." His voice was sharp, and the exasperation in his eyes put her on high alert. "Do not pretend you don't care."

The nerve of him. She crossed her arms and huffed. If he only knew how much she cared. "You better leave—"

"I made a mistake," he said, right over her words. "Not the mistake of marrying you. That might be the smartest thing I've ever done. The mistake was not realizing what I had with you."

She blinked. Was this more double-talk, or was he actually…?

Suddenly, her heart started beating hard, so afraid to hope, but more afraid not to. "What?" It was the only sound she could get out.

"You"—he pointed at her—"are more important to me than any meeting. I'll always work a lot, it's how I'm built, but never again will there be a choice. Because you'll always come first. I knew that all along, I just forgot for a while. It won't happen again, I promise you."

Her speeding heart was in her throat as she looked into his eyes….those eyes she knew were telling the truth.

"We're not strangers, Jules," he added. "And we weren't some Vegas accident. You bring me to life and you make me *crazy*. I love how I feel when I'm with you. When I'm not with you, I…" He put a hand over his heart. "It's unbearable. Please forgive me. Please don't make me live like that."

He reached for her, but she stepped away.

"I'm mad at you."

Nothing moved on him except his eyes, squinting and refocusing, trying to understand. After a moment, he lowered his outstretched hand. "Okay." He stepped back, looked down, and brushed the sawdust from his palms. "I get it. I'll leave."

"I'm *mad* at you," she repeated. "But it might pass if you give me a minute."

The taken-aback expression on his face was sincere. And heart-melting. What took its place was a tiny smile twitching the corner of his mouth. "How much longer?"

She pushed her hair off her shoulders, trying not to smile back. "Couple more seconds."

"Jules, I can't wait that long." He moved forward. "I miss you. I miss my wife."

So what if he was quoting *Jerry Maguire*, Jules charged full steam ahead, never doubting Dexter would catch her. "I missed you, too," she said, clasping her hands behind his back. "I couldn't breathe."

"Neither could I," he said, arms squeezing her tight, then he bent to kiss her. The touch of his lips was soft at first, allowing her to remember that place they fit together, intertwined, that happy nirvana carved out for only them.

"I love you," he whispered over her mouth, and Jules had to grip him tight to not fall. "I love your smile, your voice— the noisier the better."

"Dex." With a heart so surprised, so full of love it could burst, she laughed and tried to shove him, but his strong arms around her wouldn't budge.

"I love how you think and give," he added, swaying them like they were dancing to Count Basie. "How you light up a room and bring energy and color everywhere you go. You know how badly I need that." He cupped her cheek, his thumb running a trail over her skin. "I love your self-portrait hanging on the wall. How you painted your hair as a rainbow of sunlight, your eyes and heart, the way they blend together in an ocean."

On the brink of tears again, she lifted onto her toes so she could touch his face. "I'm a visual artist—I don't have the words to follow your speech."

"I don't want a speech." He kissed the palm of her hand. "I just want—"

"I love you," she blurted. Then smiled, knowing she was blushing. "How was that?"

Every trace of anxiety and worry on his face disappeared as he kissed her again. "Perfect."

Her heart pounded even harder as she squeezed him, wanting to scale him like a koala bear, but Dexter bumped into a sawhorse. "By the way, what exactly are you doing out here?"

"This?" He curled a strand of her hair around one finger. "The more I thought about it, the more I saw your point about adding on. You deserve a beautiful place."

"You said it'll ruin the resale value."

"Like *you* said a million times, doesn't matter if you're never selling." He touched his forehead to hers. "Especially since we're living here."

When her mouth fell open in delight, Dexter laughed and held her even closer. "I hope you don't mind, but when I was sketching the plans of where your art studio would go, it didn't flow right until I added another room next to it. My office. I've already chosen the paintings of yours I want to hang in there."

"Your office? Wait." She clutched the front of his shirt. "Dex, your meeting with the investors is today. Two hours ago. Call them—call them now."

"No." His voice was firm, as was his focus on her. "The second I decided *you* were more important than anything, I acted; it wasn't even a choice." He smiled. "Though I'm lucky my team is forgiving, and *very* lucky that the head investor is a hopeless romantic. He texted an hour ago when he found out why I canceled. He offered to fly to Hershey in three weeks."

"Wow, that is lucky."

"This could be big, Jules." He lowered his chin and broke eye contact. "You know better than anyone how badly I need an artist like you to make it work. Will you help me?"

With a heart about to burst, she stroked his perfect hair,

that didn't look so perfect now. "Of course."

"You'll recall how my current boss gave me the next two weeks off?" He winked. "After that, my home office will be a satellite for a while, but if it bothers you, I'll rent a place in town."

"Don't you dare. That's why we have a deck." She looked around. Half of the outside wall of the house was gone, partially covered with the frame of the addition. The other half was protected with a hanging tarp. "You did all this since yesterday?"

"Luke and Dad wanted to help, but I wouldn't let them."

"Now we'll do it together. You must've been working all night—Dex." She gripped his shoulders. "You shouldn't be using a hammer or a saw, no electric tools at all! Baby, you're sleep deprived."

"Not *that* sleep deprived." He kissed her so hard, Jules saw stars…skyrockets and meteors and rainbow rings around Saturn. When his hands slid to her hips, she felt skyrockets, too.

"I think it's time we go inside," she whispered, losing her breath. "We have a skipped honeymoon to make up for." The next second, her breath was completely snatched away when Dexter scooped her up and pushed through the hanging tarp.

"Need any apples or Hershey's bars for fuel?" he asked.

"I'm good," she said, kissing her big, beautiful husband's neck.

"Hey." He stopped walking and peered at her left hand resting on his chest. "Where's your ring?"

"Oh, um, buried under a bolder by the lake."

"Babe, no." His eyebrows furrowed in mock disappointment and his bottom lip jutted out in a sexy pout. "Hated me that much?"

That bottom lip was just too tempting. "Loved you that much," she corrected, trapping his lip between her teeth, nibbling until he moaned.

"I have a confession to make, Mrs. Elliott." His voice was hoarse and impatient as they crossed the threshold of their bedroom. "I threw the Vegas bet on purpose."

She released her lips from his neck to gaze at him, partially thrilled at hearing her married name, and partially in shock at what followed it. "No, you didn't. I remember what happened now. You *won* the bet. That's the whole reason we had to get… Ohhh."

"Crazy, huh? It all came back in a rush." Wearing a smoldering grin, he sat on the bed, keeping Jules curled to his chest. "Makes sense, though. It was the only way to keep you with me." He ran a hand down her leg, over her bare feet, his nose touching hers. "And it worked like a charm."

Epilogue

A hundred missed calls later

With a sketch pad under her arm, Jules tiptoed out of the bedroom. Enough moonlight shone through the windows to see the pile of dishes, take-out cartons and other evidence of nearly two weeks' worth of neglected housekeeping.

More than enough moonlight showed the State of Nevada wedding license displayed on the fridge. A happy thrill ran through Jules, remembering how Dex had made such a fuss about hanging it where he could see it every day.

So I'll never forget the night you took pity on me and changed my life.

She nearly tripped over the heap of towels from their early-morning swim. Had that been today or yesterday? Time was one dreamy, delicious blur. Dex's cell sat on the counter. Dead for days. No charger in sight. Halfway buried under her paintbrushes and his DIY book on how to add a room.

Every once in a while, she'd catch a nervous eye twitch or a reflexive glance at where his watch should be. Whenever she suggested he check his phone or email, he'd explain to her in slow, sexy detail why, exactly, he was a better man because of her.

She was better because of him, too. He stabilized her better than yoga, made sense, was a stunning example of how to bravely face an unknown future. *Which is always easier—* he was quick to point out—*when the leap of faith is made with someone you love like hell.*

The other day, while she'd soaked in a bath, one by one, he'd brought in her paintings, sat on the side of the tub, and asked what they meant, shared what he found interesting, learned about her art.

How could she love him more?

Holding back the tarp with one hand, she stepped onto the deck. The easel was bathed in moonlight, still angled from when she'd painted last. First, she consulted the pages she'd already filled with sketches of his profile, his steady gaze, even the nude study she'd done from memory. That was a goody, and for her eyes only.

Then she picked up a brush.

This far from the city, the stars filled the sky, reflecting off the lake, distracting her with memories of the day he'd come back. That first time he'd said "I love you." The countless times since then. Her skin warmed, stomach flipped at the thought of her legs intertwined with his, fingers interlocked, wedding rings clinking against each other.

The hours and days ran together. They'd fight it, but real-life responsibilities would return soon. She heard the bedsprings squeak, heard him beckon her by name, sending a lovely shiver of anticipation through her body.

Real-life responsibilities? Sure, whatever. Just not too soon, please. Their twelve solid days of honeymooning beat every other couple in the family.

Not that they had a bet going or anything...

About the Author

USA Today bestselling author Ophelia London was born and raised among the redwood trees in beautiful northern California. Once she was fully educated, she decided to settle in Florida, but her car broke down in Texas and she's lived in Dallas ever since. A cupcake and elliptical aficionado (obviously those things are connected), she spends her time watching arthouse movies and impossibly trashy TV, while living vicariously through the characters she writes. Ophelia is the author of the Sugar City series, including WIFE FOR THE WEEKEND and KISSING HER CRUSH; AIMEE & THE HEARTTHROB; DEFINITELY, MAYBE IN LOVE; the Abby Road series; and the Perfect Kisses series. Visit her at ophelialondon.com. But don't call when *The Vampire Diaries* (or *Dawson's Creek*) is on.

Find your Bliss with these great releases...

THE DOCTOR'S FAKE FIANCÉE
a *Red River* novel by Victoria James

Former surgeon and bachelor Evan Manning has one thing on his mind—to reclaim the career that a car accident stole from him. But when he's forced to return to his hometown of Red River, Evan comes face-to-face with the gorgeous woman who's haunted his dreams for the last year—the woman he rescued from the burning car that injured his hand. When artist Grace Matheson's sexy hero hears that she needs work, he offers her a job and a home—if she'll pretend she's his fiancée for a month. The more time they spend together, the more real their feelings become—and the more likely heartbreak is.

HER ACCIDENTAL HUSBAND
a *Sorensen* novel by Ashlee Mallory

Payton Vaughn's trip to Puerto Vallarta for her friend's wedding was her big escape from her ridiculously overbearing mother – oh, and that little matter with her cheating fiancé. Now, her flight's been cancelled, and she's crammed into a tiny car with the gorgeous-but-irritating best man. He has no business getting to know her better—not even for all the tequila in Mexico... until they wake with grande-sized hangovers as man and wife. Now Payton and Cruz must decide if they've reached the end of their journey...or the beginning of a new adventure.

UNEXPECTEDLY YOURS
a novel by Coleen Kwan

Derek Carmichael has harbored a secret crush on his best friend's older sister for years, but Hannah has always been out of his reach. Hannah is wary of Derek's player past and the rampant rumors connecting him to beautiful socialites. Still, she can't help but give in when their attraction reaches a boiling point. Trying to keep it a secret from her overprotective brother is one thing, but when Hannah finds herself unexpectedly expecting, her life is thrown upside down. She and Derek may be becoming parents together, but that's no basis for a happily-ever-after.

The Practice Proposal
a *Suddenly Smitten* by Tracy March

Liza Sutherland isn't looking for love. Not from a charity-auction date she didn't even bid on and especially not with Nationals first baseman Cole Collins, the guy she obsessed over as an awkward teenager. She won't get involved with a notorious player, no matter how attractive Cole is. When Frank makes Liza a deal she can't refuse—a bet she will fall in love with Cole or a cool half mil goes to charity—the game is on. But neither bet on the real feelings that surface. Could a fake fling turn into an official forever?

CPSIA information can be obtained
at www.ICGtesting.com
Printed in the USA
LVHW090323151221
706073LV00020B/373

9 781523 978533